MY PAGE~~ ~~ST MY HIP, AND I JUMPED.

I pulled it off my belt and checked the number. I'd been beeped to call my own office? Very strange, since I'm the only one who works there.

I flipped my cell phone open, punched in the number, and entered the answering machine code.

"This is to let you know that twenty-five monkeys have been killed out at the Happy Hunting Ranch, east of El Paso," cracked a bad imitation of Robert DeNiro. *"You'll find their bodies stuffed inside a burlap sack hidden inside the taxidermy shed. This is a one-time call. Don't blow the information."*

The message had been left only an hour ago.

I turned and stared at the body bag containing Timmy Tom Tyler, as a large raven parasailed directly over my head.

"Caaaaaaaaa!"

The jarring cry chilled me to the bone. A business card for the Happy Hunting Ranch had been in Timmy Tom's wallet.

"The characters breathe with the endlessly fascinating idiosyncracies of real people. Jessica Speart is a revitalizing gust of the southwest in a stuffy room."

Nevada Barr

Other Rachel Porter Mysteries by
Jessica Speart
from Avon Books

GATOR AIDE
TORTOISE SOUP
BIRD BRAINED

ATTENTION: ORGANIZATIONS AND CORPORATIONS
Most Avon Books paperbacks are available at special quantity
discounts for bulk purchases for sales promotions, premiums, or
fund-raising. For information, please call or write:

**Special Markets Department, HarperCollins Publishers, Inc.,
10 East 53rd Street, New York, N.Y. 10022-5299.
Telephone: (212) 207-7528. Fax: (212) 207-7222.**

JESSICA SPEART

A RACHEL PORTER MYSTERY

B●RDER PREY

AVON BOOKS
An Imprint of HarperCollins*Publishers*

This is a work of fiction. Names, characters, places, and incidents are products of the author's imagination or are used fictitiously and not to be construed as real. Any resemblance to actual events, locales, organizations, or persons, living or dead, is entirely coincidental.

AVON BOOKS
An Imprint of HarperCollins*Publishers*
10 East 53rd Street
New York, New York 10022-5299

Copyright © 2000 by Jessica Speart
Inside cover author photo by George Brenner
ISBN: 0-380-81040-9
www.avonbooks.com

All rights reserved. No part of this book may be used or reproduced in any manner whatsoever without written permission, except in the case of brief quotations embodied in critical articles and reviews. For information address Avon Books, an Imprint of HarperCollins Publishers.

First Avon Books paperback printing: June 2000

Avon Trademark Reg. U.S. Pat. Off. and in Other Countries, Marca Registrada, Hecho en U.S.A.
HarperCollins® is a trademark of HarperCollins Publishers Inc.

Printed in the U.S.A.

WCD 10 9 8 7 6 5 4 3 2 1

If you purchased this book without a cover, you should be aware that this book is stolen property. It was reported as "unsold and destroyed" to the publisher, and neither the author nor the publisher has received any payment for this "stripped book."

Acknowledgments

Thanks go to Doug McKenna, USFWS Special Agent extraordinaire; Dr. Thomas Butler of the Southwest Foundation for Biomedical Research, for his time and knowledge; Caree Vander Linden of the United States Army Medical Research Institute of Infectious Diseases at Fort Detrick, Maryland, for her technical advice; Shirley McGreal of the International Primate Protection League and Wally Swett of Primarily Primates, both of whom have dedicated their lives to the plight of primates in the U.S. and abroad; Patsy Asher, whose heart and hospitality are as big as Texas; Barbara Link and Diane Barendse, for making many calls and introductions on my behalf; Adair Margo, for giving me an insider's view of El Paso; Alex and Patti Apostolides, for those oh-so-necessary martinis.

And finally to George, who diligently read and reread my manuscript. The man deserves the Medal of Honor.

One

"I'm gonna let you in on something big, Porter. But you've gotta come out here now and see what's about to go down!"

The insistent whisper curled into my brain, gnawing like a rodent's incisors. Prying open an eye, I glanced at the clock. Five A.M. I'd been dreaming of Harrison Ford; my reality was Timmy Tom Tyler. I was tempted to hang up the phone and roll over, picking up where Harrison and I had left off.

"You're gonna owe me big time on this one." Then Tyler shrewdly dangled his bait. "Hell, this might even get you one of those cheap gold-plated stars."

Damn! Those were the magic words I couldn't resist. Harrison gave me an understanding "see ya later, kid," smile as I groaned. Timmy Tom was undoubtedly calling from some godforsaken place in the middle of nowhere. I was beginning to hate cell phones.

"Where are you?" I croaked. My tongue felt as fuzzy as a hair ball, coated with the residue of one too many frozen margaritas from last night. This was my newest approach to the "I-can't-believe-the-man-I-loved-left-me" remnants of a heartache.

"Just head out on the Anapra till you hit a dirt road after Marker 63, and hang a right. Don't worry, Porter.

1

You won't have any trouble finding me," Tyler declared mysteriously. The phone clicked dead.

Like this was just what I was itching to do at the crack of dawn: run around playing sleuth in the middle of the desert. But Timmy Tom was the first snitch I'd developed since my transfer to El Paso four months ago, and with the way things were going, I had little choice but to cultivate his good will. Fish and Wildlife refused to pay informants. Hell, from what I heard, the Service wasn't all that crazy about paying *me* these days.

I groggily dressed, made my way out the door, and pulled myself up into the monster Ford F-150 pick-up I'd inherited from the posting's previous agent. Since it was too early to stop at a convenience store for coffee, I washed my Pop-Tart breakfast down with a can of Coke that had been sitting in the cupholder since yesterday.

Then I hit the road, with the serrated peaks of the Organ Mountains rising like a set of mismatched musical pipes beside me. In the rear view mirror, the barest wisp of a cloud played hide-and-seek with a waning moon that was loath to cede the last vestige of night. But an expanding sliver of sun was inevitably winning. I raced toward where it rose, liquid as a broken egg yolk, its rays spilling onto the ebony asphalt in widely splayed fingers of warm, yellow light.

Forty-five minutes later, I veered sharply onto a dirt path studded with creosote bushes and a wide array of rocks that were "bigger than a pebble, and smaller than a breadbox." The ideal spot to practice what I'd dubbed as *driving aerobics*. Less boring than a Stairmaster, it was the perfect solution for the exercise-impaired. This morning's workout consisted of bouncing through the middle of no-man's land: a patch of bleached desert on the New Mexico–Mexican border. My body shimmied and shook as the Ford vaulted over rocks, my hips swinging from side to side. Who knows? If my career with Fish and Wildlife didn't pan out, maybe I could host an infomercial and make some bucks teaching these moves to Midwestern housewives. A few more months of jiggling around like this, and Sharon Stone would be asking *me* for some tips.

So, what was Tyler talking about? The only thing I'd seen so far was a flock of glossy starlings bolting out of the brush, resembling a bunch of cheap-suited Joes on their way to a funeral. Then I caught sight of a shimmering shape on the ground up ahead. The crumpled form caused my heart to flutter as rapidly as the wings of the avian throng, and soon crystallized into a body lying flat on the parched desert floor. A cadre of buzzards flew directly above, slowly circling lower and lower. Unless this was Tyler's way of catching a few rays, my guess was that things weren't looking too good for him right about now.

I parked my Ford and walked over to where Timmy Tom silently scowled up at me. My breakfast instantly turned to a cold, hard lump in the pit of my stomach, even though the Chihuahua desert heat could have fried a tortilla. Someone had taken the jingle "reach out and touch someone" a little too far: Timmy Tom's cell phone was rammed halfway down his throat.

My eyes traced a distant set of tire tracks that approached from the sun-baked earth of Mexico and came to a halt at a broken-down barbed-wire fence. Its rusted tines sliced across the landscape like a jagged line of stubble left after a bad shave. On this side of the border, a different set of tire marks picked up not far from the body. Their treads revealed them to be fairly new, showing little wear—so the vehicle clearly hadn't been government issue. The tracks disappeared in the direction of the Anapra Road, taking with them whatever secrets had been here. It was business as usual on the border.

I walked back to the pick-up and dug out my own cell phone, since Timmy Tom's line was out of order, and placed the emergency call to the local sheriff's department.

"Hold on to your *caballos*, lady. We'll get out there eventually." The reply was delivered in a cowboy twang.

I chalked up the laid-back response to an over-abundance of lithium in the local water supply. Not about to stand around and count rattlesnakes while waiting for the local law enforcement to show up, I decided to start my own investigation. Once the police arrived on the scene, they'd greedily claim the corpse as their own. Call it quirky, but I tend to get possessive of dead bodies that I find. Especially when the cadaver happens to be my one and only, true-blue, "boy-have-I-got-something-for-you" informant.

I swiftly emptied my glove compartment of its survival gear—a stash of Snickers and Hershey bars—grabbed a pair of latex gloves, and pulled them on. When I turned back around, I found that a vulture had already begun noshing on Timmy Tom's arm. A few deft Jackie Chan moves established that I was the one with first dibs, then I set to work, getting better acquainted with Tyler than I had ever wanted to.

A quick examination proved the corpse to be free of any bullet holes or stab wounds. In fact, the only discernible mark was a tiny red bump on the arm the free-loading buzzard had attacked. I glanced over to where the bird sat on a gnarled piece of juniper wood, bobbing his head as he bided his time. He shot back a look, sending heebie-jeebies shivering down my spine.

"Shoo! Go on! Get out of here!" I urged.

The buzzard's only response was to draw his wings,

the size of two hearses, tightly against his body, letting me know that he wasn't about to go anywhere. Well, some hump-shouldered wannabe thug wasn't going to get the better of me.

Though I excel at sticking my nose into places it doesn't belong, I'm not crazy about getting too touchy-feely when it comes to dead bodies. I put my queasiness on hold and began to rifle through Timmy Tom's pockets.

Tyler appeared to be traveling light today. Any car keys he'd had were gone. By the look of things, so was his vehicle. The only item to be found on his body—aside from the newly defunct cell phone—was a wallet. His billfold was like a mini-suitcase, and I took a dive into Timmy Tom's luggage.

Two twenties and a ten told me that Tyler's murder couldn't be pinned on a robbery. I examined his driver's license, where the photo sneered out at the world. My fingers unpacked a little further, removing a slim stack of business cards.

Hmm, there was one for the Good Luck Cafe, a greasy spoon Timmy Tom had tried to sue after eating a burger he claimed had been tainted with mad cow disease. His case was thrown out when all he offered for proof was a sorry attempt at a "moo." Another card was for a local flophouse, the No Tell Motel. Tyler had dragged them into court as well, insisting a romp on one of their mattresses had given him a permanent dose of the clap. Then there was a card for the Happy Hunting Ranch, a popular place frequented by well-heeled hunters. Its name pretty much said it all. At the bottom of the pile was a card for Timmy Tom's very own entrepreneurial enterprise, MONKEY BUSINESS. It read, "Your best bet for that special pet. Monkeys also available for the entertainment trade and private parties."

Timmy Tom had been a two-bit dealer in illegal monkeys and primates—though he'd been known to sell whatever else might crawl, swim, or in any other way cross his path. Mexico had provided him with an easy source for his trade. The country ranks high as a sieve for the flow of illegal wildlife into the United States, due to the porous border between Texas and Mexico. From Texas, the smuggled critters are easily shipped to disreputable pet stores, roadside zoos, and other black holes of greed.

I'd first met Timmy Tom after a prospective buyer had angrily lodged a complaint against him with the local U.S. Fish and Wildlife office. It seemed one of Tyler's "lovingly hand-reared" spider monkeys had introduced itself by wrapping its prehensile tail around the customer's neck, pulling its body up, then sinking its teeth into the guy's face. When the man tried to pull the critter off, the monkey retaliated by clamping down on his hand.

"What a frigging wuss!" Timmy Tom countered, when I'd stopped by to check out the complaint.

Next came the tour of his "facility," which really lassoed my interest. I spotted a group of baby spider monkeys that Tyler claimed had been captive born as a litter. The problem was, females generally produce only one baby a year, and the babies outnumbered the adults. To top it off, Timmy Tom had pointed out two neutered males as the "parents." Talk about your miracle births. I promptly shut down Timmy Tom's illegal pipeline.

More recently, Timmy Tom and his partner Juan had started a business dealing in tufted capuchins, commonly known as organ grinder monkeys. The scam was to open a school where Tyler would "train" them to do tasks for the disabled. Unless one of them had been taught to raise the dead, as of now, Timmy Tom was permanently out of business.

Tyler's wallet slid easily back into his front pocket, the worn denim fabric having molded itself to the billfold's shape. That's when I felt something odd beneath his pants. No, part of Timmy Tom hadn't sprung back to life. What I'd come into contact with was up too high for that.

I popped the waistband button out of its frayed hole and released the zipper on Timmy Tom's jeans. Well, whadda ya know? There was a money belt strapped securely around his waist. Either something valuable was secreted inside, or Timmy Tom was even more paranoid than I'd guessed.

I could barely contain my excitement as my fingers flew to uncover buried treasure. But all I found was a card for a company called Panfauna Associates, along with a dirty scrap of paper folded into a tiny square. I unwrapped it and discovered four groupings of nearly illegible characters. I stared at the soiled and wrinkled paper, determined to decipher what they meant. They were probably just Timmy Tom's weekly Lotto numbers, but you never knew.

Tyler had recently begun to call me with information on a regular basis, seeming determined to help bring other illegal dealers down. I didn't delude myself into thinking he'd realized the error of his ways; I'd tightened the noose on *his* pipeline of black-market primates, and Tyler wanted the competition toppled, too. But this time he must have crossed the wrong guy—like someone in the Mexican Mafia.

I returned Tyler's treasures and stripped off my gloves as I studied the area around me. There were plenty of different footprints in the sandy desert soil. Easily identified were those that matched the soles of Timmy Tom's shiny new boots, as well as the ones that belonged to my own broken-down, worn-out hikers. I lightly ran my fingertips over the other footprints. The imprinted soil was crusty and dry to the touch—Nature's way of letting me know the tracks were several days old.

I sat back on my heels, my face turned up to a sun drowning in a blue ocean of sky. When I glanced back down, ghostly sparks of light danced behind the orbs of my eyes. My sight cleared after a moment, but I still blinked twice, surprised to see the striations that had suddenly appeared, zigzagging through the sand in front of me. Then I remembered an old tracking trick: if you want to find a trail, it's best to look directly into the light. I immediately stood and began to follow where the path led. While I didn't know what the pattern was, I did know that the design was man-made.

I skirted some yucca and pushed past scrub, following the shine that came off the striation. Its lines were as sleekly smooth as a serpent, leading directly into a creosote bush. Around the plant's edge lay a network of broken twigs. Bending over, I examined their fractured ends. They were still fresh and green, and a quiver crept along my spine. Someone had been here recently. I gingerly lifted the foliage, prepared to leap back at the first hint of a spider's hairy leg or the crinkly sound of dry leaves, camouflaging a slithering rattler. Call me a city girl, but I was more nervous of stumbling upon a creepy crawler than of being ambushed by a phone-wielding homicidal maniac.

I steeled my nerves, got down on my knees, and carefully peered beneath the brush. Bingo! A fresh heel mark lay cleverly concealed by a network of lacy shadows. My adrenaline raced at its distinctive marking: a five-pointed star imprinted in the heel's center. From there, I followed the striations to where they ended back at the tire tracks. I picked up a large mesquite branch and dragged its limbs directly over my path. The same striated pattern appeared, automatically erasing my footprints.

The mesquite branch came in handy for something else, as well—fending off the growing number of buzzards that had gathered, intent on grabbing a McTyler snack. A few of the birds even began to cast a lascivious eye toward me. The array of heads pivoted in my direction were as bald and wrinkled as a chorus line of senior citizen Chippendale dancers. I was just starting to feel worried when the cavalry finally arrived.

The Dona Ana County sheriff's patrol car slowly wended its way towards me, its Goodyears kicking up a cloud of dirt and sand. By the time the vehicle came to a stop, a layer of dry dust coated the back of my throat. Timmy Tom didn't fare too well, either. A cloud of grit had settled upon him, enveloping his corpse in a motley shroud. Meanwhile, the deputy who stepped from his car looked like the kind of guy who would arrest a speck of dirt for loitering. His khaki uniform was so crisply pressed, I was torn between saluting and checking my reflection in his boots, which were polished to high-gloss perfection.

"Glad to see you made such good time," I dryly commented.

The vultures stood their ground, remaining unimpressed.

"What's your problem? It's not like the guy's going anywhere," the deputy answered by way of cordial greeting. Then he turned and walked away. "Be back in a minute. Mother Nature and me need to have a little chat."

A second man emerged from the car. Tall and gaunt, he slowly unfurled his body one vertebra at a time, then approached with a body bag clenched in his fist.

"Jack Purdy, county medical examiner." His lips barely moved as he introduced himself while extending a hand.

"Rachel Porter. Special agent with Fish and Wildlife," I responded.

Purdy's bony fingers wrapped around my hand and then slid down my wrist as if noting my size for future reference. "I understand you haven't met Bill Hutchins, our deputy sheriff, before. So let me give you a word of advice: he's not keen on feds. Especially ones working for agencies in the Interior Department, so it's probably best you comply with whatever he asks."

Welcome back to the West. "Thanks for the tip, but I feel pretty much the same way when it comes to dealing with deputy sheriffs who can't see around their own egos," I informed him. I suddenly remembered which direction Hutchins had been headed, and took off running after him.

"Be careful where you walk!" I called out. "I just found some important tracks over there!"

I reached Hutchins just in time to see the man tread straight through my prized creosote bush as he finished pulling the zipper up on his pants. "Don't get your petticoat in a knot—there are tracks all over this place. Besides, we rely on more scientific methods for dealing with crime here in Dona Ana County these days. Probably things your agency doesn't even know about," he drawled.

I checked under the bush and found that the print had been totally eradicated. "Too bad. There was a perfect imprint of a heel mark that might have belonged to the killer."

Hutchins shrugged. "No big deal, since it wouldn't have done you much good. That is, unless you were planning to check the heels of every Mexican around."

"You mean your scientific technique has already determined it was a Mexican who committed the murder?" I countered.

Hutchins glared, his eyes aimed at me like two .45 revolvers. "Why don't you tell me what you're doing out here, anyway?"

"The corpse over there is Timmy Tom Tyler from El Paso. He was one of my informants," I replied coolly.

Hutchins pulled out a Marlboro, lit up, and inhaled deeply. "Okay. What say we try this again. What were you doing out here in the first place?" he repeated slowly, as if I might not understand English.

I was tempted to slow-mo the guy right into the next county. "He called me with a tip that something was about to go down, and asked me to meet him here."

Hutchins squinted hard, trying his best to intimidate me. "Yeah? Well, I'm waiting. You wanna tell me exactly what *was* going down?"

His *mucho macho* attempt to extricate information nearly prompted me to suggest he take a refresher course in Interrogation 101. "I wouldn't know. As you can see, he never got the chance to tell me."

Hutchins turned his head and cracked his neck as we walked back to the murder scene, where Jack Purdy was busy checking out Timmy Tom's body.

"So, you think this low life was calling you about some kind of puppy-napping?" Hutchins asked, transferring his snide attitude to the corpse lying at his feet.

Okay, so Tyler might have been a low life. But he was *my* low life, damn it, and nobody else's. "Tyler put his life on the line this morning by calling me. I think he deserves a little more respect than that."

Hutchins drew tightly on his Marlboro. "But you believe Mr. High Class here was calling you about animal smuggling that was going down?"

"Of course. What else would it have been?" I responded.

"That's crazy!" Hutchins scoffed derisively. "Nobody's going to risk a murder rap over a bag of snakes or tarantulas. Drugs are the only thing that make sense in this kind of situation."

I could have clued Hutchins in on the staggering sum of moolah commanded by the sale of endangered species, but I placed the lesson on hold as Jack Purdy finished bagging Timmy Tom and started to zip the sack closed.

"Wait! Tyler's wearing a money belt. You'll probably want to check out its contents," I reported, ever the good Samaritan.

Hutchins leaned in towards me, his pupils cocked and ready for action. "And just how would you know about that, unless you'd been messing around with the body?"

What did the guy think I was, a closet necrophiliac? "A vulture pulled down his zipper and opened his money belt. So I decided it wouldn't hurt to take a peek."

"You know, I've heard about you, Porter," Hutchins said in a low, menacing tone.

"Only good things, I trust."

"What I've heard is that you're considered a loose cannon who likes to poke her nose into other people's investigations. Well, you're not going to get away with that around here," he warned, jabbing the air with the tip of his Marlboro. The ember burned red hot, devouring what little was left of the filter.

"How often do you ride out this way?" I queried.

"Only when I have to," Hutchins replied, taking a last drag on the fiery stub.

"Well, then. Since you didn't know Tyler and you don't regularly cruise the Anapra, you might want to thank me for handing you this case." If I was going to be termed a loose cannon, I might as well enjoy it.

"Yeah. Right. Like I need to waste my time on more paperwork," Hutchins responded, stomping the remains of his Marlboro into the ground. "Hey, Purdy. Find the money belt and dig out what's in it."

Purdy's bony fingers loosened Tyler's pants, and dove into the hidden belt. They resurfaced with the articles for Hutchins' perusal.

"Panfauna Associates, huh? Never heard of 'em." Hutchins quickly dismissed the business card and moved on to the second piece of paper. "Congratulations, Porter. Looks like what you've got here is a bunch of mumbo jumbo numbers," he huffed. "I advise you to leave the hard-core investigative work to real police and keep yourself busy with your critters. And that goes for any other case you happen to stumble upon here in Dona Ana County."

"Aw, shucks—I bet you sweet talk every federal agent like this. Or should I consider myself special?" I inquired.

"I also expect you to keep me informed if you stumble across anything else involving this case," Hutchins responded, blatantly ignoring my question.

"You'll be the first deputy sheriff I call," I assured him.

Purdy replaced Timmy Tom's papers and began to zip the body bag closed once more. Tyler sullenly glared up at me as he slowly disappeared from view, as if to make sure I understood he'd died on my behalf. Then Purdy grabbed a roll of yellow evidence tape, and carefully wrapped it around the sack three times in a coroner's version of a lock and seal storage bag. "Dr. Jack Purdy" was printed in black letters every few inches on its surface, and he used a magenta Magic Marker to sign his initials wherever the tape overlapped.

I was silently saying good-bye to Timmy Tom when my pager started vibrating against my hip. I instinctively jumped, bumping into Purdy who in turn collapsed on top of Timmy Tom's corpse. A low groan issued from inside the bag, almost as if Tyler were getting in the last word.

"Excess air making its way out of the body," Purdy stiffly remarked, doing his best to appear unperturbed.

I pulled the pager off my belt and checked the offending number. I'd been beeped to call my own office? Very strange, since I'm the only one who works there.

I flipped my cell phone open, punched in the number, and entered the answering machine code.

This is to let you know that twenty-five monkeys have been killed out at the Happy Hunting Ranch, east of El Paso," crackled a bad imitation of Robert DeNiro. *"You'll find their bodies stuffed in a burlap sack hidden inside the taxidermy shed. This is a one-time call. Don't blow the information."*

The message had been left only an hour ago.

I turned and stared at the bag containing Timmy Tom Tyler, as a large raven parasailed directly over my head.

"Caaaaaaa!"

The jarring cry chilled me to the very bone. The Happy Hunting Ranch business card had been in Timmy Tom's wallet.

"Caaaaaa!"

The strident call hung in the air, patient as a waiting noose, then transformed into a cold laugh emanating from Timmy Tom's corpse.

I knew the noise was nothing more than the desert up to its tricks, yet a ghoulish premonition rose within me. What had Tyler been involved in? Why had he been murdered? And what were monkeys doing on a hunting ranch deep in Texas?

Two

Hunting ranches are big business in Texas these days. Dubbed the exotic game capital of the world, the state is more than just a home where the buffalo roam. It's also where everything from Nubian ibex to African scimitar horned oryx are kept under lock and key at over one thousand private ranches. While the deer and the antelope may play on the Lone Star's open range, so do 50 varieties of unusual trophy-class critters, all available year round to be mown down purely for your hunting pleasure. Throw in a few snappy slogans, such as "No Kill-No Pay" and "If you don't like him, don't pull the trigger," along with luxury accommodations, and game ranches have morphed into the Great White Hunter's ultimate dream vacation.

But such privilege doesn't come cheap. Shooting an American bison runs a mere $3,000. But nab a markhor from the mountains of Afghanistan, and it will set you back a good twelve grand. If you get a hankering for something even more exceptional—say, a trophy-quality African bongo—be prepared to fork over a hefty forty-thousand smackers. It's no wonder that raising cattle for McDonald's quickly loses its appeal once ranchers hear prices like these. Exotic animals have become the Lone

Star's gold-plated cash crop, raking in a cool $100 million a year.

I followed the set of tire tracks from Timmy Tom's body across the desert floor, to where they disappeared on the asphalt. The lick of black top trailed off in the distance like a long mourning veil. I pointed the Ford east toward Texas, and sped down a two-lane road so desolate there weren't even any telephone poles flying past to be counted.

I was once again in the Southwest, thanks to some powerful politicos whose feathers I'd ruffled during my last assignment. Apparently, I'd upset them so much they hadn't just wanted me banished from Miami, but run clear out of the state of Florida. After conducting a thorough search, they came up with the perfect place to bury me—a spot where I couldn't possibly cause any trouble.

My former boss, Charlie Hickok, had called upon hearing the news. "Congratulations, Bronx. Sheeeet! You must be doing something right to have gotten that scrawny ass of yours dumped on the border. You just gotta remember, the greater the odds are against you, the harder you gotta fight," he'd said consolingly. "Tell you what. Seeing as how you're probably ready to high-tail it back to civilization right about now, I'll do what I can to get you transferred down here to New Orleans."

Charlie was a wise man. He knew how much I appreciated having my ass called scrawny. But a recent break-up with the love of my life, New Orleans police detective Jake Santou, put the kabosh on any idea of moving back to Louisiana just yet. Seeing Santou would have been more than I could bear. I'd turned Charlie's offer down, and chalked up his blizzard of curses as being his way of wishing me well on the border.

Crossing into Texas, I hopped on to Highway 180,

grateful for the distraction of playing tag with an inter-
minable number of traffic lights. I passed billboards
trumpeting everything from discounted Tony Lama cowboy boots to Mexican saddle blankets, tacky hot pink
taco stands, and other comforting signs of Western civilization. It helped keep Timmy Tom's image at bay.
Soon, the traffic lights grew fewer and the billboards
more sparse as I headed deeper into rugged west Texas
ranching country.

The Happy Hunting Ranch was an elite stomping
ground for many of the world's wealthiest hunters. Or,
as the ranch liked to advertise, "We've got 15,000
critter-filled acres of pure happiness, all trigger-ready for
those discerning enough to want to shoot the very best."
Equally well known was its eccentric owner, Frederick
Ulysses Krabbs.

Frederick Ulysses was the scion of an old El Paso
family which professed to trace its lineage back to the
battle of the Alamo. That claim had been disputed by a
San Antonio newspaper, which insisted there was no
record of a Krabbs having ever fought there.

The Krabbs clan immediately sued the paper, then
bought it. Renaming it the *Alamo Bugle*, they next proceeded to broadside history. A week-long series of front
page articles trumpeted an exciting new discovery: it
wasn't Davy Crockett who'd heroically gone down fending off Santa Anna's men. New, "reliable" sources revealed that to be a bald-faced lie pumped up to promote
a 1950s television series. The real hero of the Alamo
had been none other than Frederick Ulysses' great
grandfather, the esteemed Francis Uriah Krabbs. Sup-
posedly Francis' pivotal role had been ignored all these
years due to the fact that the Krabbs family had left San
Antonio, preferring to reside in El Paso.

The Krabbses instantly became West Texas heroes,

venerated for their loyalty to El Paso. The clan was celebrated with a parade whose route passed the largest bank, insurance company, and investment firm in town—all Krabbs-family owned. Frederick's father, Filmore Udall, had gotten into the three businesses early on, establishing a Krabbs tradition of pillage and plunder. Promising to keep El Pasoans' money safe from harm, Filmore had also sold life insurance policies to the men of each household—conveniently allowing him to better bilk their widows and orphans through shady investments.

Frederick Ulysses had continued the family's entrepreneurial tradition by jumping on the exotic critter gravy train.

The entrance to the Happy Hunting Ranch was impossible to miss, marked by a giant billboard that featured an elk jauntily standing in the center of a bull's-eye with its ankles crossed and a thumb cocked rakishly toward the access gate.

I drove through, passing a camera mounted onto a post. I'd heard the ranch ran a tight operation. Translated into every day hunter-speak that meant U.S. Fish and Wildlife agents were definitely considered persona non grata.

I followed a winding dirt road, guided by markers bearing shiny white hoof prints. The last sign was a cartoon drawing of a deer leaping joyously in the air while proclaiming, *"You're Here!"*

I pulled into a lot and parked next to a row of open-sided Jeep Scramblers painted with black and white stripes, clearly meant to resemble a battalion of motorized zebras. As long as one ignored the tires, shape, and size, it was quite the camouflage job. I was certain the resident critters were equally impressed.

Each Jeep was missing its front windshield. Situated

where the windshield wipers normally would have been were brown leather mounds touting the logo "Bucks Bull Bag"—custom-made bean bags upon which hunters propped their rifle barrels. How convenient: customers didn't even have to rouse their rear ends from the comfort of their vehicle's lushly padded seat to snag a world-class trophy. It made you stop and wonder what the phrase "sport hunting" really meant.

I turned away from the gas guzzling zebras and focused on the stone and timber lodge which loomed before me. Obviously plenty of greenbacks had gone into building the place. It exuded an easy air of elegance and privilege, in silent acknowledgment that the bucks could be traced to old money.

I bounded up a set of rough-hewn stone steps and went inside, which evoked East Africa in all its colonial glory. I half expected to spot Karen Blixen and Ernest Hemingway discussing the merits of a lion hunt over a glass of sherry.

The main room was filled with enough exotic wildlife to make any zoo lustful with envy—except this collection was composed of decapitated heads mounted in a variety of frozen expressions. There were addax, water buffalo and aoudad ram, sable, eland, and gemsbok. A lynx's taxidermied form was balanced on a large wooden support beam overhead. Next to it stood a dainty black and tan springbok, posed as if to take a death-defying leap into space.

I'd have given anything for a dose of Merlin's magical wizardry in order to zap every single creature back to life. Suddenly, a swell of power seemed to race up my toes, my feet, and my legs. My veins began to tingle and my blood started to rush, fed by a high-voltage electrical current.

Out of the corner of my eye, I was sure I caught a

ripple of movement. My breath froze and I remained perfectly still. A flurry of whispers murmured softly in my ear, then I spotted the flicker of an eye, and the twitch of a nose on a Grevy's zebra. Next came the explosive bang of an angry kick as a powerful hoof ripped through the wooden panels and jettisoned past my head. The menagerie's previously silent screams built to a roaring crescendo, followed by a torrent of movement. The hunting lodge's taxidermied zoo had come alive!

Gazelles and black-faced impalas sprang off the walls. A family of javelina squealed in joy at their freedom. I cheered on a herd of red stag deer which raced out the door, the thundering of their hooves rattling the stone and timber lodge. My brain pounded as more and more creatures galloped by until a full-scale stampede was in progress.

The next instant, the room was wrapped in deafening silence, the gallery of heads motionless on their plaques as before. But each pair of eyes scorched through my skin, piercing straight into my heart. I knew the only place these animals would ever be set free was in my prayers.

A long corridor loomed ahead and I followed, curious to see where it would take me. My expedition was interrupted when a woman the size of a bulldozer abruptly appeared, as if I had triggered a silent alarm. She planted herself directly in my path, placed her hands firmly on her hips, and stared at me, her nostrils flaring fiercely. The message was loud and clear: *I dare you to come any closer.*

Just one look at her was more than enough to stop me dead in my tracks. Her mound of fiery curls rose skyward in that Texas tradition of "the higher the hair, the closer to heaven." Meanwhile, Maybelline and Revlon staged a wild West showdown on her face. Bright blue eyeshadow weighed down a pair of lids which were fringed with "I Wanna Be Tammy Faye Baker" eyelashes, while a bright slash of tangerine lipstick competed with the "Like a Virgin" pink blush applied generously on her cheeks.

There was no question that some poor mustang was no longer out galloping over the plains; its hide had been pulled, stretched, and distended into a jacket that dripped with a generous shower of fringe. The woman was weighed down with enough turquoise jewelry to make one suspect she'd raided an Indian reservation.

An icy smile, taut as a brand new rubber band, informed me this wasn't going to be easy. "Sorry. But only registered guests are allowed in this area. Why don't you tell me who you are, and exactly what it is you're doing here?"

Hmm . . . I wondered what had given me away. Probably the fact that I wasn't toting a loaded bazooka under one arm, while dragging a dead buck through the place.

"I'm here to see Mr. Krabbs," I politely responded.

Her eyes stayed on me like a smart bomb.

I waited a beat, and then pretended to take notice of something over the woman's shoulder. She glanced around, and I made a quick feint to the left, followed by a fast dodge to the right, but my opponent nimbly blocked my Texas two-step with a simple shift of her hips. All this gal needed was a helmet and the Dallas Cowboys would scramble to sign her up for their defensive line.

Big Red glared, silently informing me that she didn't appreciate my under-handed tactics. "I'm Mr. Krabbs' personal assistant, and I know for a fact that he doesn't have any appointments today. So unless you want to tell me what this is about, you don't stand a chance in hell of making it any further." She folded her arms across an ample Texas range of chest.

I crossed my own arms in the hope of sending back a similar message. "I'm a special agent with the U.S. Fish and Wildlife Service, and this is official business."

"All the more reason you need an appointment," she countered. "Mr. Krabbs isn't partial to being bothered by trespassing federal agents."

I was about to hit Big Red with a return volley when a shock of white hair, sculpted into an Elvis pompadour, floated into view. Perched on top was a zebra-striped ball cap with a slap-happy elk embroidered in a bull's-eye.

The cap's owner was a dead ringer for one of my very own favorite, finger-licking trademarks—the legendary Colonel Sanders. Except this Texas cowboy was casually attired in jeans, a red checkered shirt, and a pair of pointy lizard skin boots handtooled with red, white, and blue American bald eagles.

My western colonel continued to amble toward us, having apparently taken no notice of the skirmish. He stumbled slightly as he passed me, so that his arm deliberately brushed against my chest.

"Howdy there, miss," he drawled in a voice as smooth as aged bourbon, his cornflower blue eyes twinkling.

Wow! A cowboy who didn't call me "ma'am." Just goes to show, the older I get, the easier I am to impress. Gut instinct told me this was the guy I was after.

"Mr. Krabbs?" I'd decided not to deck him for the 'accidental' quickie feel, since he'd called me "miss," but the over-the-hill Don Juan kept right on strolling past. Hey! What did he think I was, some easy case of hit-and-run?

I whirled around only to have Big Red cut me off at the pass.

"I believe I already said Mr. Krabbs won't be able to see you today," she said between clenched teeth.

"Well, that's too bad—because today is just perfect for me." I turned sideways and body-slammed Big Red, shoving her out of my way.

I sprinted down the hall, but my colonel was nowhere in sight. I shoved open the lodge door and dashed outside, with Twinkle Toes hot on my heels.

Krabbs had already climbed into one of the motorized zebras, and started its snorting engine. This was no time to worry about manners. I made a mad dash for the Jeep, jumped inside, and set my fanny on the seat beside him.

Krabbs instinctively pulled back in surprise. The next instant, his mustache twitched in delight and his eyes lit up like a pair of sparkling Christmas balls.

"I gotta tell you, Cupcake: I got me a wife. But if that don't bother you none, maybe we can work something out."

I was about to respond, when my redheaded shadow beat me to the punch.

"Don't say another word, F.U.! The woman's a goddamn fed!" Big Red screamed at the top of her lungs, her fringe shaking in an out-of-control hula.

Jeez! It wasn't as if she needed to yell; the two of us were sitting right here. And what was the term 'F.U.' supposed to be? A polite abbreviation for a curse word?

Krabbs leaned across my chest and yelled back, "What's that you say? She's a vet?" He picked up my hand and stroked it. "Well, we already have one of those, but I'm sure we can find something else for you to do around here. I know of at least one thing that could use some tending to," he added, giving my fingers a squeeze.

Big Red scurried over to the driver's side of the Jeep, where she bent down and placed a finger behind each of his ears. It took a moment before I realized she wasn't tickling his fancy, but boosting the volume on a pair of old-fashioned hearing aids.

"Goddammit! I said she's a fed! This woman's here to nail your ass to the wall." By now, her blush had turned from "Like a Virgin" pink, to "Madder Than Hell" red.

Krabbs slapped her hands away in annoyance. "What the hell are you talking about, Velma? Why, this gal was just coming on to me! We were beginning to get all nice and cozy."

Krabbs started to scoot closer, then jerked back as if having received an electrical shock. "Which is why you got here just in the nick of time," he continued, his tone turning unexpectedly gruff. "You know how I'd hate for the missus to think anything improper might have been going on between us."

Though his eyes remained glued on Velma, his fingers glided over to me in an easily interpreted dance. He followed that up with a sneeze, which allowed him to turn his head and throw me a sly wink.

"I believe I got me a tissue around here somewhere." Krabbs fumbled about and then made a dive down toward my legs.

I deftly pushed him away with an arm. "*Gesundheit!*" I warned in stern reprimand.

I wondered if there was room for two more heads on the Happy Hunting Ranch's wall. "Mr. Krabbs, I'm Rachel Porter with the U.S. Fish and Wildlife Service, and I'm here about a call I received. There's been a report that a number of monkeys were killed on your ranch, and that the bodies are in your possession."

"Monkeys? Hell's bells! What in tarnation are you talking about, gal? That's the most ridiculous thing I've ever heard. No hunter in his right mind would fork over a plug nickel to gun one of those miserable things down."

Krabbs gave an involuntary shudder, as if an invisible monkey's paw had grabbed him by the scruff of the neck. "Hell, they're nothing but goddamn filthy critters, all full of germs and stuff. Here at the Happy Hunting Ranch we only present the best, top-notch, grade-A wildlife to be shot."

It was nice to know the man had his standards. "I'd still like to take a look around the grounds. Nothing personal, but when this kind of call comes in, it's my duty to check it out," I calmly responded.

"That's nothing but a big ol' pile of cow patties!" Krabbs grumbled. "You know yourself that monkeys aren't any good for mounting on a wall. And nobody's gonna eat the damn things with all that AIDS crap going around." Krabbs' hand wandered up to his cap, where his fingers idly caressed the embroidered rump of Happy Hunting's trademark elk. "Tell you what. You forget this nonsense and I'll give you a hat just like mine. How's that sound?"

Now, *there* was a bribe for you. "Tempting as that is, I'll go for the guided tour," I informed him.

"You don't have to let her do that, F.U.!" Velma fumed. Her fingers tightened on the driver's side window ledge as if she were about to rip off the door. "She knows damn well this is private property. Which means that if little Miss Busybody wants to nose around, she'd better have herself a search warrant."

Krabbs gave her hand an approving slap, followed by a pat on the cheek. "By golly, honeybunch here is right! But that's what I pay this heifer the big bucks for."

Velma blushed, and her lips trembled slightly.

"So now, tell me. Have you got yourself one of those

hide-and-seek papers she's talking about?" He flashed a wide smile, displaying receding gums.

I had about as much likelihood of getting a search warrant from the local court as Krabbs had of receiving an award from the Humane Society. "I don't see why there should be any problem with my taking a look around the place. Unless you have something to hide, that is."

Krabbs picked up an empty bullet shell casing near the gear shift, and popped it into his mouth. He rolled the object around with his tongue while he thought the situation over.

"Don't get me wrong. It's not that I've got anything to hide; it's just that I don't see what's in this for me. Making things all nice and easy for you, I mean. Tell you what. You show me yours and I'll show you mine," he suggested flirtatiously. The metal casing clacked against his teeth.

Cute. If this was the game he wanted to play, I was more than happy to oblige. "Let me put it this way, Mr. Krabbs. I'll get a search warrant, if that's what you want. The only difference will be that I'll take the place apart inch by inch when I come back, since you'll have had plenty of time to hide whatever evidence there is. And trust me, I'm very good when it comes to finding what it is that I'm looking for," I archly warned.

Krabbs nearly swallowed his bullet. "Who the hell do you think I am? Saddam Hussein, running around concealing stuff?"

"No," I answered. "I think you're a man who's smart enough to let me poke around as discreetly as possible, in order not to rile up your guests."

Krabbs slowly rolled the shell in his mouth once more before spitting it into the palm of his hand. "I've decided I like you. You've got gumption, gal." I caught his eye roaming down over my form before coming back up to meet my gaze. "Besides, you're pretty good looking for a fed. You can call me F.U.," he said, with a wink. "It's short for Frederick Ulysses, which is just too damned big a mouthful to say." He threw the zebra's throttle into drive.

"Where are you going?" Velma asked in alarm, firmly holding on to the jeep with both hands.

Krabbs looked over at me.

"I'd like to examine the taxidermy hut," I firmly replied.

"Then that's where we're headed," he answered.

Velma pulled her tangerine lips back to reveal a set of choppers which gnashed together with the fury of an attack dog. "I've got to warn you, F.U. You let some Fish and Wildlife agent come prancing in here to do as she pleases, and I guarantee she'll keep coming back demanding more."

"Hell, that's what I'm counting on," F.U. chuckled. He gave Big Red a pinch on the cheek, and then pried her fingers off the door. "Don't you worry, honeybunch. I've got everything under control."

As we pulled away, Velma's ill-tempered vibes were as sharp as a set of Ginsu steak knives being flung at my back. Krabbs' Detroit zebra countered Velma's psychic attack by throwing back a small storm of gravel.

Three

West Texas is a land of wide, open spaces, most of it privately owned. Throw in the warm climate, and a ride through a hunting ranch is somewhat like being in Africa. Except that the wild animals you encounter on the African veldt don't act as if they've been munching on Prozac.

"I've got 15,000 acres here, Cupcake. If you like, we can spend all day together and mosey through every single one of them," F.U. obligingly offered.

"Since I don't have all day, let's just head right to the taxidermy hut." I already envisioned Velma scurrying back inside the lodge and calling every available worker. It wouldn't have surprised me to find the hut in pristine condition by the time we arrived there.

Krabbs steered our mechanical zebra to the right and headed down a long, bumpy dirt path. We finally arrived at a game-proof wire fence that stood a good ten feet high. A weatherbeaten wooden sign bearing the name *Hatari* hung over its gate. Krabbs drove up to a push button alarm pad mounted on a cement pole and punched in a numerical code. The gate compliantly swung open, then automatically slammed shut behind us.

"Wait till you see this place. These critters here lead

a nice, peaceful life, just as if they were in a zoo," F.U. said, his eyes getting all misty.

Right. Until somebody picks them off like ducks in a shooting gallery.

I spotted a herd of doe-eyed Thompson gazelles which looked like a bunch of extras hired for a remake of *Bambi*. The gang didn't run away as we passed. Gathered around a feeder, they were intently chowing down on mounds of cracked corn. I noticed that a timer controlled the food supply. By the look of it, this place was more of a petting zoo than a ranch. Where else would you find "wild" animals lured to baited areas at designated times, clearly expecting to receive a hand-out?

"Now, look at that. What could be a sweeter sight?" F.U. sighed. "I got me forty different kinds of horned and antlered herbivores from all over the world, living on fifteen fenced-in pastures. Each pasture is a thousand acres of paradise."

"And I wager the other fourteen pastures have feeding stations exactly like these," I replied.

"You bet your boots they do!" Krabbs confirmed. "Hell, we don't get the prices we charge for keeping a bunch of scrawny critters running around the place!"

We exited *Hatari* and drove through another coded gate to enter a pasture designated *Out of Africa*. The main attraction in this section of paradise was a herd of long-maned wildebeest furiously jostling for space around giant bales of hay. They had no fear of people either, probably because they'd been hand-raised in captivity. It must be quite a feat for some guy with an automatic rifle the size of a small cannon to drive out and blast a couple of these critters off the face of the earth.

"Why does the ranch have fifteen different gated areas?" I asked, curious if there was a practical reason, or if Krabbs nad merely come up with fifteen different cute names.

"It's because I run this place like a science." F.U. arched a fluffy white eyebrow that would have filled Colonel Sanders with envy. "This way I know exactly which animals are where, at all times." His fingers idly plucked a stray hair from his goatee. "Say, I have a hunter who's got a hankering to shoot a water buck, but doesn't want to take all day doing it. Well, I know we got us a record-class critter grazing over in *Kilimanjaro Pass* that's worth thirty-five hundred smackers. I'll have Dr. Dick geared up and out on the range before he's finished sipping his first Diet Coke. By the time he's halfway through his second, a guide will have tracked the critter down and set it in Dr. Dick's gunsite, ready for him to shoot. Then the good doctor can move on to bagging himself the next critter on his list, if he wants."

Talk about efficient. "You must get some real conservationists coming to the ranch," I remarked caustically.

"You betcha!" F.U. eagerly agreed. "Every trophy hunter out here is a real conservationist at heart. Hell, they want to make sure there are plenty of animals around, so that they can come back and shoot more of them next year."

I was tempted to comment, when something off in the distance caught my eye. An adult blackbuck antelope stood framed against the solid blue Texas sky, its luxurious coat as deeply rich as a pool of dark chocolate. The Zorro of the antelope world, the creature had mask-like rings of snowy alabaster encircling its eyes. But what made this blackbuck so highly prized was the impressive thirty-inch horns which flared out in a V-shape, their spiral twists braided tightly as corkscrews. Though I knew blackbucks were among the fastest animals on earth, it quickly became apparent that this particular antelope wasn't about to go anywhere.

The creature buckled down onto its knees while frantically twisting its head, where a convoluted tangle of wire was snarled around the buck's magnificent horns. The critter's front legs were entwined in another jumble of razor thin metal. The sun's liquid fire highlighted one more slender, lethal strand: a single loop was coiled around the antelope's neck in a hangman's noose, where it wound tighter and tighter with each convulsive jerk. Another few minutes of this and the distraught animal would be strangled.

"Stop!" I cried in terror.

But either Krabbs' hearing aids were on the blink, or his mind was elsewhere. I threw my left leg over the gear shift, slammed my foot down hard on the brake, and switched off the ignition.

F.U. reacted by snatching my leg and pulling me toward him. "See that? I just knew there was a spark 'bout to burst into flames between us!" he exclaimed.

"For God sakes, look over there!" I commanded, grabbing hold of his chin and pointing his face toward the buck.

"Holy NRA! That don't seem good." Krabbs quickly reached for his walkie talkie and pushed the speaker button. "Velma, this is Papa Bear," he called, holding the unit close to his mouth.

The reply was a dense wall of static. I was ready to leap out of the jeep and cut the creature loose myself, but I knew the buck would only hurt himself further in his ensuing panic.

"For chrissakes, Velma! Stop your sulking and pick this thing up!" Krabbs shouted.

Apparently Velma was giving Krabbs a dose of some good old-fashioned silent treatment.

"Goddammit," F.U. muttered to himself. He paused, took a deep breath, and brought the mouthpiece to his lips once more. "Please, sugarplum. This is really important," he cooed, his fist quietly pounding on the steering wheel. "I know I forgot about Secretary's Day this year. So, how's about you and me having a nice lunch together later on? Just the two of us. Only there's this one itty bitty thing I gotta take care of first."

"Are we going out someplace nice, or do we have to stay here?" Velma's voice crackled through the air with all the gentility of a rocket launcher. "And while we're at it, let's get this cleared up once and for all. I'm not your damned secretary. I'm your personal assistant."

"Whatever you say, puddin'."

"All right, then. What is it that you want?" Velma grudgingly relented.

"I need someone in the northwest quadrant of *Out of Africa*, on the double. We got us one of them blackbuck males all twisted up in some damn loose wire, and the sonuvabitch is down on the ground." F.U. was about to hang up, when he thought better of it. "Thank you, sugarplum," he added.

"You're welcome. I'll make reservations at Chez Bull 'n' Bear for noon. Over and out," she brusquely replied and hung up.

In less than four minutes, a black and white striped "jeepra" came hurtling across the Texas plains and headed straight for the injured buck. It came to a halt about twenty yards away from where the animal knelt, with its neck awkwardly contorted and its hind quarters rearing up in the air.

The vehicle's door flew open and a man bolted out holding a .22 caliber rifle with a stainless steel spotting scope attached to its barrel. I pushed open my own door, determined to stop him.

"Where are you going?" F.U. asked, latching on to the back of my jeans.

"Where do you think? I'm going to stop that idiot from shooting the buck!" I roared.

"Whoa! Hold on there a minute!" Krabbs cried, grabbing my arm as I was halfway out the door. "He's not gonna kill the critter; what he's got there is a dart gun. He's gotta immobilize the buck so he can cut it loose. Besides, you can't get out of the Jeep. None of the hunters do—it's too damned risky out there," he reprimanded.

"You've got to be kidding," I didn't bother to hold back my laughter. "You consider these animals out here to be dangerous?"

"No," Krabbs snapped. "What's treacherous are all the damn rattlers crawling around this place. We're right next to *Rattlesnake Run*."

I followed his finger in the direction of the next fenced-in pasture.

"Anyway, you don't really think I'd have that critter shot, now, do you?" he asked. His tone turned coy, and his hand snaked over toward me. "I can charge a client four thousand bucks for that privilege. That's how I make my living, Cupcake."

I picked up his hand and firmly placed it back on the wheel. "You know what I've decided?" I asked, keeping my tone as softly seductive as his own.

"No. What's that?" F.U. asked hopefully.

"That unless you keep your hands to yourself and stop calling me Cupcake, I might have to use that dart gun on you." I hopped out of the Jeep, more than willing to take my chance with the rattlers, when the crack of a rifle shattered the ranch's orchestrated sense of serenity. I caught sight of the red-tailed dart lodged solidly in the creature's rump, and breathed a sigh of relief. F.U. hadn't lied to me, after all.

The buck's hind quarters gave way as the critter crumpled down to the ground. I walked over to where he lay drifting on a cloud of muscle relaxant. The ranch hand arrived soon after, toting a tool box along with his dart gun. He dropped both and knelt beside the dazed antelope.

The man was as ruggedly built as a linebacker, with hands the size of bear paws. His thick mane of brown hair was loosely pulled into a long ponytail, matched by a beard that spread like urban sprawl over his lower face. Grizzly Adams paid me no mind as he flicked open the tool kit and pulled out a wire cutter. Then he bent over the buck and gently lifted a thin metal strand. He proceeded to cut each one, being ever so careful not to nick a single hair on the sleeping antelope.

"Is the buck going to be all right?" I asked in a whisper, afraid anything louder might somehow break the spell.

But Grizzly Jr. didn't speak, intent on his task. He removed the metal wire on the buck's horns and neck, then carefully clipped the jumbled fencing from its legs. Once finished, he checked for superficial cuts, as well as any deeper, camouflaged wounds on the blackbuck's hide.

"He'll be fine in a few days. He just needs time to recover," he said, in a powerful, deep bass.

"You mean you're actually going to give him a reprieve before bringing someone out here to gun him down for his horns?"

I instantly regretted my remark as a pair of piercing brown eyes pivoted in my direction, their gaze as intense as a kettle on low boil. The man didn't need to say a word; he burned with the ardor of someone on a mission,

like a newly anointed John the Baptist. Either that, or
the guy was a closet serial killer. F.U.'s Jeep pulled up
behind us, drawing an invisible curtain over Grizzly's
gaze. The ranch hand turned his attention back to the
antelope.

"How's it look? My champion buck is going to survive, isn't he?" F.U.'s voice sailed toward us, filled with
concern.

"He ought to be fine," the ranch hand responded in a
voice as flat and empty as a patch of bare desert.

"That's just great," F.U. replied, pulling the jeep
around in front. "But we'll give him a day or two to rest
up anyway," he announced magnanimously. "After all,
we believe in fair chase here at the Happy Hunting
Ranch. Isn't that right, Dan?"

Grizzly's gaze captured mine and the curtain fluttered.
"Sure thing, Mr. Krabbs," Dan responded coolly. His
focus settled again on the dozing antelope. "There's no
need for the two of you to wait around. I'll stay here
until the sedative wears off, just to make sure a coyote
doesn't come by and get him. Wouldn't want you to
lose your investment."

"Let's get going then," F.U. cheerfully responded.
"The other thing I don't need is for some damned snake
to take a nip at this Fish and Wildlife agent I got here."
Krabbs motioned to me. "So, why don't you hop on
back into the Jeep and we'll mosey along?"

Grizzly's head never made a move, but I noticed his
eyes slide my way. I didn't care if he was an Elmer
Gantry wannabe or the Son of Sam dressed up as a cow-
poke; I wasn't about to let this guy spook me.

"My name's Rachel Porter," I said, holding my hand
out toward him.

Dan bent down and placed the wire cutter inside the
toolbox before standing back up to face me.

"I'm afraid I didn't catch your full name," I prompted.

He hesitated, the grip of his hand taking stock of my own. I was surprised to discover that his skin wasn't as rough and weathered as I'd expected.

Grizzly stared at me with a tinge of apprehension before finally responding. "The name's Dan Kitrell."

There was something odd about the man. Perhaps he was on the lam, which would help to explain his uncertainty. For all he knew, I was using the identity of a Fish and Wildlife agent as a guise, when in reality I was actually a bounty hunter.

"We'd better get a move on. We still gotta make it to the taxidermy hut, what with Velma waiting for me back at the lodge," Krabbs anxiously coaxed.

Kitrell dropped my hand and turned his back without another word.

I rejoined Krabbs and we tore through *Out of Africa*, edging along *Rattlesnake Run* before gaining entree into the fenced-in area named *Dr. Livingston, I Presume*.

"Has Kitrell worked for you long?" I asked.

Our jeepra passed a group of giant African eland that started to follow us down the dirt road, refusing to believe we wouldn't play Pied Piper and feed them.

F.U. chuckled at the sight as he pressed down hard on the gas pedal, leaving the herd in our dust. "I hired Kitrell a while ago. Not much in the way of references, but he's a hard worker—and in my book, that's what counts. Why?" he asked, turning to catch my expression. "Something about him you don't like?"

I shook my head. "No. Just curious."

Krabbs tugged on the brim of his cap, causing his embroidered elk to give a quick wiggle. Then he pointed straight ahead. "There you go. That's our taxidermy hut."

The plain wooden building was so nondescript it

could have been anything from the Unabomber's cabin to a caretaker's lodge. The giveaway was the cable line stretching across its pathway: hanging upside down from the heavy wire was the carcass of an Axis deer. Next to it hung a Corsican ram and a North American elk.

"Those are some of the record-class critters a couple of our clients shot this very morning," F.U. bragged. "Randy should be along pretty soon to gut and get them ready for posterity."

"Then you do your own trophy work here on the premises?" I inquired.

Krabbs nodded. "Yep. We like to think of ourselves as a full-service operation. What I find is that our customers always tend to feel a sense of regret at the end of a hunt, as if there's something that's missing."

My guess was that *something* were a few formerly living, breathing four-legged creatures.

"Think of all those critters we saw on our way over here, and how beautiful they are," Krabbs waxed poetic. "Well, that's what our clients want to take back home with them. A little bit of nature that they can appreciate and remember forever."

I looked at the dead elk, which hung upside down by its hooves with its tongue hanging out. "How about just letting your clients buy a videotape of them feeding the antelope?" I suggested.

F.U. snorted. "That's a good one. No, what I mean is that everyone wants to show off a beautiful trophy of what they've paid good money to shoot. That's what hunting trips are all about: man proving his dominance over the four-legged beasts of the kingdom."

I silently questioned who the civilized creatures really were and which was the brute.

We parked and skirted around the lifeless carcasses to head inside the cabin, which was filled with critters of a very different sort. Row upon row of animal "manni-kens" stood as stiffly posed as department store models, fiberglass forms representing every type of species that was to be found on the Happy Hunting Ranch.

There was something oddly zombie-like about the molds, which ranged from life-size figures to truncated busts of shoulders and heads. They were as smooth and featureless as newly hatched pods from *Invasion of the Body Snatchers.* Some partially finished models, tightly cocooned in tanned hides, patiently waited in a corner for a few finishing touches.

But there was far more. Packed inside large bottles, glass eyes glared out at me like a prize-winning collec-tion of ghoulish marbles, their irises a spectrum of colors in a variety of shapes and sizes. Other containers were filled with an assortment of plastic tongues that could have been sold as souvenirs at a Kiss concert.

Another group of jars held nothing but teeth in a vi-sual ode to lost and found dentures, while boxes over-flowed with claws formerly belonging to black bears and mountain lions. The pièce de resistance was the large blood-stained table in the middle of the room. I was beginning to feel as if I'd stepped into some crazed un-dertaker's cellar—only this one was brimming with an excess of grisly animal parts.

Come into my parlor and let me dismember you, whis-pered the taxidermist to the nosy Fish and Wildlife agent.

"This here is like a real artist's studio," F.U. boasted. He walked over to a cabinet and flung open its doors to display an impressive array of seeming S&M instru-ments. "Here we've got us some scalpels and tail skin-ners, along with lip tucking tools. And I believe these are ear openers. Or maybe they're a pair of stretching pliers." He picked up an implement in each hand and began a mock duel, in a charade of a Punch and Judy show. "Fact is, we've got just about every kind of skinning and defatting knife that's made."

"What about the original skulls and skeletons from the animals that are shot? Why don't I see those here?" I inquired.

"Because we don't use that stuff. The real critters would just get bugs and smell, or rot. This way, the animal stays looking good forever. Hell, I've even had husbands ask if they could haul their wives in here and get 'em done: *'Keep 'em looking hot, keep 'em looking young, and while you're at it, get their traps wired shut,'* " he added with a chortle.

"That's probably just frustration on their part after their Viagra didn't work," I responded.

F.U. snickered and threw me a wink. "Well, that's something I wouldn't know nothing about. Fact is, I'm still looking for a gal who's woman enough to handle me. But for those men who've got problems, we can always build 'em a pair of these."

He tossed a fiberglass testicle form my way.

"Why don't you keep the balls in your court?" I pitched them back to him. Turning away, I began to poke around a stack of boxes.

"You ain't gonna find nothing in there except for a big old pile of furs," F.U. volunteered. "But let me know if you spot something you like, and I'll see what we can do about it."

"Is that a bribe?" I inquired.

"Hell, no. Just a neighborly offer," F.U. said, throwing up his hands in mock surrender.

I finished digging through a box stacked with the skins of Himalayan tahrs, and moved on to one spilling over with the heavy coats of Mongolian yaks.

"Oh, I think we can do better than them old things if

you're looking to find yourself a fancy coat," F.U. chuckled.

I spotted a burlap sack hidden behind some boxes in one of the corners and quickly moved toward it.

"What the hell?" Krabbs muttered in annoyance, and started to follow.

"If you don't mind, I'd rather you stay where you are and let me take a look first," I instructed.

"Listen here, missy. Don't you forget that I'm letting you do this without one of those warrants." The bourbon edge to his voice was turning decidedly sour.

The fact that his Texas charm had taken a sudden dive made me all the more suspicious. I pushed the boxes out of my way. There was no question that something was inside the sack; the rough material bulged, as lumpy as an old mattress. Even more alarming were the dark stains leaking through the fabric. The fluid felt sticky to the touch.

A sick flutter careened in my stomach, bringing what little was left of my Pop-Tart popping back up into my throat. I couldn't decide whether to rip open the sack and check out its contents, or cut to the chase and give Krabbs a head start before making him the target of my own private hunt. My mind reeled at the thought of hunters who would not only partake in killing monkeys, but then have them stuffed and mounted. I held my breath, steeled my nerves, and pulled the burlap bag wide open.

The first thing to catch my eye was the feathery white tail of a colobus monkey, its limbs entwined in the thick, red-maned ruff of a golden lion tamarin. I reached in and a wave of relief hit me, along with a generous dose of astonishment. The fur I was feeling wasn't real, but a cheap synthetic. This had to be some sort of sick joke, with me as the butt.

Out came a cuddly ring-tailed lemur, closely followed

by a capuchin with cute black button eyes. If I were a child, I'd have thought Christmas had come early. But as an adult, I was growing more furious by the minute. Orangutans and squirrel monkeys sailed through the air. A macaque nailed me with a silly grin, followed by a roly poly gorilla. I pressed on through the sea of soft bodies until my fingers finally hit rock bottom. They wrapped around the last wet, furry limb to emerge with a jolly toy chimp dripping with red paint.

"Is this your idea of fun? Exactly what are you pulling here, besides trying to make me look like a fool?" I angrily demanded.

"Whoa! Now, hold on there a minute, Cupcake. I'm as much a victim here as you are," Krabbs protested.

"That's it! That's the last time you call me Cupcake!" I looked around for something I could use to pummel the man.

F.U. derailed me by letting out an angry yelp, while stamping the heels of his "God Bless America" bald eagle boots. "Goddammit, I know what this is! It's those hare-brained animal rights nuts at it again!" he crowed.

A trickle of red paint had dripped off the chimp, forming a pool of make-believe blood. "What are you talking about?" I asked skeptically.

Krabbs pulled his cap off his head and began to beat it against his leg, as if to give the embroidered elk a good spanking. "There's a few of them troublemakers that act up around here every once in a while. Just a coupla weeks ago they dressed up like Bambis and laid down outside the gate, doing their darndest to stop a group of hunters from coming in."

F.U. grabbed hold of a rag and tried to wipe the paint off my arm, then walked over to the boxes that were piled up next to the sack.

"Aw, goll darn it! Wouldn't you know they'd have to go and throw paint in here, too!"

"Do you have any idea who they are?" I still wasn't sure whether to believe him.

Krabbs continued to gaze at the mess. "Yeah, I do. Hell, I sure hope Randy can clean up this stuff."

I was surprised Krabbs wasn't demanding that the intruders be lynched at the very least, if not gassed, shot, and electrocuted. "I take it that you intend to press charges." Aside from trespassing, who'd ever gotten in here had thoroughly damaged some very expensive skins.

But F.U. deliberately ignored my question. "God knows, I've done my level best to try and make 'em understand that what I'm doing here is helping to save wildlife. Hell, if this place didn't make the money it does, I'd be tempted to sell it off to a developer who'd slap up shopping malls and yuppie ranchettes faster than you could lasso a steer. For chrissakes, *I'm* the damned environmentalist around here!"

I already knew Krabbs well enough to suspect there was a practical reason for his wanting to protect the identity of the intruders.

"I'm going to have to file a report on this," I bluffed. "I'll also be starting a formal investigation, which means any arrest charges will show up on the perpetrators' permanent records." F.U. flinched. "Unless you care to cooperate and tell me who's responsible, of course. Then I'll be able to skip the process."

"Aw, hell and tarnation!" Krabbs exploded. "It's my idiot son and that low-class, no-class girlfriend of his."

Sometimes you just had to laugh over life's little ironies. "Your son's an animal rights activist?"

F.U. glanced around as if afraid someone might hear. "Can you believe it?" he groused. "My own flesh and blood turning on me. I imagine it's something I must have done wrong when he was a young colt growing up," he contritely admitted in Oprah-like fashion. "I should have taken him out hunting on the ranch more often, is probably what it is."

Yeah. There's always nothing like a little blood sport to help bond a father and son. F.U. suddenly caught a peek at his watch and took a White Rabbit hop.

"We gotta get outta here! I'm gonna be late for my lunch!" Krabbs high-tailed it outside.

By the time I made it through the front door, he'd already hauled ass back to the jeep and was waving for me to hurry. Just the thought of Velma's wrath had the man quaking in his boots. I wondered if I could pay her to give me lessons.

"I'm curious. Where do you get most of your animals from?" I asked upon joining Krabbs in the jeepra.

F.U. turned toward me with a grin licking at his lips, as he drove like a bat out of hell. "Tell me something first. Do you still think I'm such a bad fella?" he asked coquettishly.

"Now, why would I ever think that?" I parried, playing the game to get my answer.

Krabbs pushed his lower lip out in a mock pout. "'Cause you suspected me of pulling some sort of funny business with shooting a bunch of monkeys. But now that you know I didn't, what do you say? Do you and me stand any kinda chance?"

"I've got to tell you, F.U., I'm just not that kind of woman," I demurely replied, folding my hands in my lap. "First of all, you're a married man. Second, there's Velma to consider." I figured that ought to scare some sense into him.

F.U. reached over and patted my hand. "Don't you worry. I'll figure something out."

So much for playing the sweet, old-fashioned girl. "That's great. In the meantime, you were going to fill me in on who supplies you with animals," I prompted.

"Well, some of them we breed right here on the ranch," Krabbs replied, skirting the issue.

"And the rest?" I persisted.

"What do you want to know for, anyway?" Krabbs suspiciously countered.

"Because I think it's important that we have an open and honest relationship." I hoped the trap would prove vague enough to ensnare him.

F.U. visibly softened. "Well, just between you and me, I'm working with a dealer by the name of Admiral Maynard these days."

There was no need for me to ask where Admiral Maynard got *his* supply. The vast majority of critters gunned down on hunting ranches are the very same animals which folks flock to visit in zoos—a dirty little secret that's been going on for years.

The majority of zoos produce a flood of surplus critters. The more cute babies there are, the higher attendance records go up. The problem is, there's only so much room at each zoo for any one particular species. So guess where the older animals end up getting dumped?

A Noah's ark of creatures are continually hauled off to be sold on the auction block. Documents are changed to hide a critter's origin and gender, while a minimal papertrail assures that the sales of everything from lions to water buffalo are nearly impossible to trace. Add it together, and you begin to get a picture of the well-oiled network dealing in the zoo surplus trade.

"You know, I got me a little chalet up in Lake Tahoe. Maybe you'd like to use it to go skiing sometime," F.U. suggested.

"No, thanks," I demurred. "I'm not one for cold weather."

"Tell you what, then. I usually head to Vegas once a month." He playfully bumped his shoulder against mine. "I got a little bit of a weakness when it comes to playing the slots. What say you and me take a trip on up there together?"

I shot him down with a shake of my head. "I used to live in Las Vegas. Since then, I never go near the place."

"In that case, how about I set you up right here at the ranch with what we call our 'Get Acquainted Hunt'? You get to go out and shoot an aoudad, a mouflon, and one Texas dall ram. Usually we charge ten thousand dollars for that package. But for you it would be free, of course." F.U.'s cornflower blues sparkled.

"To tell you the truth, I prefer my animals alive and kicking," I responded.

"Well heck, gal. Then all I've got left to offer is a well-paying job whenever you're ready. Same as I gave to one of your predecessors. He took me up on my offer, and let me tell you-me, that he's real happy about it too," F.U. confided.

Hold on a minute—back up there! "You've got a former Fish and Wildlife agent working here at the Happy Hunting Ranch?" I inquired in disbelief.

Krabbs grinned and gave my arm a little squeeze. "Now, don't you go getting all jealous. He's not here; he's working on a cattle ranch I own nearby, just over the border in New Mexico. Heck, maybe you even know him."

My mind went blank, unable to imagine who it could be. "What's his name?" I asked.

"Johnny Lambert. I hired him on for the job of ranch manager out at the Flying A. But don't you worry none—I'd keep you right here at Happy Hunting with me."

Johnny Lambert. The name sounded familiar. But no matter how hard I tried, I couldn't figure out why.

Four

I departed, leaving Krabbs to face his lunchtime rendezvous with Velma. It was time to head into El Paso and break the news of Timmy Tom's demise to Juan, his significant other, more commonly referred to as "Fat Boy."

El Paso is a city of contradictions, the main one being that it's not really part of Texas. Situated on the state's westernmost outskirts, the place is so isolated it's even in a different time zone. Nor is it totally Mexican in character, though its personality *is* more salsa than ketchup. El Paso is a completely different country with an identity all its own.

Forty-eight million cars travel on the city's main highway every year, but most of them keep driving right on past. If they bother to pause at all, it's usually only for gas, making El Paso the state's most glorified truck stop. What these travelers are missing is a canvas in progress—one whose personality is defined by its people.

El Paso's cast of characters covers a wide spectrum ranging from car thieves and smugglers, to godfearing church goers, bankers, and high-powered industrialists. The result is a spicy stew of the powerful and the powerless seething on a frontier border filled with mystery, magic and myth. Part militarized zone, part carnival, the place is a ticking time bomb in a land of the forgotten. In lots of ways, El Paso is the ultimate loner's hideaway. Which is probably the reason I felt comfortable here.

Since landing in El Paso, I'd tried my best to behave. Even I was surprised at the major attempt I was making to play by the rules these days. I'd gone so far as to sit and quietly listen while a bunch of pencil-pushing bureaucrats drummed the Service's mantra into my head.

Big cases, big problems. Little cases, little problems. No cases, no problems.

Otherwise known as the "if-there's-no-shit-it-won't-hit-the-fan" philosophy. It was hoped that I'd learn from my punishment, and so far, there hadn't been any upsets. Probably because nothing big had come along to kick over their apple cart yet. But I was beginning to tire of apples and starting to search for oranges.

I turned off I-10 and drove through El Paso until the Tortilla Curtain came into view. Then I swung a hard right onto Montestruc Street to enter the barrio called Little Chihuahua. My landmark was a warehouse adorned with the mural of a Mexican peasant weeping tears that formed the Rio Grande. Defined by narrow streets and even skinnier alleys, the neighborhood was filled with houses once painted as bright as children's *piñatas* but now faded and peeling. An array of colored bottles dangled off the battered fences surrounding each run-down dwelling. The local belief was that they helped prevent roaming dogs from peeing in people's yards. They looked like glistening charms on a chain link bracelet.

Timmy Tom's house had an aqua facade as lusterless as yesterday's hot internet stocks. I parked and let myself in through the gate. That action instantly set off a home-made alarm—the recording of an angry Chihuahua yapping at the top of its lungs. Fat Boy responded by sticking his head out the front window to investigate. He motioned me inside without a word.

I made my way past his collection of yard art. A couple of rickety grocery carts stood next to gnome-sized figures of all Seven Dwarfs; nearby was Mother Goose, along with Mary and her little lamb, closely tailed by Jack and Jill hauling their buckets. Statues of the Three Wise Men brought up the rear, their arms laden with dirty plastic flower pots. I ducked beneath a clothesline that drooped under the weight of Juan's blue jeans, and slipped in through the door.

There was no problem finding Fat Boy; all I had to do was follow the sound of music. It was obvious Juan had already received the bad news. His body, the size of a sports utility vehicle, was dressed in black from head to toe.

Most people fight the battle of the bulge at some point in their life. But Fat Boy had long ago zoomed past heavy to enter the realm of the enormous. Juan believed the fatter he was, the longer he'd live, and did whatever he could to nourish his condition. That fortitude was put to the test when he'd landed in the hospital after a bad car accident. It didn't matter that his jaw had been wired shut; by the time Juan was released, he still hadn't lost an ounce of fat. Rumor had it that he'd received a barrage of high-caloric liquids. I preferred to believe he'd managed to suck cheeseburgers down right through his straw.

Juan stood before me now with tears streaming down his face, and a wooden organ grinder hanging around his neck. Lola, his monkey, sat perched on his shoulder dressed in a somber black skirt.

"I'm an asshole from El Paso, but that don't get in my way. 'Cause I've learned to use a lasso, and I'm hopin' that'll pay off some day."

Juan's voice cracked as he cranked out the last few notes of music, then he wiped away a trail of tears. "That was Timmy Tom's favorite song. We wrote it together, and were gonna take it out on the road. I'd even been teaching Lola how to twirl a lasso for our show."

Juan pulled two Tootsie Rolls from his pocket and unwrapped them. Popping one in his mouth, he handed the other to Lola, who'd excitedly begun to squeal, swaying from side to side on his shoulder. She shoved one end in her mouth and frantically began gumming down on it. Lola was doing a hell of a job, for not having any teeth.

"I didn't have a choice. They had to come out!" Fat Boy whined when I'd first confronted him about her toothless state. "Timmy Tom said otherwise she'd bite someone for sure when we were out on tour, and we'd get sued for everything we own."

From what I could see, that amounted to Three Wise Men and a few fairytale characters who'd seen better days.

Fat Boy hastily slipped a second Tootsie Roll in his mouth, after glancing over to make sure Lola wasn't watching.

"We were gonna dress Lola up like a cowgirl for our tour," Juan said shakily. "You wanna see her outfit?"

I shook my head no, and Fat Boy burst into a loud wail.

"Maybe later," I relented.

But he wasn't in the mood to be consoled. "My life's ruined! We were even planning to cut an album. What am I going to do now?"

"Go solo?" I suggested helplessly.

Fat Boy surprised me by blowing his nose and agreeing. "Yeah, I'm considering that. After all, I still got Lola to think of."

So much for my stab at grief counseling; it was time to get down to business. "We need to talk, Juan. I don't know if anyone told you, but I'm the one who found Timmy Tom."

Fat Boy sank onto a couch whose upholstered red roses sagged beneath his bulk like a well-worn hammock. "Yeah, I know. The police called me. Jeez, Timmy Tom loved that cell phone." Juan broke into another round of tears.

"Timmy Tom had asked me to meet him early this morning near the Anapra Road. Do you have any idea why?" I asked, raising my voice over Juan's wail.

He shook his head and eased his pain with another Tootsie Roll. Lola shrieked in rage.

"All right. Then tell me what Timmy Tom was involved in these days. Had he gone back into smuggling?" I pressed.

Fat Boy shrugged his shoulders, and Lola clung onto his shirt for dear life. "Don't know that, neither," he responded noncommittally. But his left eye had begun to wander, which was a sure sign that he was lying.

"Don't fib to me, Juan," I snapped.

He handed Lola another Tootsie Roll, which only aggravated me more. I'd been secretly hoping he'd toss one to me.

"I'm not fibbing," Fat Boy stubbornly insisted.

"I know when you're jerking me around, Juan. What's the deal? Timmy Tom's lying on a slab over at Memorial Medical Center with Ma Bell climbing halfway down his throat. And it's not from choking on his phone bill, either. Don't you think he'd want you to tell me the truth so that I can find his killer?" I persisted, hoping to break him down.

Juan obstinately stuck out his jaw, the size of a pork butt. "How do you know when I'm fibbing, anyway?"

The last thing I'd ever do was tell him. Knowing Fat Boy, he'd resolve that problem by knocking out his eye and having a glass one implanted.

"I have my ways. Now, tell me what was going on."

"All I know is that Timmy Tom recently lost a big client," Fat Boy sulked.

"What kind of client?"

"What kind do you think?" Juan fired back. "It sure as hell wasn't a producer for organ grinder music."

"You know what I mean." I was tempted to punish him by taking away his candy. "What kind of animals was he dealing in?"

"Monkeys," Juan sullenly replied. "What else?"

I figured that had to be true; Timmy Tom had been a big believer in specializing. Besides, Fat Boy's eye hadn't moved.

"Let me see the paperwork on what he was bringing in and who the client was," I demanded.

"How should I know where Timmy Tom kept that kind of stuff?" Juan's fingers nervously played with the ends of his straggly hair, which were drawn back into what resembled the tail of a piglet.

"Because you were his bookkeeper, damn it!" Grieving was one thing; taking me for a fool was another. Especially since I'd already played that game this morning.

Fat Boy laboriously worked his rear end to the edge of the couch, one massive cheek at a time. Then, using his palms for leverage, he gave the cushions a hard shove and launched himself up on his feet. Lola hastily abandoned ship, springing into the air with the grace of an acrobat to land on top of the venetian blinds. Fat Boy shot her a reproachful look as he shuffled into the next room, huffing and puffing while grumbling under his breath.

I wondered what I could quickly snoop through, when something hit me on top of the head. Unless the sky was falling, it had to be Lola up to no good. I glanced down to spot a Tootsie Roll at my feet, as if in answer to my prayers. Then I looked at Lola, who grinned devilishly, with another candy roll gripped in her paws. She must have pilfered them without Fat Boy's knowledge. We removed the wrappers and simultaneously placed the candy in our mouths.

I was swallowing the remains when Fat Boy trudged back into the room with a suspicious glare. Clenched in his hand were some crumpled sheets of paper, their left sides ragged. I figured they must have been hurriedly ripped out of a loose-leaf notebook that probably contained all sorts of goodies.

Juan reluctantly handed me the pages, and I eagerly scanned them. A large number of spider and squirrel monkeys had been shipped from South America to the One World Zoo, but the facility had no address or phone number listed.

"Where can I find this place?"

Fat Boy's left eye started sliding like a greased pig at a 4-H Club fair. "How the hell should I know? You're the animal police. Aren't you supposed to have the drop on where all the zoos are?" He precariously lowered himself back into his seat.

"All the legit ones," I retorted.

"Well, as far as I know, that's exactly what One World is." Fat Boy's wandering eye picked up speed.

Right. And I beat out Cindy Crawford when it came to looking hot in a bathing suit. Timmy Tom must have gone back to smuggling monkeys for the pet trade to make a few quick bucks. Unless he'd been involved in something else illegal for which a nonexistent zoo made a dandy cover. Either way, I was smack up against a frustrating dead end.

"So why did One World Zoo drop Timmy Tom as a supplier, anyway?" I casually queried.

Fat Boy didn't reply, but pulled out more of his candy stash. The response was Pavlovian. Lola swooped down and balanced on Juan's head before scrambling onto his shoulder, and snatching the mini-log out of his hand. Then she cartwheeled over to the opposite end of the couch.

"I taught her to do that trick," Juan disclosed, unsure whether to be pleased or upset.

"We were talking about Timmy Tom," I reminded him.

Fat Boy discreetly extracted one last Tootsie Roll and shoved it into his mouth. "I think they wanted some animals that Timmy Tom couldn't get for them."

His eye hadn't budged an iota.

"And what kind would those have been?" I persisted.

"I don't remember anymore," Fat Boy pouted. But his eye told a different story. It swung to the side of his head, as if pulled by the force of a magnet.

I clearly wasn't going to get anything else out of him today. "Let me give you a piece of advice," I warned him. "It would benefit you to remember what Timmy Tom was involved in. In the meantime, don't get any funny ideas about picking up where he left off."

"Yeah, yeah. I'll keep that in mind, Porter," Juan irritably responded.

He turned back to the organ grinder, and cranked out the tune he'd been playing when I'd walked in.

"I'm an asshole from El Paso, but that's okay by me. 'Cause I got a gal named Lola, and she don't monkey around on me."

I let myself out the door.

* * *

It used to be that Fish and Wildlife agents worked out
of the official U.S. Fish and Wildlife building in El Paso.
Of course, once upon a time, there was also more than
one Fish and Wildlife agent assigned to the area. I drove
past the compound, where a mere two inspectors were
now housed. The Bridge of the Americas spanned the
nearby border, along with a legion of trucks and cars
that were backed up twenty-four hours a day, seven days
a week.

I continued driving along the Border Highway, with
the Rio Grande running through a steeply walled concrete ditch off to my left. During monsoon season heavy
rains turn this stretch into a raging, wet 'n' wild amusement ride. That's when people usually drown attempting
to cross the river from Mexico into El Paso. Yet in other
areas, the Rio Grande is little more than a pathetic brown
dribble, the majority of water sucked out for irrigation.

After jumping on to I-10, I crossed into New Mexico,
then swung onto Highway 136. Ahead was an eight-mile
stretch of desolate asphalt I'd dubbed the "ghost road,"
mainly because I was usually the only one on it.

These days my "office" was an eight-by-ten room in
Santa Teresa, New Mexico, in what had been coined a
"permanent-temporary" assignment. What was permanent was that there would never be a fax or copy machine at my disposal. The temporary part was that I'd
been given a laptop for the moment. For all intents and
purposes, I was a hermit in a one-person station. The
big boys in Washington must have reasoned that the
further they kept me away from any action, the less trouble I was bound to get into. So far, they'd gotten their
wish.

I flipped on my laptop and checked my messages.
Surprise, surprise. Once again, my boss in Albuquerque

hadn't liked the way I'd written up my latest case report and demanded that I re-do it. I suspected he considered this part of the indoctrination to mold me into the perfect government servant. Boy, was he ever in for a rude awakening.

I closed the laptop, slipped the chore onto my mental "to do" list, and stored it away until later. Right now, something more vital was calling for my attention: sitting in the corner of the room were a set of old files just begging to be examined. It was a task I'd dodged since my arrival, damned if I'd waste precious time dredging through someone else's outdated paperwork. Who knew it would suddenly become so appealing? What I was hoping to dig up was information on the prior Fish and Wildlife agent F.U. Krabbs had told me about—the mysterious Johnny Lambert.

The previous agent might not have done much in the way of investigative case work, but he'd certainly been diligent when it came to keeping his own J. Edgar Hoover–type file. Slumbering inside was a Xeroxed collection of dirt on just about everyone in the Service. I headed straight for the middle of the alphabet, and pulled out a well-thumbed folder.

Well, well. Wasn't this interesting? Johnny Lambert had been a busy man when it came to serving his government. He'd bounced from Border Patrol to the Forest Service before landing a job with U.S. Fish and Wildlife, where he'd maintained a low profile. That is, until the Service stumbled upon blatant evidence which couldn't be ignored: Lambert had received steady kickbacks from a local exotic boot company. In exchange, he'd turned a blind eye to truckloads of illegal caiman skins surreptitiously hauled in over the border. Not only had Johnny been amply rewarded in greenbacks for his cooperation; he'd obtained free expensive footwear to boot. I thought

back to my meeting with Krabbs this morning, and realized that probably wasn't all Lambert had been paid
off to ignore. I was starting to understand why a former
Fish and Wildlife agent would be in F.U.'s employ.

My stomach rumbled. Then it groaned, and kicked
and roared—a gentle reminder that it was nearly noon,
and all I was running on was one measly Pop-Tart
topped off by a Tootsie Roll. It was time to head home
for lunch.

I got onto the Camino Real highway, and followed
the Rio Grande as it hooked its way north. The noontime
desert air was as hot and pungent as a bowl of green
chiles, the light as crisply bright as freshly minted gold
coins. Off to my right lay enormous fields of Egyptian
cotton, thick with buds the color of buttery popcorn.

The cotton was replaced by acres of peppers, with an
occasional pick-up truck which sat decorated in garlands
of red, as if in preparation for an early Christmas. Sometimes the strands of dried chile peppers lay draped across
the vehicle's hood, while others snaked along fenders.
Most hung from a procession of tailgates, but all were
temptingly offered for sale. Eventually the peppers disappeared, and I landed in the tiny town of Mesilla.

I'd decided to forsake city living this time around,
choosing instead to reside where Pat Garrett had once
been sheriff and Billy the Kid spent time rotting away
in jail. The town was still filled with an array of outlaws
and vagabonds—only these days, they consisted of ec-
centrics and artists determined to make a killing on the
tourist trade.

I drove past the old San Albino Church and through
the heart of the plaza, where a local cop sat in his white
Chevy Corsica, snoozing a lazy day away. I turned down
Calle de Parian and parked in front of what I'd come to
call home—a squat chunk of adobe smaller than most

other places I'd lived, but still large enough for all my belongings. The rent was right, even if that was due to a certain amount of disrepair.

The owner, Sonny Harris, was a retired tracker with the Border Patrol, and one of my neighbors. He'd originally purchased the place with high hopes that his son would move in. The problem was, he'd never bothered to ask his offspring how he felt about it. Harris received his answer when Sonny Jr. promptly skedaddled as far away as he could get. According to my landlord, his son got exactly what he deserved: Sonny Jr. was now freezing his butt off up in the Alaskan tundra. I viewed his son's departure as my own good fortune. Not only was the place cheap, but it also came fully furnished. I'll admit I wasn't all that crazy about the decor, which could best be described as "Wild West extravaganza."

A morbid gallery of animal skulls lined the walls, while the lighting fixtures were gaudy plastic antler chandeliers. The Roy Rogers wagon wheel coffee table that had nearly broken up a relationship in the film *When Harry Met Sally* was now residing in my living room. The remainder of the furnishings were Early Cowboy/ Salvation Army.

The most challenging part of my day was trying to find anything remotely edible in the house. I confronted the refrigerator—an energy guzzling antique that guaranteed the freon police would knock on my door for helping to accelerate the destruction of the planet. My campaign to prod Sonny into buying a new fridge was a bust. Explaining the hazards of the growing hole in the ozone layer had only made him more ornery. As for the greenhouse effect, Sonny told me it sounded like a damned good idea: it gave God a chance to start over again from scratch.

I opened the refrigerator in the hope of scavenging

something partly digestible, and a muffled scream escaped my lips. Sitting on the top shelf was a large cow's head, freshly skinned and bloody. A pair of startled eyes stared unblinkingly at me while my gaze was drawn down to the tongue hanging out of its mouth, heavy as a sodden sponge.

I abruptly slammed the fridge shut, took a few deep breaths, and grabbed a dingy dish towel. After flinging the refrigerator door back open, I quickly threw the cloth over the head like a shroud, and carefully transferred it on to a plate. Then I rocketed out of the house with it.

The thing about having neighbors is that not only can you rarely choose them, but they also seem to come in odd pairs. I headed toward the adobe house on my left, where I high stepped through a desert garden doubling as a homeopathic medicine cabinet. My neighbor, affectionately known as "Tia Marta," was waiting in her doorway as if she'd been expecting me.

"Rachel, my dear! You have perfect timing. Amaya is just about to leave." Tia Marta gave me a light pinch on the cheek as I squeezed past her with the cow's head in my hands.

"Now, remember. You're to take those herbs only once a day. No more! Or you'll have that husband of yours dropping dead from too much desire," she teasingly advised her client.

Soon after moving in, I'd learned Tia Marta was one of the most renowned curanderas in the entire Southwest. She was part healer and part psychic hot line, with a large dash of Dr. Joyce Brothers thrown in. Over one hundred true believers gathered at her house every day, eagerly clamoring for her services.

A preconceived notion of what she looked like had taken seed in my mind before I'd even met the woman: plainly dressed, with a mane of silky, white hair meticulously pinned up in a bun. Then of course, there was the walking stick she'd need in order to get around. And definitely, no make-up would sully the skin of my southwestern Mother Teresa. Boy, had I ever been wrong.

Tia Marta jumped out at the world as if she'd sprung directly from the opera *Carmen*. Curly jet-black hair flowed down onto outfits that were as flashy as a traveling gypsy's. And when it came to make-up, Elizabeth Taylor was clearly her model. A heavy layer of kohl was painted around each of her cat-shaped eyes, dramatically flaring out into wings that would have rivaled Cleopatra. As for her lips, they were as red as Dorothy's ruby slippers. Dangling silver earrings danced as she spoke, complementing the rings which adorned each of her fingers. The final touch was nails which glittered the color of gold, her joy for life exuding straight out through the ends of her Manchu-length fingertips. Just being in her presence energized me more than downing a container of espresso. On top of which, the woman had to be at least eighty years old.

"You're just in time for lunch, my darling. Wait till you see what I've cooked for us today!" Tia Marta clapped her hands in delight.

That was the other thing. Tia Marta loved to cook, and lived alone. I lived alone, and loved to eat. It was a match made in heaven.

I held the guillotined cow's head towards her. "Forget Amaya's husband. You're going to give *me* a heart attack one of these days. I nearly plotzed when I opened my fridge and caught this thing gawking back at me."

Tia Marta burst into a hearty laugh which wiggled its way down my body to tickle my toes. Damn it! The woman's happiness was contagious. She leaned in and gave me a buss on the cheek.

"My dear, what can I tell you? So many of my clients

brought me food this morning that my refrigerator ran
out of space. I stuck some in yours since I always cook
for the both of us, and there's never anything in there,
anyway. I plan to smoke the head tonight. That way
we'll have good barbacoa for our dinner tomorrow."

In Tia Marta's backyard sat a refrigerator whose interior had been gutted and fitted with a smoke pipe, specifically for cooking the delicacy to perfection.

Tia Marta suddenly stiffened and I prepared myself,
knowing what was next. I closed my eyes as she proceeded to sniff loudly at my arms, my neck, and my
face, like a blood hound latching onto its prey.

"I'm not sure where you've been, but you're in need
of a good cleansing," she firmly announced.

My stomach vocally disagreed. "How about some
lunch first? I'm starving," I protested.

"Don't be crazy," Tia Marta scoffed. "By that time
the evil spirits will have settled in but good, and it will
take me twice as long to get rid of them. No. First we
cleanse, then we eat."

My stomach responded with an angry growl.

"You hear that? The evil spirits are upset because
they're afraid of what is coming," she smugly predicted.

Silly me—and here I just thought I was hungry.

Tia Marta led the way to her altar room, the Home
Depot of religious tchotchkes. A string of miniature
white lights blinked on and off in the doorway, as if
announcing a two-for-one sale. Inside, over fifty religious statues were arranged on a cluster of tables and
shelves. I seriously doubted the Devil would ever dare
set foot in this place.

We headed over to a table filled with prayer candles.
A black velvet reproduction of the *Last Supper* hung
directly above it. The rest of the walls were festooned
with the largest collection of Virgin Mary paintings this

side of the border. Best of all was the plastic Madonna picture which transformed into Jesus with each of my slightest moves. The only tchotchke in the room that made no sense was a framed portrait of Lucy and Desi from the old *I Love Lucy Show*. Naturally, it was my favorite.

A Bible lay beside the candles, along with a stack of lottery tickets waiting to be played. Nearby were dried herbs, a dish of rose petals, a bowl of holy water, and a carton of eggs. Tia Marta picked up one of the eggs and rolled it over my head, across my shoulders, and down my back as she said a prayer. Then she cracked it open and emptied its contents into a dish. A black speck lay motionless in the yolk's yellow center before it slowly began to spread, like a spider extending its legs.

"You see!" Tia Marta announced triumphantly. "I told you something was there. *Now* we can eat."

A shiver ran through me faster than feet scurrying across a hot griddle as the black mark continued to disperse. I admit it; there were times when Tia Marta's rituals totally gave me the creeps.

We headed back into her kitchen, and I sat down at the rough-hewn wooden table. This was the area of the house which I loved best. There was something about the salmon painted stucco walls that always made me feel warm and cozy, while the turquoise window frames added a light-hearted dash. A stream of light danced on the uneven brick floor as Tia Marta placed a steaming bowl of *caldillo* before me. I dug into the savory beef stew with such zest it was possible two or three evil spirits were still lurking inside, just as hungry as I was.

Tia Marta sat down and joined me, placing a cup of hot liquid by my side. I sniffed it and glanced at her.

"It's broomweed tea for that hangover you woke up

with this morning," she responded, dipping a warm tortilla into her stew.

I didn't bother to ask how she knew. Instead, I quietly drank the liquid, and my small twinge of headache went away. Since meeting Tia Marta, I'd come to accept that if you think it, and believe it, the most amazing things can happen. It was then that I noticed a slight bump on her forehead. She followed my gaze with her fingertips and gently massaged the skin.

"What caused that?" I inquired.

Tia Marta shook her head like a war-weary soldier. "I should have known there'd be trouble last night after I spotted that black owl outside my window. But I was so tired, I couldn't stay awake. The next thing I knew, a spirit grabbed my leg and yanked me out of bed, while a demon tugged at my hair, and third ghost slapped me on the rear end."

There were times when I felt certain Tia Marta had to be pulling *my* leg. This was one of them. But she continued on, deadly serious.

"I tried to pray out loud, but the spirits wouldn't let the words leave my mouth. So, I said the Lord's Prayer in my mind. After that, I told them to get out of my house, first in English and then in Spanish, in case they didn't understand." She gave a nonchalant wave of her hand, as if that's all it took to brush the ghouls and the goblins away.

"So, what did it all mean?" I asked, wanting a good wrap-up to the story.

Tia Marta glanced behind me. "It means that someone possessing *mal ojo* is around," she whispered hoarsely.

I understood enough Spanish to know *mal ojo* meant evil eye. As of this morning, I was in search of someone who gave evil phone. I opted against filling Tia Marta in on that juicy tidbit; she'd probably start rubbing eggs over every piece of communication equipment I owned.

Lunch was formally declared over as Tia Marta's afternoon crowd began to appear. I grabbed the cow's head, promising to keep it entombed in my refrigerator until later, and headed out the front door. As I crossed through a patch of creosote, a woman hiding behind a pair of fashionable DKNY sunglasses appeared. She tottered past decked out in a hot pink satin top, tight black capri pants, and high-heeled platform shoes. I heaved a sigh of resignation, aware that my fashion sense extended no further than scruffy jeans and a pair of dirty hiking boots. Maybe I could strike a deal with Tia Marta's spirits, and get to play fashionplate next time around. It wasn't until I was knee deep in a bunch of honey mesquite—terrific for conjunctivitis and peptic ulcers—that I heard the clipclopping of platforms race up behind me.

"Rach?"

Great—not only did I feel like Courtney Love on a bad grunge day, but I was stuck with a dead cow's head in my hands.

"Don't you recognize me?" the fashion maven asked. A bittersweet smile tugged at the corners of her mouth, as if I'd disappointed her.

I moved a step closer and nearly dropped Elsie on Miss Vogue's hot pink painted toenails. The woman bore a resemblance to someone I'd known. Still, it couldn't possibly be. The friend I remembered was definitely younger.

I received my answer as she whipped off her sunglasses with a theatrical gesture. "Rach! It's me, Lizzie!"

Both Elsie and I stared at my old pal, Lizzie Burke, in astonishment. Gone was the young girl I'd known in Las Vegas, replaced by a more mature and much altered version. Her unruly dark curls had been teased and sprayed to conform into a Dolly Parton clone. But something more essential about Lizzie was different. The carefree sense about her was gone, making her seem far older than her thirty years. Lizzie had worked as a computer programming whiz for Clark County, with dreams of becoming a dancer. What was missing was the spirited bounce there had been to her walk. I quickly set Elsie on the ground.

"I thought you were in Miami!" Lizzie exclaimed, giving me a warm hug.

"Well then, we're both surprised. As far as I knew, you were still in Vegas." I returned her embrace. She clung for a second too long, her hug containing the slightest air of desperation. Or maybe it was just my imagination.

"I *was* in Miami. That is, until I got hold of a case which made the wrong people angry," I admitted.

"That seems to be your specialty." Lizzie giggled, revealing a hint of her old self. "Don't tell me: you've been stationed here as your penance."

"You've got it." I chuckled, pleased to have bumped into her once more. Then I caught sight of the ring on her finger. She sported a diamond large enough to have made Elizabeth Taylor envious.

"Did you win that playing the slots in Vegas, or is there something else I should know about?" I asked mischievously.

Lizzie flashed a quicksilver grin and threw her arms around me once more. "I got married, Rach! In fact, there's heaps of stuff that I have to fill you in on." She gave me a curious look. "Were you just at Tia Marta's for a cleansing?"

The ominous black speck with legs began to crawl into my mind. I quickly shoved it away.

"No, we're just neighbors. I live next door." I pointed to my ramshackle abode.

Lizzie gave it a passing glance. "I have to run, or I'll be late for my cleansing. But why don't you come for dinner this evening and we'll catch up with each other then?"

She wrote down her address and then cheerfully waved as she ran inside, her platform shoes pounding out an oddly disturbing beat.

Five

I headed toward El Paso for dinner that evening as the sun gave a last gasp. The Franklin Mountains pushed up through the land like a great spine, their ridges sharp as quills perforating the sky so that they bled blood red from the setting sun. I wasn't sure what to expect as I wound my way up the curving mountain road, but Lizzie had clearly traveled quite a distance since her days of dreaming about fame and fortune in Las Vegas. According to the address, her house lay situated on Crazy Cat Mountain, one of the poshest sections in El Paso.

My Ford chugged skyward as the night bloomed, providing me with a spectacular view of El Paso and her Mexican sister city, Ciudad Juarez. This was when the magic of twilight kicked in. The first hour of darkness swallowed up the poverty that lay on both sides of the border, and turned the twinkling lights below into shimmers of fairy dust. Up ahead loomed an immense structure painted brilliant shades of yellow and green. I checked the address, and turned into the driveway of the colorful monstrosity. I had arrived at Lizzie Burke's house.

I parked my truck under an orange overhang and headed to the front door, where I rang the bell. In response, the music of *42nd Street* gleefully pealed through the evening air, bringing a smile to my lips. Lizzie had always practiced her tap dancing to that tune in her Vegas bungalow. The chimes ended, swallowed up by dense silence. I rang the doorbell again. This time, the ensuing melody was drowned out by a voice as grating as harsh sandpaper.

"Will somebody get the damn door!"

The only noise to be heard above the screech was the shrill yapping of a dog.

"For chrissakes! What the hell's wrong with you people, anyway?" yelled the voice, distinctly more irritated as it drew closer.

The door abruptly flew open, and a tiny terror of an old woman glared out at me. She leaned on a walker, her fingers gripping its aluminum rails as if the contraption might take it to mind to make a run for the border. One glance made me wonder what the walker was mainly used for: to support the frail frame underneath the elaborate dress, or to keep the woman from crumpling beneath her cotton candy tower of blue-tinted hair?

She paused for a moment, giving me the once over. "And just who the hell are you?" she snapped.

The clip clop of Lizzie's platform shoes came to the rescue.

"Mother! I told you that my friend was coming for dinner this evening," she chided. Her hip nudged the walker out of the way as she opened the door to let me in.

"Then you should have told her to dress better, while you were at it," the old woman barked, stomping off with the help of her walker.

Lizzie stuck her tongue out at the receding figure, reminding me of the girl I'd known in Vegas—until I caught sight of the outfit she wore. A blue satin shirt, studded with enough rhinestones to form its own glit-

tering Milky Way, was tucked inside a pair of bejew-
elled, white satin pants. I was barely through the door
when a red ball of fur flew up off the floor, like a frantic
junkie hopped up on crystal meth.

"Down, Ten-Karat! Down!" Lizzie commanded.

The Pomeranian paid no heed, but kept right on jumping and nipping at me as Lizzie turned and led me
through the entrance way. I followed, doing my best not
to gawk. Between the marble floor, the mirrored walls,
and the massive crystal chandelier, it was all I could do
to not whip out my sunglasses and slap them on to cut
out the glare. I was grateful when Lizzie steered me into
a room that wasn't paneled in mirrors.

"Was that your mother?" I asked. The frenzied pooch
leapt up again and this time came close to French kissing
me. The damned dog was proving to be more persistent
than most of the men I knew.

Lizzie caught the bouncing ball of fur neatly in one
arm as she handed me a glass of champagne. "Bite your
tongue. That witch is my mother-in-law, Crazy Krabbs.
That's what I call her—though not to her face, of
course."

Lizzie turned her attention to the dog cradled in her
arms, her voice melting into baby talk. "And this little
sweetie here is Ten-Karat." She presented her mouth to
the pooch, which Ten-Karat obediently licked. "I named
her after the size of my diamond. Not bad for a girl from
Jersey, huh?" She flashed a smile and clinked her champagne glass against mine with a tad too much enthusi-
asm.

But what had caught my attention was the name
"Krabbs." That, along with the taxidermied heads which
littered the walls.

"The only Krabbs I know is the owner of a place
called the Happy Hunting Ranch. He wouldn't happen

to be any relation, would he?" I asked, hoping against hope she'd say, "It ain't so."

"What a small world!" Lizzie exclaimed. "Why, that's my husband, F.U.!"

Well, hit me upside the head and drag me on home. Sometimes life was just stranger than fiction.

"How do you know him?" Lizzie asked.

"I received an anonymous call this morning claiming some dead monkeys were stashed at the ranch. So I dropped by and your husband took me on a tour." Referring to F.U. as Lizzie's husband left a sour taste in my mouth, as if an express elevator filled with bile were rising up in my throat. "The monkeys turned out to be a bunch of stuffed toys someone had planted in the taxidermy shed."

Lizzie rolled her eyes, as if not surprised by the story. "Then, I take it you met Velma, F.U.'s attack dog. That bitch scares me silly. You'd think *she* was married to the man, the way she stands guard over him." Lizzie swirled her champagne and a little splashed over the rim. "Sometimes she even questions *me* when I call and ask to speak with him. I swear, someday I'm gonna punch that broad's lights out," she fumed.

"F.U. believes his son was responsible for the anonymous call." I took a sip of the champagne. Mmm. Good stuff. I glanced at the bottle. Of course: it was Dom Perignon.

"Yeah. How do you like that? Not only did I inherit a crazy mother-in-law, but I also managed to get a pain-in-the-ass kid in the bargain. And F.U. wonders why I'm always running off to Tia Marta's for a cleansing."

"Does F.U.'s son live at home?"

Lizzie nearly snorted a stream of champagne out her nose. "F.U., Jr.? No way! That was settled before we got married. I told him he could have either his mother or his son live with us, but there was no way I was gonna deal with them both. Even a twenty-karat diamond couldn't have bribed me on that one," Lizzie responded.

"What the hell's going on in there? Let's eat already!" Mother Krabbs yelled, as if on cue.

"The gorgon calls." Lizzie refilled both our glasses. "Here, you'll need more of this to make it through dinner."

I followed her back to the entrance hall, where she dropped Ten-Karat and picked up a mallet, its round head covered in felt. Lizzie took the stance of a slugger at bat, then whacked a large Chinese gong near the staircase. A resounding *"ohm"* resonated throughout the room. The next thing I knew, my body was oscillating in rhythm with it. Hmm. Maybe this was something worth investing in.

"This is how I call F.U. down for dinner. It's better than having to scream, and it's one of the few things he can detect when his hearing aids are turned down," she explained. "All that damn shooting he's done over the years has really taken a toll on him."

I felt certain all the animals he'd shot weren't too crazy about it, either.

"But what drives me nuts is that he's so damned stubborn," Lizzie continued. "He refuses to give up those old hearing aids and buy a new, updated pair."

I caught sight of a seat mounted on the bottom of the staircase handrail. It had a lever on its side like those used in manually operated elevators.

"What's this for?" I inquired.

Lizzie lifted the mallet, as if inclined to give it a whack. "That's how my mother-in-law gets up and down. Personally, I'd just as soon rip the damn thing out and leave her stranded upstairs."

The Krabbses were beginning to give a whole new

meaning to the term "dysfunctional family." The Colonel Sanders of hunters was already bounding down the stairs, obliviously muttering to himself before he caught sight of the two of us standing together. He froze in place with a horrified expression on his face, as if he were a deer caught in his own gunsites.

"I've never seen that woman before in my life!" he sputtered, holding a hand to his heart as if to keep it from jumping out of his chest.

Lizzie clipclopped over to his side and turned up the volume on his hearing aids. "This is my friend, Rachel Porter, who I told you about. Besides, you did so meet her! She came by the ranch this morning."

Lizzie turned and whispered in my ear. "He's getting a little forgetful lately. I swear, it must be all that Viagra he takes. It *has* made him more chipper, but I'm afraid it's beginning to affect his memory."

F.U. caught my eye and gave a sly wink. Right. He was about as forgetful as a two-timing horny toad on the make.

"F.U., is that you out there? Get your ass in here now! I'm starving to death!" Mother Krabbs demanded from inside the dining room.

"We have one more guest coming, Mother Krabbs. He should be here any minute," Lizzie responded for F.U., who gave a slight cringe.

"Are we waiting for F.U., Jr.?" I ventured.

Lizzie rolled her eyes. "No way. F.U., Jr. refuses to come here anymore. It seems we're too bourgeois for his taste."

I was beginning to think the kid had a point. The doorbell rang, prompting F.U. to check himself in one of the mirrors before he strode over and opened the door.

Standing in the entrance was a slight man with a copper-colored Afro, way too big for his head. It took a moment before I realized the shag rug was actually a cheap wig. Dressed in double knit bell bottom pants, the visitor also wore an olive green Nehru jacket, with a red ascot tied around his neck. Someone should have told him the sixties ended over thirty years ago.

Atop his long nose, Coke bottle lenses perched like a bird on a wire. The bottom of his face sloped off abruptly, due to the lack of a chin, and his complexion was the color of skim milk. But most perturbing of all was his smile. It appeared to be permanently etched on his face.

Lizzie kissed him on each cheek as she pulled him through the doorway. "Rachel Porter, meet Dr. Martin Pierpont," she gushed. "Our resident genius."

I was in for an even bigger surprise: in place of hands, Dr. Pierpont sported a pair of prosthetic aluminum devices which resembled the claws on a crab. Each device split open and closed, working much the same as a thumb and forefinger. Pierpont held out a hook and I shook it.

"A pleasure to make your acquaintance," he murmured. His smile remained plastered in place.

F.U. led the way into the dining room as Lizzie clasped Dr. Pierpont's arm like a smitten schoolgirl. A highly polished table awaited us, laden with enough crystal, bone china and silver to make me feel I'd wandered into Windsor Palace. But the true showstopper was a large oil painting of F.U. dressed as a Spanish conquistador, wearing a helmet and bearing a cross and a sword.

F.U. sidled over to me. "I've always had this thing for Don Quixote. Personally, I think I look pretty hot that way. How about you?"

What I thought was that I needed a lot more champagne. I took a seat beside Lizzie. Pierpont crossed to the opposite side of the table and sat next to Mother Krabbs, who shot him a sour look. He lifted her hand to his mouth and gently gave it a kiss, holding it captive in one of his hooks

"Yeah, yeah. Let's eat already before I drop dead from hunger," she dourly responded.

Lizzie rang a crystal bell and an elegant butler appeared. It wouldn't have been far off the mark to bet that Jeeves was better bred than the rest of us. He slowly made his way around the table, ladling cream of green chile soup out of a large silver tureen into our Limoges bowls.

"What kind of doctor are you?" I asked Pierpont, curious to know in which field his genius resided.

Lizzie piped up before the good doctor could remove his soup spoon from his mouth. "He's a brilliant scientist."

Pierpont's smile never wavered. I took that to mean Lizzie had answered correctly.

"That's wonderful. In what field of science do you work?" I noticed Pierpont had the same eyeglass frames as Elvis Costello.

Dr. Pierpont placed the tip of his hook against the bridge of his glasses, which slid up his nose as if gliding on an escalator. "I'm a doctor of veterinary physiology and pharmacology, with a specialty in embryo transfer. And what exactly is it that *you* do?" he countered.

"I'm an agent with the U.S. Fish and Wildlife Service," I replied, wishing I could add "with a Ph.D. in nuclear bullshit-ology."

"Oh, F.U.! Pleeeeease let me tell her!" Lizzie begged.

F.U. pulled on his goatee, causing a white hair to fall and daintily float in his cream of green chile soup.

"She's such a good friend. Besides, I want her to

know just what a sweetheart you are," Lizzie cajoled, throwing him a kiss.

That seemed to do the trick. F.U. tickled her under the chin, and a chuckle rose to his lips. "You know I can never deny my baby doll whatever she wants."

"Oh, for chrissakes, I'm trying to eat here!" Mother Krabbs groused.

"Are you certain you want her to know? We don't need any unnecessary problems," Pierpont added cautiously.

"Don't be silly," Lizzie responded. "Rachel would never do anything to hurt me, would you?" she asked, squeezing my hand in excitement.

"Of course not." I was seriously beginning to believe I'd stepped into a roomful of lunatics.

The butler quietly removed our soup bowls, replacing them with paper-thin dinner plates.

"We're having Ten-Karat cloned so that I'll never have to be without her—not even when she's dead and gone. And Dr. Pierpont is the man who's doing it for us!" Lizzie exclaimed, nearly bursting with the news.

I remained silent for a moment, not quite sure how to react. "This is some sort of joke, right?"

"You see! That is *exactly* why I didn't think she should know," Pierpont pounced.

"And just why is that?" I challenged.

"Because as soon as the word 'cloning' is mentioned, every government lackey wants to tie it all up in some absurd set of rules and regulations," Pierpont spat back, while retaining his grin.

The butler silently re-appeared and placed a slice of roast beef on Mother Krabbs' plate.

"Personally, I think all elected officials should be spayed and neutered so they can't reproduce their own kind. Speaking of which, have you got any kids?"

Mother Krabbs asked, grabbing hold of the butler before he could leave.

"I'm not a government lackey or an elected official," I said in my own defense. "I'm a Fish and Wildlife agent. And no, I don't have kids."

Mother Krabbs nailed me with rheumy eyes as she forked another three slices of rare beef off the platter.

"What makes any of you certain that cloning a dog can actually be done?" I inquired.

"Because Dr. Pierpont says it can. Isn't that right, Martin?" She turned her gaze in his direction.

"Anything is possible. All it takes is money and time. But especially money." Pierpont's grin spread a little wider.

"And we have plenty of that," Lizzie cheerfully added. "Why, F.U. has already given three million dollars toward having Ten-Karat cloned."

F.U. affectionately pinched her cheek. "Anything my little sugar plum desires."

"What a pile of bull dookey!" Mother Krabbs declared between mouthfuls of beef. She put down her fork long enough to dish a helping of mashed potatoes onto her plate.

"Just think of all the good things that can come from Martin's work. For all we know, his research might even help save endangered species!" Lizzie chattered.

"It does sound intriguing," I admitted. "Tell me, Dr. Pierpont. Where did you work before this?"

"Martin used to work for the government in one of their programs. That is, until there were some of those budget cuts, and his lab was shut down." Lizzie seemed unable to relay the information fast enough.

"No wonder you're not crazy about government officials. What was the program you were involved in?"

Pierpont focused on cutting his roast beef into precise,

even squares, after which he attacked a piece with front teeth as small and sharp as a rodent's. "It's really nothing I can talk about," he answered after carefully swallowing.

"Top secret?" I prodded, suspecting where this guy's real genius lay was in the art of making himself sound important.

"So then, he opened his own business," Lizzie broke in. "But you know how hard that is, raising capital to try and get projects off the ground, and all."

"I don't think Rachel's real interested in all the nitty gritty workings of the business world, sugar," F.U. remarked, patting her hand.

"Sure I am," I offered.

"No, you're not," F.U. corrected me. "Women in Texas never are."

"So now Martin works for us here!" Lizzie summed up.

"Where's the dessert?" Ma Krabbs demanded, drumming her spoon on the table.

"I'd be interested in visiting your lab sometime," I ventured, as chocolate mousse was served all around.

Pierpont fixed his Elvis Costello glasses on me like a pair of high-powered telescopes. "I'm afraid that won't be possible."

Man! Was this guy ever getting on my nerves. "Don't worry, I'm not planning to steal your secret formula. It's just that your work sounds fascinating." If Pierpont was some sort of genius, I didn't need to alienate myself from the possible savior of endangered species.

Pierpont shook his wig in refusal. "You're very kind, but the answer is still no. My work is terribly demanding, and I don't like to be disturbed. Therefore, I've made it a policy that no visitors are allowed."

"Don't take it personally, Rach. Even I haven't been there," Lizzie attested.

"Well then, can I inquire where your lab is located? I imagine you're working in conjunction with a university in the area," I hazarded a guess.

"Sorry, but that information is classified, as well," Pierpont responded, slipping a spoonful of mousse into his mouth.

"Well, this conversation is about as exciting as a worn out dog trying to hump my leg," Mother Krabbs announced, pushing away from the table. "I'm calling it a night."

She clomped down the hall with her walker, followed by a series of squeaks and hums as she successfully launched herself up the stairs.

"I should be going, as well. I was up at the crack of dawn this morning," I said, pretending to stifle a yawn.

"Let me walk you to the door," Lizzie offered, jumping up from her chair.

"Me, too." F.U. eagerly joined her.

Pierpont remained seated, but cordially extended a hook. "It's been a pleasure, Agent Porter. Let me know if there's ever anything you'd like to have cloned."

I looked at the man sitting in front of me, and knew of at least *one* thing I could live without having reproduced. "I'll do that," I responded, and slipped my hand around his hook. The sleek steel burned bitterly cold into my flesh, almost as if he'd somehow managed to regulate the temperature of his prosthesis.

I walked into the hall accompanied by Lizzie and F.U., along with Ten-Karat, who bounced up and down as if she had springs under her paws. Lizzie wrapped her arms around me, her body heat helping restore the warmth to my skin.

"You don't know how much I've missed you, Rach.

Let's get together. Just the two of us," she whispered in my ear.

I nodded, then turned to F.U. "Thanks for an interesting evening. I'm sure I'll be seeing you again." I had no doubt it would be due to some sort of hunting violation.

F.U. responded by pulling me into a body cast of an embrace. "Don't you worry, Cupcake. I'll be in touch," he whispered in my ear.

Then Ten-Karat leaped up and nailed me smack on the mouth with her tongue. Gee. Just how lucky could a girl get?

I headed for my Ford, glad the evening had come to an end, when something lobbed me on the back of the head. Unless Lola had escaped from Fat Boy, I was the target of a lunatic Krabbs attack.

"Psst! Up here!" came a raspy voice.

Mother Krabbs leaned out her bedroom window, throwing bath oil beads my way.

"What are you doing?" I called up, wondering why F.U. hadn't yet had her legally committed.

"Shh! Keep it down! I don't need Dum dum and Dodo to hear us," she commanded.

"What do you want?" I asked again.

"Well, it's not as if I'm waiting for you to recite the balcony scene from Romeo and Juliet. So, what do you think?" she fired back.

"How the hell am I supposed to know?" I snapped.

"My, my. You've got quite the little mouth on you, don't you?"

Like she was one to talk.

"Since you can't figure it out, I'll give you a clue." She waved for me to come closer. "Pick me up at noon tomorrow. You're taking me to lunch."

"And why would I want to do that?" I retorted suspiciously.

"What have you got? A Ring Ding for a brain like that daughter-in-law of mine?" she sniped. "You want information about Pierpont, don't you? Well, who do you suppose you're going to get it from?"

"You?" I inquired incredulously.

"I'd say that all depends on where you take me to eat," she replied with a dash of Greta Garbo mystique.

"What about Lizzie? Won't she be home when I pick you up?"

"Nah. She'll be at that gym of hers. Or out shopping and spending my money, while F.U.'s fooling around at the ranch. By the way, I have to eat by twelve-thirty sharp or my blood sugar goes crazy. So don't be late," she instructed.

Mother Krabbs pulled her head back inside and shut the window before I could respond.

I drove home pondering what Lizzie had gotten herself involved in.

Sometimes thinking too much does more harm than good. By the time I reached Mesilla, I was in bad need of a drink. El Patio, the local bar, was just the type of down-and-dirty dive I was looking for after an evening at the Krabbses' mansion. It had two pool tables, a juke box, and a black and white checkerboard floor, along with a flickering Budweiser light that hadn't been dusted since the first Superbowl.

I took my regular spot, slipping onto the stool next to another staple of El Patio's run-down decor—my neighbor and landlord, Sonny Harris. Hovering in his late sixties, Sonny hated having been forced to retire from the New Mexico Border Patrol. Partly, it was a matter of pride. The number of men he'd captured during his career had set a record high. Sonny felt that due to this, his skill was a tool which should be treated with respect and taught to the next generation of agents. His superiors at Border Patrol had disagreed, believing the agency needed to catch up with the times.

"The only thing their trackers rely on these days is a bunch of shiny gadgets and snooty, high-falutin' technology. Heaven forbid something happens to those fancy Japanese instruments of theirs. A bunch of wet-behind-the-ear trackers will be helpless as newborn infants. Hell, you need more than that to catch desperate men on the run," he'd told me with a contemptuous sniff.

The other reason Sonny hated retirement was because he was bored out of his gourd with not much to do but drink. He sipped his shot of house whisky as I ordered a cold draft beer.

"Guess what? I put those tracking skills you taught me to good use today," I informed him, signaling the bartender to refill Sonny's glass.

He immediately perked up, his Yosemite Sam mustache twitching in excitement. "Oh yeah? And where'd you do that?" he asked eagerly.

"Out along the Anapra Road," I replied.

"Hell, you're talking about smugglers paradise. So, what'd you find?"

"Not much besides a dead informant. Whoever else was there had wiped their tracks away with a mesquite branch."

Sonny glanced over at me, his face etched with as many lines as trails he'd tracked, each telling a different story. "Anything else?"

"Yeah." I smiled, eager to reveal my coup de grace. "I found a freshly made heel mark hidden beneath a creosote bush."

"Good girl," Sonny said proudly.

"The only problem was the sheriff who came out to investigate. He stepped on it and destroyed the evidence."

Sonny shrugged. "Figures. Did you note the size of the footprint?"

"No," I admitted. "I didn't remember to do that."

"See? You already forgot the first lesson. Always keep a stick with you to mark things like length and stride. Otherwise, all your hard work won't amount to more than a dog lifting his leg and peeing in the dirt." Sonny polished off his whisky, and the bartender automatically refilled his glass.

He was right. In my excitement, I'd overlooked one of the most basic steps. My sense of dejection must have showed, for Sonny proceeded to buy the next round of drinks.

He clinked his glass against mine. "Don't worry, you'll get it right next time. Besides, life ain't that bad. You could always be a black cow standing out in the summer heat of the desert." It was his standard toast. "Sounds to me like a drug deal gone sour."

If so, then why had Timmy Tom bothered to call me out to the scene? The unspoken question reverberated inside me like the vibration from Lizzie's Chinese gong. I polished off my beer, bought Sonny another round, and hit the road for home.

The moonlight shone bright, making lunar love to a bunch of bleached skulls scattered across Sonny's front lawn. I quickly strode past, afraid the taint of death might be catching. I had yet to understand what was so decorative about a pile of dead critters.

I opened my front door and walked inside, where it felt dark and lonely. Santou's image unexpectedly swamped my mind, and I lunged for the TV, hoping for a distraction. What I got was a country western singer crying of a good love gone wrong. I was tempted to pull my revolver and shoot the messenger, but opted to save some bucks and turned off the set, putting one of us out of our misery.

I had vowed to keep no photos of Santou lying around. Little did I know it wouldn't matter. Every love song, every sunset, every lousy couple were constant reminders of what I was missing. No matter how hard I tried, Santou remained permanently seared in my heart.

I combated my attack of the blues by heading into the bathroom and jumping in the shower. However, no amount of soap and water could wash away Santou's ghostly image, which mercilessly teased me like an unforgiving lover. I knew each hard-earned line in the man's face as intimately as if I were studying my own reflection in a mirror.

I stepped beneath a coursing stream of warm water, where the shower's spray turned into the sensual touch of Jake's fingertips. Closing my eyes, I felt his lips blaze a trail across my mouth, my cheeks, my nose. The warmth of his breath caressed my breasts, my stomach and hips, as the memory of his scent rushed over my senses with the force of a tidal wave, pulling me down as I gasped for air. I held on for dear life by winding my fingers in his black tousled curls, only to have his deep set eyes lock me tight in their embrace, his lopsided grin sending the message that there was no escape.

I reached out and upped the volume of cold water, chasing all thoughts of Santou down the drain.

Then I turned the water off and the pipes let out a groan. In the silence that followed, I heard the sound of shoes creaking across the floor. My skin turned deathly cold at the knowledge that I wasn't alone—an intruder was in the house.

I grabbed a towel and quickly wrapped it around my

body. Then I ran straight for the living room desk, where my gun was stashed. I slid open the drawer, and my fingers instinctively wrapped around the .38's handle. I held the revolver before me as I listened for the telltale sound of steps. But all I heard was the whisper of silence beckoning me forward, daring me to enter the next room.

The wet towel clung to my skin like a jealous lover as I approached the kitchen and slowly walked in. A shaft of light hit the dreary linoleum floor. My eyes followed its trail. The refrigerator door was ajar.

I pulled open the door. Gaping out with blind eyes was yet another skinned cow's head—but in place of a lifeless tongue, a black cell phone was sticking out of the creature's mouth.

A wave of dizziness caused me to sway towards the flayed beast, but the smell of raw flesh brought me back to my senses. That, and the cold shiver which crept up my back. I suddenly knew there was someone standing behind me.

My breath tore through my lungs as I spun around. A shadow lurking in the corner ran through the darkened hall and out the front door, disappearing into the black of night. I followed as far as the walkway, my gun trembling in my hands, but couldn't see anything. I went back inside and bolted the door. Every cell in my body shook, as the cry I'd been holding back ripped its way out.

Grabbing a plastic garbage bag, I walked in to confront the warning that had been left for me. The cow's eyes held a stunned expression, not yet having come to terms with its own death. I gingerly removed the phone from the critter's mouth, and found it was a plastic toy.

I made one final trek outside with the bag, then polished off a bottle of cheap wine before crawling into

bed. The smell of barbacoa crept through my window
from Tia Marta's smoker. As the hooting of an owl kept
me awake, I thought about decapitated heads and prowl-
ers. It took the low whistle of a distant train to break
the spell. Its lonesome cry pierced my soul as it split the
air, and I rode it to sleep, my restless dreams gliding
along on the silvery wail of the Atcheson, Topeka, and
the Santa Fe rail.

Six

I woke up to the commotion of Tia Marta pulling out pots and pans in my kitchen. The other sound was my pager vibrating on the night table where it nervously jerked, as if threatening to jump up and bite me. I checked out the number and saw that it was Fat Boy calling. I leaned over, picked up the phone, and dialed his number.

"Where were you? I was calling all night! What's the matter with you, anyway? Don't you know what a beeper is for?" Juan fumed, sending a full head of steam through the receiver.

I'd mistakenly left my pager at home when I'd headed off for dinner at Lizzie's. In hindsight, it appeared to have been a wise move.

"I'm here now. So, what's up?" I inquired, conjuring at least six different ways I'd have chosen to start off my day.

My question was met by a pause. If Fat Boy had been so anxious to get hold of me, what was the hold-up about?

"Well?" I prodded. "Why did you call?"

"I want to know if you got Timmy Tom's phone back yet," Fat Boy blurted out.

Well, well. Wasn't *this* the grief-stricken significant other?

"His cell phone is rather difficult to get hold of at the moment. But I'm sure it'll be removed when the autopsy is done," I explained to Juan.

A shiver rippled through me as I remembered the phone which had been left in my refrigerator last night. I firmly squelched it.

"And just when is *that* going to happen?" Fat Boy asked waspishly.

"I couldn't tell you. Timmy Tom's body first has to be shipped up to Albuquerque, where the exam will take place," I informed him. "But you should be aware there's a good chance you won't get the phone back."

"What! What kind of crap is that? That's my private property," Fat Boy erupted.

"I thought that was Timmy Tom's cell phone."

"Yeah, but when he died I inherited it," Fat Boy replied indignantly. "Which means that it's legally mine now, and I'll be damned if some government official is going to get it for free."

"It also happened to be the murder weapon," I reminded him. "Besides, what do you want that phone for, anyway?"

I could hear the wheels turn as he thought. "I need one for when I'm out playing my organ grinder, so that I can make and receive calls. Why else do ya think?" Juan huffily retorted.

"You actually want to use the same phone that was shoved down Timmy Tom's throat for conducting your business?" I wondered how Juan could be so ghoulish.

"Listen, Porter. I don't owe you any explanation. All you need to know is that it's got sentimental value. Being that it was the last thing Timmy Tom used," Juan added, with a well-placed sniffle.

I didn't answer immediately, letting the information sink in. Evidently, pauses were a no-no when it came to Fat Boy's busy schedule.

"Besides, I'm the one who paid for damn thing. Which means it rightfully belongs to me!" He slammed the phone down hard, making me wince.

Some mornings you just had to wonder why you even bothered to get up and shave your legs. This was clearly turning out to be one of them. On top of which, I had to make myself look more than routinely presentable. Lunch with Ma Krabbs was looming ahead later today. I jumped out of bed, showered, threw on some make-up, and donned a clean top and pants. Then I headed into the kitchen, where Tia Marta was whipping up a breakfast fit to keep a coven of vampires away. The scent of chili powder and garlic permeated the air in a Mexican potpourri. I'd taken the precaution of pulling out a large bottle of mouthwash in the bathroom, knowing an after-breakfast gargle would be a "Miss Manners" must.

Tia Marta was humming merrily as she fried up a batch of chorizo sausage in one of my "you'll-never-get-this-thing-clean" pans. Marta smiled at the sight of my wet hair, already beginning to dry into its standard red frizz.

"I don't suppose you've got anything in your garden that will permanently sedate the frizzies, do you?" I wistfully asked.

Tia Marta added a dash more chili to the chorizo, and reached for the carton of eggs. "I'll mix something up, but it won't do much good. Your hair is just like you, my dear: it's got a mind all its own," she chortled.

She was just about to break open an egg when her *mal ojo* monitor zoomed into overdrive. She rushed over with egg in hand, and began rolling it up and down my body as she hastily said a prayer. Much more of this dairy action, and the biggest problem I'd be facing would be a case of spiritual high cholesterol.

"That's odd. I must have missed something when I did your cleansing yesterday," Marta muttered.

Cracking the egg open, she dropped the contents into a dish. A speck of blood winked up at us from where it floated, crimson as a maharaja's ruby.

"Something more than usual is going on in your life. What have you been up to lately?" she questioned.

I suddenly felt like a mischievous child who'd been caught red-handed. Even worse, I relished the feeling of impishness. "Well, I discovered a dead body yesterday morning, and had dinner with a mad scientist last night." I decided not to mention the surprise waiting for me when I got home. My hunger-driven adult self chided me to behave, longing to eat a couple of those fortune-telling eggs.

Tia Marta gave a no-nonsense snort. "Hmph. That must be it, then." She focused her attention on breaking four eggs into a pan, until her tongue finally rebelled. "But let me warn you. I'm going to make you drink an extra strong cup of licorice weed if you plan on bumping into anymore corpses today!"

I grinned and gave her a kiss on the cheek. "I'll have to check my appointment book and let you know," I teased, my fingers going for a piece of chorizo.

Tia Marta swatted my hand away with her spatula. "Enough play. I have breakfast to cook so that you won't starve," she scolded, and began to scramble the eggs.

I grabbed a couple of Goodwill plates, along with utensils, and arranged them on my dilapidated kitchen table, placing two large mugs of freshly brewed coffee beside them.

"I went to Lizzie Burke's for dinner last night," I casually mentioned.

Tia Marta glanced at me questioningly and I realized she had no idea who I was talking about.

"Sorry. Lizzie Krabbs, I mean." God! How I hated that name. "We used to be friends and neighbors when I worked in Las Vegas. I didn't know she'd moved here until we bumped into each other outside your house yesterday. I forget. How long is it that Lizzie's been coming to see you?" I inquired, doing my best to sound nonchalant.

Tia Marta gave me the eye, as if knowing what I was up to. She dished the eggs and sausage on to our plates, then sat down to join me. "That girl has been coming for cleansings at least once a week for over a year. But hers is a very difficult case. She always has lots of bad spirits hovering around."

I didn't doubt that for a second, what with F.U., Velma, and Mother Krabbs buzzing about like three Grade-A, certifiable wackos.

"She does seem to be a completely different person from the one I knew in Vegas," I offered.

"How so?" Tia Marta asked, popping a slice of chorizo into her mouth.

"Well, the Lizzie I knew was feisty, and funny, and ambitious. *That* Lizzie would never have taken guff from anyone. From what I can tell, that spark in her is gone."

Tia Marta nodded her head knowingly. "Unhappiness and too much money can do that to a person."

Perhaps it was hearing it out loud that helped clarify my suspicion. "Do you really think she's unhappy?" I asked.

"Isn't it obvious?" Tia Marta retorted.

I was nearly finished with breakfast when a flock of

chattering birds flew by, helping to jump-start my memory. "By the way, did you catch the hooting of that owl last night? I swear the thing was perched right outside my window, serenading me for hours."

Tia Marta blanched, her skin turning ghostly pale. Her fingers darted with the speed of a hummingbird's wings to skim her forehead, chest, and shoulders.

"It's a good thing I gave you another cleansing this morning. What you heard was an omen of death."

I sat in my office filled with paperwork, pondering last night's dinner and the mysterious Dr. Pierpont. The mere thought of Pierpont was enough to send my scam detector soaring straight into the stratosphere. I'd bet his promise of being able to clone Ten-Karat was as empty as a ruptured balloon. More likely, Pierpont planned to leave F.U. with lighter pockets and Lizzie with a broken heart.

The other item eating away at me was Fat Boy and his insistence on recovering Timmy Tom's cell phone. What was that bit of insanity all about? Acting on an off-the-wall hunch, I picked up the phone and placed a call to the Dona Ana County medical examiner.

"Jack Purdy's office. How may I help you?" intoned a bored-sounding female voice.

"I'm a relative of Timmy Tom Tyler." I threw in the right note of sorrow. "He's recently deceased. The victim of a terrible crime. Could you please tell me if his body has been sent up to Albuquerque yet for that autopsy they perform?"

"Who did you say you were again?" the secretary asked, sounding as if she'd rather be anywhere than on the other end of the phone.

"I'm his sister." I said, letting the hint of a sob slip out. "Tammy Taylor Tyler."

Silence filled the telephone wire. I figured I'd give it to the count of ten and then call back, pretending to be Timmy Tom's mother.

"I don't see anything here about his having relatives in the area," she finally replied, her tone tinged with a shade of suspicion.

"That's right, he doesn't. Which is why I've just flown in from Nashville," I half sang the info, stirring in a hefty dose of country western twang. "Me and Timmy Tom hadn't been real close these past few years. I can't tell you how bad that makes me feel—but I guess it's just something I'm going to have to learn to live with." Who said I'd lost my touch when it came to impromptu acting? "That's why I'd at least like to know if his body is still here. I only pray that his soul is at peace, floating somewhere up there in heaven."

"I'm sorry, but we're really not supposed to give out that kind of information," Purdy's secretary responded. However, her voice had begun to waver.

I moved in for the kill. "I gotta confess that it's not being allowed to know where Timmy Tom is that's breaking my heart in two." If Fish and Wildlife didn't work out, I could always try my hand at being the next Tammy Wynette. "Then there's Mama to think of, what with her high blood pressure condition. And to top it all off, she's about to run out of her cardiac pills!" Move over, Meryl Streep! I'd almost forgotten how good I could be.

"Well, I don't suppose it can do any harm," the voice on the other end crumbled. "His body is still here, but it's scheduled to be shipped up to Albuquerque after two o'clock today."

"Bless you," I sighed. "By the way, does the medical examiner happen to be in? Just in case I have any questions?"

"No, he's out at the moment. But I expect him back within the next hour," she replied.

I hung up, knowing I'd have to act fast if there was any chance of retrieving the information I wanted. Approaching Sheriff Bill Hutchins with my request would only impede my investigation. Quickly deciding upon a course of action, I jumped into my pick-up, set my mental fuzz buster on high alert for cops, and sped off.

At the medical examiner's office I tried to veer into one of the few available parking spaces, only to find none was large enough to for a pick-up. This was one of those times when there was no choice but to redefine what handicapped spaces were for.

I walked inside the medical examiner's office and came face-to-face with Purdy's secretary. She couldn't have been more than twenty years old, and looked exactly the way she'd sounded—bored and indifferent. The girl sat behind a desk littered with up-to-date issues of *Cosmopolitan*, *Elle*, and *In Style Magazine*, along with a hefty disarray of papers. The set-up was perfect.

"Hi, I'm Shirley Bassey. I have a ten o'clock meeting with Jack Purdy," I said. I figured she was too young to ever have heard the song "Goldfinger."

She looked at me curiously, one tweezed eyebrow arched ever so slightly. "Hey, weren't you the one who called on the phone a few minutes ago?"

"Wasn't me," I replied innocently. Damn! I was going to have to work on my accents.

Purdy's secretary continued to gaze warily at me. It was time for my New York roots to kick in. I took a deep breath and got pushy.

"My appointment? Ten o'clock? Remember?" I prodded.

Miss Cosmo's reaction was one of annoyance. She pushed her magazines about in no apparent hurry. I decided to help move things along by pulling the date book out from beneath her stack of reading material. The girl's gratitude couldn't have been more subliminal. Her press-on fingernails crawled through the calendar pages like a sloth on valium. My foot tap, tap, tapped an impatient beat, hoping that the rhythm might be catching.

"There's nothing scheduled here," she smugly told me.

"Hmm. That's odd. Jack left a message on my answering machine that he urgently needed to speak with me this morning. In fact, he specifically said he'd placed a note on your desk concerning our meeting."

Miss Cosmo's fingers rifled through the mess for another nano-second before she gave up and shrugged. "Well, since Mr. Purdy's not here right now, it doesn't much matter, does it?"

"It seems this place could use some better organization." I flashed a patient smile. "In any case, the rest of his message was that I should wait in his office if he hadn't yet arrived."

Our Gal Friday pointed toward two chairs standing on either side of a beat-up end table. "Feel free to sit over there. It's our waiting room."

"Thanks, but I'll just go into Jack's office as he suggested, since there are some calls I need to make," I countered.

The girl tugged at the hem of her skirt, as if some length would give her more authority. "Why don't you just make your phone calls from out here?"

My expression hardened into grim determination. "Because what I have to say requires total privacy." I pulled out my badge, quickly flashed it in Miss Cosmo's direction, and just as swiftly tucked it away again. "I'm a federal agent and the calls are highly confidential. So, if you'd just point the way to Jack's office, I know he'd appreciate it."

She silently nodded, having fallen for the bait. I felt bad about conning her, but figured it would teach Our Gal Friday an important life lesson. When you're a woman in this world, the one thing you can never do is to let hell, high water, man, beast—or in this case, another female—get the better of you.

I followed her down the hall and entered Purdy's office, shutting the door behind me. Clearly there wasn't a moment to lose, and I began to search for a roll of the same tape which had been used to seal Timmy Tom's body bag closed.

My pulse raced as I spotted a box that promised to hold the motherlode, my fingers fumbling as they opened the lid. But instead of tape, it contained magnets, key chains, and other knickknacks, all designed to resemble the chalked outlines of dead bodies. Great. A guy with a sense of cadaver humor.

I moved on to the filing cabinet, but it held nothing but files. The only item left to be exhumed was a free standing locker in the corner of the room. Naturally, it turned out to be locked.

"Is everything all right in there?" Purdy's secretary called from down the hall, apparently dubious as to what I was up to.

My eyes made a quick scan of the room. Damn! I'd forgotten to lift the phone off its hook! "Fine, thanks. I'm just organizing my notes. I'll be making my calls in a minute." I placed the phone's receiver on top of the desk and punched in the number to the twenty-four hour nationwide weather report. That ought to tie up the phone for a while. Then I pulled my ever-trusty Leatherman multi-tool out of my purse, walked back to the locker, and went to work.

I initially attempted to use the drop point blade, but the lock stubbornly refused to budge. Next, the screwdriver failed to pass the test. Heck, I even gave the awl a shot. My time was running out, and I hadn't had one iota of luck. I was almost ready to bite the proverbial dust, but there was no way some damned piece of hardware was going to screw me up. Grabbing the file, I steadied the blade and plunged its tip straight into the tumbler's heart.

Click! The lock released and sprang open.

Gotcha! I gloated, my spirits soaring on a high-octane current of toe-tingling exhilaration.

I victoriously grabbed the handle and pulled, only to have the locker door eject a loud *creeeaaak.* I held my breath and froze, but all remained quiet on the secretarial front. I continued on with my mission, trying to keep the door's squeaks to a minimum as I coaxed it open.

Eureka! Inside was the Fort Knox of evidence tape, with Purdy's name boldly emblazoned on each roll. All were neatly stacked in piles. A stash of his special magenta Magic Markers lay precisely lined up on the shelf below. I grabbed a roll of tape from the furthest stack, and filched one of his markers. Mission accomplished, I closed the locker and made a beeline back to my purse. I had just finished hiding my cache when the door to the office flew open. Purdy's secretary scrutinized me narrowly, her acrylic nails curling around the door frame ominously.

"Excuse me. But what did you say your name was again?" she asked. Her tone screamed that the time had just run out on my meter.

A glimpse at the phone provided the clue. The hold button for the second line flashed a warning red. Its message, *"You've been caught,"* flickered over and over.

"Angela Massey," I quickly improvised.

She scurried out the door. I grabbed my bag and ran after her, determined to cut her off at the pass before she picked up the receiver.

"I'm afraid I won't be able to stay any longer; there's another appointment I need to get to." I did my best to appear cool, calm and collected, considering that two pilfered items were burning a hot little hole in my purse.

"You're leaving so soon? But, Mr. Purdy's on the line. In fact, I was just about to tell him that you're here." A smarmy smile flitted about the corners of Miss Cosmo's mouth, while her hand hovered above the phone as if it were a bomb waiting to be detonated.

I leaned in towards her, prepared to do whatever was necessary to defuse it. "That's something you might want to reconsider. I've decided not to mention this little incident to Jack, but let me give you a word of advice. It'd be best if you cleaned off that desk so you can find the messages he leaves. And the next time I have an appointment? Make sure to write it in Mr. Purdy's date book. Otherwise, I guarantee that what spare time you have won't be spent reading magazines, but out hunting for a job."

I quickly turned on my boot heels and hauled ass out the office door. The first thing I did was to jump into my Ford. The second was to make sure I hadn't been followed. Only then did I place a call to Sonny Harris.

"Border Patrol tracker at your service," growled a voice with all the warmth of a pissed-off grizzly bear. "And make it snappy—I'm about to eat breakfast."

I heard Sonny take a large gulp of something that most likely wasn't a protein drink.

"Hi. It's me. Rachel." My greeting was answered by a distinctly loud slurp. Not a good sign. I needed Sonny bright-eyed and sober to set the rest of my plan into action. "How about I buy you a cup of coffee?" I offered.

"I've got a better idea: save that dollar for your retirement fund. Believe me, you're gonna need it. Why don't you just cut the crap and tell me what you're after?" he countered.

I've always had a soft spot for men who don't like to spend my money. "I need your help. Remember that dead informant I found yesterday? Well, I want to pay him another visit. The catch is that it's got to be done without anyone knowing."

"Why's that?"

"I didn't exactly hit it off with Sheriff Hutchins yesterday." I was counting on the fact there was no love lost between Sonny and the local sheriff's department, either. Especially since they'd rejected his recent offer to serve as a tracker. "I'm sure he's spread the word that I have no business getting involved in the case."

"And have you?"

Damn! "First off, Timmy Tom was *my* informant. *I'm* the one he woke up at five A.M. And *I'm* the one who fought off a band of vultures while Hutchins took his good old time getting there after I called him. So, yes. I think I've got every right to know what's going on with this case."

"You're quite the little spitfire when it comes to marking your territory, aren't you?" Sonny chuckled in amusement. "Okay. You're probably gonna have to break into the morgue. Must be you've chosen me to play the part of the patsy who gets to wield the crowbar."

"Sonny, do you really think I'd ask you to do something that was illegal?" I pretended to take offense.

"Only if you couldn't figure another way to get whatever you're after. Why don't you fill me in on the game plan?"

Sonny knew everyone at the morgue from his thirty years with the Border Patrol.

"I need your natural talent as a charming escort," I told him.

"Boy, are you ever desperate," he snorted.

"Personally, I prefer to think of myself more as relationship challenged," I countered. "So what do you say? Will you do it?"

"Sure. What the hell else have I got to do with myself all day? Besides, I can think of worse ways to spend my time than with a not-so-bad-looking redhead."

"Yeah. I know. You could be that black cow standing out in the sun in the middle of the desert," I said with a smile.

"You got it," Sonny replied.

I knew that was his way of saying he was totally looking forward to our adventure. We agreed to hook up at Memorial Medical's parking lot in half an hour.

Sonny arrived on time, swerving alongside me in his Mitsubishi pick-up. He was dressed in his usual attire of jeans, a blue flannel shirt, and dingy suede vest.

"How do I look?" Sonny asked, giving his bolo tie a slight tug.

"Like you're the John Wayne answer to my prayers," I replied, amply stroking his ego.

"Good," he said gruffly.

We walked inside and Sonny ambled up to the reception desk. Behind it sat a woman with a body the shape of a pear.

"Well, well. If it isn't Sonny Harris. You're looking mighty handsome these days." She bestowed a smile on him.

"Howdy there, Miss Mae. And aren't you the pretty

sight to behold walking into this place? I swear, if I were sick, I'd be feeling better already," he purred, piling on the charm.

Miss Mae's complexion turned candy apple red, and a girlish giggle came from her lips.

"This here's my niece, Clara Sue. She's visiting from back East, so I'm showing her around town."

Clara Sue? I flashed him a dirty look, and saw his mustache twitch.

Miss Mae pulled her gaze away from Sonny long enough to throw a bone of a nod my way.

"It's funny you should stop by today. It just so happens I've been thinking about cooking up a pot of that chili you love." Miss Mae paused, and coyly batted her eyelashes. "The problem is, I always tend to cook too much. It's near impossible for one person to eat it all by her lonesome."

The keyword here was "near." All it took was one look at Miss Mae's waistline to know she'd managed to overcome the impossible.

"Why, Miss Mae. If that's an invitation I hear, I'll be over quick as a longhorn steer heading for the cow pasture, spurs on and ready to do it justice," he bantered.

Miss Mae's gaze slid my way, and she gave a half-hearted simper. "Of course, you're welcome to come for dinner, as well."

Sure. I was about as welcome as a flock of disease-ridden vultures. "Thanks anyway, but I'll be heading back home real soon," I told her.

Miss Mae instantly brightened, warming up to me like a long lost cousin. "Oh, that's too bad! What a shame! How soon did you say you'd be leaving?"

"Day after tomorrow," I responded.

She turned and zoomed in on Sonny with the intensity

of a heat-seeking missile. "How about coming to my place the day after that?"

Sonny reached over and patted the dimpled flesh of her hand. "I'll bring the wine. You're in charge of dinner. By the way, you don't mind if I take Clara Sue to the morgue and introduce her to Harry Walters, do you?" he casually inquired.

"Why, of course not! You go right on down. And don't forget. Six-thirty Friday evening at my house." She blushed.

"It's a date," Sonny said with a wink.

"My bet is that she plans to whip up more than just peach cobbler for desert," I whispered as we walked away.

"You hush up!" Sonny scolded. But he couldn't hold back the grin that lit up his face. "It just so happens that I'm considered one of the more eligible bachelors around these parts."

Oy vey. I didn't want to think about what that said for my prospects in the dating marketplace. "Then I guess I better start brushing up on my chili recipe."

"Don't bother, Porter. You forget I've already tasted your cooking," Sonny responded.

Sonny pointed me toward the ladies' room. "Wait in there and give me five minutes before you head to the morgue. I'll haul Harry off for coffee in the cafeteria," he instructed, and took off.

Five minutes is a long time to wait when you're counting each second that goes by. I wasted a few minutes in carefully studying my face, and spied a brand new line. This could mean only one thing: the alpha-hydroxy moment had finally arrived.

With that thought, I headed toward the elevator and pushed the button for the basement floor. The car lurched and groaned, as though uncertain the cellar was a place it really wanted to go.

"Lingerie, ladies' apparel, and newly refrigerated cadavers!" sang a voice in my head.

The door opened and I trod down an empty hall, narrow and bare, a worn linoleum floor its only decoration. The echo of my footsteps held a disembodied, hollow sound.

The entrance to the morgue loomed ahead, its door as white as a freshly scrubbed surgical gown. I pushed it open to be greeted by a silence so loud, I could nearly hear the air itself breathing. The room was empty but for the shiny steel autopsy table which patiently stood waiting. Row upon row of drawers lay recessed inside the walls like neatly stacked cafeteria trays.

I dragged a pair of latex gloves from my bag and tugged them over skin that felt cold and clammy. Then I started in on the drawers.

Knock, knock, knock. Anybody home?

I pulled one compartment after the other open, ever so cautiously checking the toe tag on each permanently sleeping occupant. There was a John Smith, a Jane Doe, and a Luis Vasco.

"Pleased to make your acquaintance," they moaned.

I picked up my pace, knowing there was no time to dally. The guy I was looking for wasn't snoozing au natural under a sheet, but lying incommunicado inside an airless body bag.

I finally came upon a bag swaddled in evidence tape signed, sealed and delivered by none other than county medical examiner Jack Purdy. I double checked the tag to confirm this indeed was the booty I'd been searching for. Yep. Timmy Tom Tyler was listed as the bag's sole resident. It was time to pillage and plunder.

I carefully pulled off all three evidence bands that

sealed Tyler's body bag closed, and slowly undid the zipper. All the while, I wondered if I'd find anything different. Nope. Timmy Tom was still inside. So was his phone. All that had changed was his skin color. Oh, yeah—and the odor emanating from his body had definitely gotten stronger.

Tyler's eyes locked onto mine. *Stop screwing around and get on with it.*

I took a deep breath, and leaned in closer. The phone's mouthpiece end had been shoved down his throat. If his cell phone operated like my own, the power button would be situated on the bottom row. I slipped a finger inside Tyler's mouth. The next moment, a noise spewed out of Timmy Tom's throat.

I sprang backward in terror as he silently laughed at my fear. What I'd heard was the sound of Tyler's phone having been successfully activated.

Very funny. I went back to work, not pleased with Timmy Tom's post mortem sense of humor.

I stuck my finger back inside his mouth, this time hoping to locate the function button to the phone menu.

Beep, sounded a deep bass. *Blip,* sang out a higher soprano. My fingers randomly pressed a series of buttons in a sensory game of blind man's bluff. As two messages flashed on the screen, I felt like Aladdin, having hit the magical key to Tyler's cell phone kingdom. On the plus side, I was presented with a choice of menu options. On the negative side was the intermittent flash, "low battery."

Don't do this to me, Timmy Tom!

I opened the cell's phone book to scroll through its directory, tripping upon an index of Tyler's favorite haunts. All the while, the screen grew progressively dimmer.

Come on! Come on! I urged, silently praying to the

Eveready bunny. Where was he when you needed him? *Not here,* the low battery signal informed me.

Finally, something besides a restaurant or strip joint appeared. The name "Admiral Maynard" floated in and out of view, sounding familiar. I tried propping Timmy Tom's head up higher in an effort to get the phone closer to a source of light, as the letters "F.U." next slithered onto the screen. That took me by surprise, but there was no time to ponder their connection. Two listings still remained and the screen was now seriously flickering.

My arm ached from holding the dead weight of Timmy Tom's head, but the pay-off proved well worth it. Johnny Lambert's name arose in Tyler's A-list of contacts. Who'd have thought he'd be making a guest appearance?

My finger frantically stabbed at the scroll button, and one final name flashed into sight just before the screen faded to black: Dan Kitrell, the employee I'd met at the Happy Hunting Ranch. Then I remembered where I'd heard the name Admiral Maynard before: he supplied the ranch with good-enough-to-shoot critters.

I was about to zip Timmy Tom back up when I remembered the papers cached inside his money belt. Since Sheriff Hutchins had referred to them as being totally worthless, I figured he wouldn't mind if I removed them. I opened the money belt and claimed the paltry treasures, then zipped Tyler back up.

Pulling out my roll of filched evidence tape, I wrapped it around the duffel bag in exactly the same manner as before. Once finished, I initialed the letters "J.P." with magenta Magic Marker wherever the tape was crossed.

Then I slid the drawer closed and removed my latex gloves. Hopefully, this was the last morgue I'd have to see for a long time to come. After slipping out the door,

I hopped on the elevator and hitched a ride upstairs to join the world of the living.

Sonny and Harry Walters were heading in my direction just as the elevator door creaked open. I exited and walked a short distance away.

"Good seeing you again, Harry!" Sonny slapped him on the back while throwing me a harried glance.

"Stop by anytime, Sonny. God knows, you're better than the usual company I keep," Harry cracked. He stepped inside the elevator and pushed the button, and its doors slid closed.

Sonny swung around to face me. "Do you realize how close a call that was? You sure as hell like dancing close to the edge of danger, don't ya, Porter?"

I watched as he struggled to keep a straight face. Finally, he gave up and broke into a grin. "I gotta admit, that's also what I like best. I'm having myself a great time."

That was good to hear, because dancing on the edge is the only way I know.

We walked past Miss Mae, who reminded Sonny once more about dinner on Friday night, and cheerfully wished me a good trip home. Then we headed outside into the parking lot.

"So, did you get everything you needed back there?" Sonny asked.

"Yes," I replied, not yet sure. "Thanks, I couldn't have done it without you."

Sonny grunted. "Listen, I might want to take a look around for myself in the area where you found that body."

"What are you, checking up on me?" I asked, knowing he'd most likely come across something I'd missed.

"I won't bother to clue you in on whatever I find, if it makes you feel any better. Course, the thing to remember is that a pat on the back is only this far from a kick in the rear," Sonny cheerfully reminded me.

I knew I could use whatever help the man was willing to offer. "Just call me Grasshopper, master, willing to learn at your feet," I ribbed him.

"Cut the crap and just give me some landmarks to go by," Sonny instructed.

I watched him take off in the direction of the Anapra Road, wishing I could go with him. But I was already running late for my next appointment. And after last night, I knew Mother Krabbs wasn't one to be kept waiting.

Seven

The road to Crazy Cat Mountain undulated as sinuously as an exotic dancer. As I drove, I noticed how different the view looked in the daytime. El Paso's streets stretched out below like the neatly gridded lines of a waffle iron. Not so the case with Mexico. Poverty slouched like a rabid beast through snarling streets, and spread into densely packed hillsides awash with make-shift villages of squatters. The tin roofs of their shacks caught the sunlight and reflected it back, so that the mountains seemed to scintillate in a conflagration of mini bonfires.

I parked my vehicle at the Krabbs mansion, the disparity in wealth overwhelming. But that's what the border has always been about: the struggle between those with power and those without. The front door flew open and Mother Krabbs clomped out with her walker.

"Where the hell have you been? It's a quarter after twelve. We've got fifteen minutes before my blood sugar drops lower than my rear end," the tyrant barked. "You might as well come inside while I finish getting ready."

I followed, knowing I had to be as crazy as she was to have come back here today. At least Ten-Karat was happy to see me. All twelve pounds of her jumped up and down, the mini-trampolines on the bottoms of her paws in perfect working condition. But her high-pitched yapping was as irritating as a four A.M. car alarm.

"Jesus Christ! Shut the hell up already!" Mother Krabbs yelled. Ten-Karat responded by leaping up into the air and licking her on the mouth.

"Yecchhh! I don't suppose you could get rid of this thing for me? I'll make it worth your while if you make the pooch disappear."

"I don't think that's something you should be joking about," I told her sternly.

"Who's joking?" She snorted. "Hell, does Fido look like she's worth spending three million bucks on, to you? Even worse, imagine having ten of these damned things jumping around the place like a hyperactive herd of yo-yos. I'll give you fifty bucks to take the mutt off my hands. No questions asked," she snapped.

"Don't even consider it," I retorted.

"Well, aren't you the moral one." Ma Krabbs gave me the eye. "Either that, or the government is paying you people more money than you're worth."

It's always nice to know the public is so firmly behind us. I sighed, wondering if I could cite her for trying to bribe a federal official.

"Since you're apparently making the big bucks, lunch is on you today," she informed me. Ma Krabbs grabbed a purse the size of a small suitcase and headed out the door, where she caught sight of my mode of transportation.

"You've got to be kidding. You don't expect me to ride in that thing, do you?" she asked.

"Sorry, but my Mercedes is in the shop today," I said.

"A Mercedes?" Mother Krabbs scoffed, looking up her nose at me. "I wouldn't be caught dead in one of those Nazimobiles. My fanny only rides in something that's one-hundred-percent American made." She impatiently tapped a foot clad in a gold peek-a-boo sandal. Its design indiscreetly exposed a set of toenails that were as thick as a deep dish pizza. "What the hell. If we're going to lunch, we might as well do it in style."

Mother Krabbs rummaged around in her purse. "Here. Hold this stuff for me," she commanded.

Out came a comb, some lipstick, and a small can of hairspray. A toothbrush and denture cleaner followed closely behind. A hefty stack of coupons held together by an ancient rubber band followed, along with a large change purse, and her Krabbs First National Bank pass-book.

"Don't try and snitch any money either, because I'm watching," she warned.

The last thing she added onto the growing pile was a metal container in the shape of a cowboy boot.

"Those are F.U., Sr.'s. ashes in there," she informed me. "According to the terms of his will, I have to take him with me wherever I go."

Finally, Ma Krabbs pulled a slim black gadget from her bag, and pushed its button. One of the mansion's four garage doors instantly arose to reveal a baby blue Cadillac DeVille.

Ching, ching, ching! sang a set of car keys.

I looked over and saw a key chain dangling off the tip of Mother Krabbs' finger.

"I buy a new one of these babies every year on my birthday, and then never seem to go anywhere. Since I'm not getting any younger and you sure as hell aren't ever going to be rich enough to own one, we might as well take it out for a spin and put some miles on this thing." She threw me the keys. "Let's hit the road and head out of here."

After getting Mother Krabbs settled I sank back into the Caddy's soft leather seat. Wow! No wonder senior citizens liked to drive around in these things, even if they could barely see above the steering wheel.

Mother Krabbs directed me into the heart of downtown El Paso to a squat pink cinder block dive. Not only was the place situated on a run-down corner, but it came with its own wino.

"*That's* where you want to go?" I asked in astonishment.

"Hmph! Apparently clothes aren't the only thing you're lacking taste in," she haughtily responded. "Garcia's just so happens to have the best burgers in town."

Well, tie me up and throw me down. Who'd ever have thought it? As soon as I'd slid into one of Garcia's stained and ripped booths I discovered why she was really so fond of the dump. This was probably the last place in town where she was still allowed to come without getting kicked out.

"Hey! I'm starving over here! Do you think someone could wake up long enough to hop to it?" she barked.

A waiter languorously made his way over to the table, wearing a smirk, a grease splattered shirt, and a thin pair of pants.

"And what can I get for you two lovely young ladies?" he inquired, running his tongue along his lips.

"Save it, Miguel. The only thing I want from you is some food. Of course, *she* might be interested in whatever else you're offering," Ma Krabbs retorted.

The springs in my seat were already so shot, it was impossible for me to slink any further down without my rear end hitting the floor.

"The name is Jose," the waiter coldly responded.

"Whatever you say, Pepe. I'll take a green chili cheeseburger, juicy and rare, with a large side of fries. And the redhead there"—she pointed a finger in my direction—"will give you an extra big tip if you make it snappy. My blood sugar's heading south of the border."

"And what can I get for you?" Jose asked me.

It was probably safest to order something Ma Krabbs wasn't having. I could only imagine what extra nasty ingredients Jose might throw into her food.

"I'll have a bowl of tortilla soup," I answered politely.

I waited until Jose had left before turning my attention to the demon sitting across from me. "Okay. We're here. So, what's this information you've got?"

But Mother Krabbs stubbornly shook her head. "Uh, uh. That's not the deal. First we eat. Then we talk."

Whatever Jose added to Mother Krabbs' meal apparently agreed with her. She grabbed the plate from his hands and enthusiastically bit into the burger as if it were the first food she'd eaten in days.

Once our plates had finally been removed, I asked, "*Now* can we talk?"

"After I order desert," she loftily informed me.

The hot fudge sundae arrived, and I waited until Mother Krabbs' spoon was raised in mid-air before pulling the dish away from her.

"Hey! What the hell's up?" she demanded.

"Start talking, or I'll let this thing melt," I threatened.

Ma Krabbs broke into a sly smile. "So, you like to play hardball, do you?"

"Another five seconds and *I'm* the one eating the sundae," I warned.

"All right! You win," she pouted.

I pushed the ice-cream back towards her.

Ma Krabbs instantly dug in. "It's that flimflammer Dr. Scissorhands. The way I read it, he plans to bilk that dolt-headed son of mine out of every last dime he can get his hooks on. I know bull dookey when I smell it, and he's cooking up a big, old steaming pile of it. That's what I want *you* to look into." She emphasized her point by jabbing a spoonful of Rocky Road ice cream in my direction.

"You're son's not a stupid man. Maybe you're just not giving him enough credit," I said, playing devil's advocate.

"Now *that's* a pile of horse crap, if ever I heard it. You know as well as I do that F.U. couldn't count to twenty-one if he took off his boots and unzipped his fly. His problem is, he's pussy whipped, and there's more than one feline in the barn that's doing it."

There was no question that Mother Krabbs was a royal pain in the rear. However, she was also sharp enough to be aware of everything going on around her.

"What you're looking for is a private investigator. I only deal in cases involving wildlife," I reminded her.

"Don't you think I would have gotten someone other than you already, if I could have?"

Mother Krabbs certainly knew how to stroke a gal's ego.

"F.U. knows every living soul in this town. There's nobody else who'll take on this case without him learning about it. Besides, that obnoxious, yapping ball of fur is wildlife. I don't see why you should have any problem taking that mutt on as one of your clients."

"I deal only in *endangered* wildlife," I clarified.

"You want endangered? Well, the pooch is *numero uno* on my hit list. How's that for zooming the little fleabag right up to the front of your priority file?" she retorted. "And if you still won't take the case, I'll sue you for animal discrimination. Just because Ten-Karat is nothing more than a poor little Chihuahua, shouldn't mean she doesn't deserve your professional assistance. Besides, my tax dollars pay your salary."

"Ten-Karat is a Pomeranian," I corrected her.

"Whatever! All I know is that the damn thing barks, has fur, and is costing me a fortune."

I was surprised she didn't try to throw in that Ten-Karat had also fought at the Alamo.

"Here's my final offer: if it's info you want on dirty dealings with critters, then my grandson is the one you need to talk to."

She'd lost me.

Mother Krabbs shook her head impatiently. "I swear, I'm surrounded by a bunch of nitwits."

I was beginning to think F.U., Sr. had died just to escape her.

"You remember, he's the animal rights nut with too much free time on his hands. He's always hearing about some kind of shenanigans. I'll make sure that he gives you an earful. In exchange, you help me out," she bargained.

The woman had a pair of cojones larger than a stud bull's during mating season.

"Maybe I'm missing something, but what do I need you for? I can deal with your grandson directly."

"Not if I instruct him not to speak to you," she responded. "Trust me. F.U., Jr. isn't stupid enough to piss off his grandmother, especially since I'm the one holding the purse strings to his inheritance."

"And what is this information your grandson has?" I asked curiously.

"Ah! Now that's the sixty-four-thousand-dollar question, isn't it? Or the three-million-dollar question, to be more precise." Mother Krabbs slid the sundae between us.

"There's still one problem: I have no idea as to the location of Pierpont's lab."

"Scissorhands is holed up on F.U.'s cattle ranch, the Flying A, just over the border in New Mexico."

Talk about your strange occurrences. The Flying A happened to be the very same ranch that former Fish and Wildlife agent Johnny Lambert was working on. Ma Krabbs had just snagged me hook, line, and sinker.

"If Dr. Pierpont isn't working on a cloning project, then what do you think he's really doing?" I asked.

Mother Krabbs rolled a spoonful of ice-cream deep into a pool of rich chocolate. "I think he's jerking all of us around while he's busy draining me of my fortune." She held the fudge-drenched ice cream toward me, as tempting as if it were the forbidden apple. "So, do we have a deal?"

The bowl of Rocky Road whispered to me not to say no. I took hold of the spoon and brought it to my mouth.

I dropped Mother Krabbs at the mansion, got directions to her grandson's abode, and plunged back down into the heart of El Paso. I drove until I reached the Border Highway, North America's version of the Berlin Wall. F.U., Jr. resided directly across the border from Mexico in a run-down, abandoned warehouse. I walked to the front door and pressed the buzzer.

An angry voice bellowed, as if I'd been ringing the bell for hours. "Yeah. I hear you. What is it?"

"My name is Rachel Porter, and I'm a Fish and Wild-life agent," I responded. There was nothing but silence. Either F.U., Jr. wasn't overly anxious to meet me, or had passed out in sheer exhilaration at the thought.

I waited another moment, then decided to find out just how much power Mother Krabbs actually had. "Your grandmother sent me."

She was apparently able to kick ass all the way across town, for F.U., Jr. miraculously regained the use of his tongue.

"Haul it up to the second floor," he snarled.

He'd clearly inherited his grandmother's charm. A buzz pierced the air and I pulled the door open, then walked into a darkened hall.

Grunge clung to the filthy walls, matched by a layer of grime which coated the floor. I entered the decrepit freight elevator. The gate creaked closed, and the machine gave a metallic death rattle before slowly beginning to ascend. I held my breath, fearing that any movement on my part would result in certain calamity. I exhaled as two black canvas sneakers finally appeared slightly above me, then a pair of black cotton pants, a black tee-shirt, and lastly, F.U., Jr.'s perfectly shaven head.

He looked like the poster boy for a body piercing store. An array of hoops hung from his ears, eyebrows, and nose. But his body decoration didn't stop there. A trail of ball bearings lay buried beneath the flesh of both forearms, running from elbow to wrist, like the entombed spine of a prehistoric beast.

"F.U., Jr.?" I ventured.

"F.U., Jr. is dead. My name is Rage." He threw back his head and roared.

Was the whole family certifiable, or had I just entered the twilight zone known as the Generation Gap?

"You said my grandmother sent you?" F.U., Jr. turned and led the way into his loft.

"Yes. She thought it would be a good idea for us to meet." I was beginning to think Mother Krabbs was more off her rocker than I had imagined.

I walked across rotting floor boards which softly sagged with each step I took, as though my feet were treading upon a sea of sinking graves. For lighting, F.U., Jr. had decided to go the simple route. Bare bulbs hovered overhead, precariously suspended by a ganglia of electrical wires. Alongside them, an abundance of paper streamers swayed in the stale breeze of an ancient fan, filling the air with ghostly whispers. As I drew closer I saw they were long strips of fly paper, festooned with hundreds of trapped insects. Mainly flies, the bugs ranged from alive and kicking to dead and decaying. Maybe it was time for someone to suggest that Metal Boy call in an exterminator.

"You seem to have a problem with fly infestation in this place," I noted dryly. "If I were you, I'd complain to the landlord."

F.U., Jr. shook a head as shiny as a cueball. "What you're looking at is my art. I get my flies through a mail order service and then release them inside the loft. Its purpose is to show man's struggle with the shit that goes on in our lives every day," he condescended to explain.

Okey dokey. From my point of view, it simply looked like the kid was hell bent on giving a bunch of flies a hard time. Either that, or the insects had chosen to commit mass suicide rather than live here.

Leaning against the walls was an assortment of ten-foot-high canvases, each bearing a variation on a single theme: fully erect penises. One exploded in a display of colorful fireworks, while another took on the shape of an automatic rifle ejecting what I imagined were bullets. No wonder Mother Krabbs wanted to keep track of her money. F.U., Jr. was going to be needing it for some heavy duty therapy.

"Is this your work, also?" I asked.

"No. My girlfriend Cassandra paints those. But I'm the model," he said proudly.

Like I couldn't have guessed. A third painting depicted a penis as the Eiffel Tower, with one extra addition: a column of silver ball bearings ran up the entire length of its shaft. F.U., Jr. had apparently found his soul mate.

So much for psycho small talk; it was time to get to the real reason why I was here. Rage sat down at a rickety metal table filled with herbal supplements, and I joined him.

"Your father claims you're the one responsible for that bogus call to my office about monkeys being shot at his place," I informed him.

"You mean that stop-'n'-pop drive-through slaughterhouse he calls a hunting ranch? Let me guess: I'll bet he offered you a fun-filled free weekend package of food, booze, and blood-letting massacre. Did you take him up on it?" Rage taunted.

Nobody could ever accuse the kid of masking his true feelings. I decided he deserved the same treatment from me.

"I'm not a big supporter of hunting ranches, but I also don't appreciate having my time wasted on a wild goose chase. So, take this as a warning: don't do it to me again."

"I guess that means you're not interesting in learning the real truth, then," F.U., Jr. challenged.

I pushed aside a few bottles of his herbal path to happiness and planted my elbows on the table. "What say we cut the crap and get down to business? Any action I take depends on whether you've got concrete information that I can investigate. Or are you only interested in jerking me around and spouting philosophical drivel? We can sit here all day discussing the ethics of hunting ranches, while you continue to play hide and seek with a bunch of toy monkeys, or you can tell me whatever you know, and actually do something useful. Saving wildlife is the only thing I'm interested in. If you want to help, that's great. Otherwise, stay out of my way."

F.U., Jr's his face took on a dark reddish glow. But instead of detonating, the kid took a deep breath and nodded. "Yeah. I've got some information for you. One of my father's ranch hands has been inquiring about monkeys."

Monkeys! If the kid was fooling around, I fully intended to throttle him. On the other hand, his father *had* been listed in Timmy Tom's cell phone directory. And there was no question that if Krabbs were in the market for monkeys, Tyler was the man he'd have gone to.

"Maybe the guy's looking for some pets," I casually suggested. "What kind of monkeys is this ranch hand trying to get hold of?"

F.U., Jr. didn't answer. I waited a full minute, but nothing. The only response came from the elevator, which groaned its way back down to the main floor. The sound echoed off in the distance. Okay, game time was over. I got up and began to walk away.

"Chimpanzees," he said.

"What's that?" I asked, wanting to make sure of what I'd heard.

"My father's ranch hand. That's what he's after—chimpanzees."

My blood began to stir. Suddenly, I didn't even care if the kid was lying. This was the first bit of intrigue I'd hit upon since being kicked out of Miami, and I fully intended to savor every blessed moment of it. I sat back down.

"How do you know this employee has been asking around about chimps?" I began.

"Because Cassandra told me," Rage replied.

Now, *there* was a reliable source.

"She overheard it," he added.

"Are you saying your girlfriend just happened to be hanging out at the Happy Hunting Ranch, where she overheard one of the workers talking about this in passing?" I asked skeptically.

"Of course not," Rage responded. "She was at her father's house when the guy paid a visit."

"And just who might Cassandra's father be?" I asked, my doubts beginning to solidify.

"He's a guy by the name of Admiral Maynard. Ever hear of him?"

The name had popped up a few times over the past two days. Not only had Maynard appeared on Tyler's phone directory, but he also supplied F.U.'s ranch with its critters. Interesting, that F.U. and Maynard's offspring were romantically linked.

"Yeah, I have. Why is he called 'Admiral,' anyway?" I inquired. "Did he serve in the Navy?"

F.U., Jr. grunted. "Nah. It's a nickname that's stuck with him. You'll know why when you get a load of his cap."

I needed Rage to fill in more of the gaps. "How does Cassandra know this guy works for your father?"

"Because that's what he told Maynard. Also, Cassandra's seen him at the ranch before," Rage replied.

"I don't understand why your father would be interested in obtaining chimps," I prodded. "They're not your typical trophy animal." Shooting a chimp for sport would be the equivalent of killing man's nearest relative. But then, maybe that was its allure.

It was Rage's turn to shrug. "Who knows? My father has his own agenda. After all, look at the gold digger he married."

"Hey, watch it. That's my friend you're talking about," I warned.

F.U., Jr. looked momentarily startled. "You know Lizzie?"

"That's right."

"Sorry," Rage muttered. "In any case, that's why I placed that anonymous call to your office. I figured having you stop by the ranch might shake the old man up enough to make him ditch whatever it is he's involved in. Besides, I needed to get your attention, and it worked, didn't it?" he grinned.

The only thing worse than a wise-ass kid is a wise-ass kid who's actually smart.

"I've got something else you'll be interested in." Rage stretched his arms, letting the bait dangle. "Cassandra also heard her father calling around, trying to get hold of a black rhino. Is that enough of a trophy animal for you?"

"It'll do," I diffidently answered, resolved to remain cool.

My stomach was turning topsy turvy cartwheels in excitement. If Rage's information was correct, I hadn't just hit a vein of illicit activity, but a major artery.

I had one last question. "Did Cassandra happen to catch the name of the ranch hand asking about chimps?"

Rage smugly nodded his head. "The guy's name is Dan Kitrell."

Bingo! Grizzly Adams, the last entry on Timmy Tom's cell phone 'who's who' of skullduggery.

"Thanks, Rage." I began to head out, and pushed the button for the elevator. "Hey, have you met Dr. Martin Pierpont?"

Rage nodded, grabbing at a fly in the air.

"What's your impression of him?" I queried.

"Just that he makes Dr. Strangelove look like your normal, average guy," F.U., Jr. responded.

"Your grandmother mentioned Pierpont's lab is at your father's cattle ranch in New Mexico." I figured this was a good time to double check the information.

F.U., Jr. shot me a look which telegraphed that something wasn't quite kosher. "Grandma must have lost a few more of her marbles. My old man gave the Flying

A to an environmental group over a year ago, as a land trust."

I got into the elevator, which began to sink beneath my feet of its own accord. Weird. "But your father spoke as if he still owned the ranch."

"He thinks of it as his, because he didn't get any money for it. My father claims he gave away the fifteen thousand acres to prove that he's really a conservationist. But that's nothing but a pile of crap."

If he'd actually given the land to be preserved, he deserved credit for it. "Lots of environmental groups take on ranches to save them from development. Personally, I think it's a good thing."

I pushed the elevator button, and the gate closed with a rasp.

"True," Rage grudgingly agreed. "Except my old man didn't give away the ranch out of the goodness of his heart; he wanted the tax break."

The lift suddenly dipped, then moaned as if in complaint of my weight. God, these old things were spooky. Maybe this was a good time to ask if there were stairs?

"So what's the name of this environmental group?"

"It's called The Southwest Heritage Trust," F.U., Jr. responded.

The elevator began to descend, suddenly lurched, and then let loose a loud shriek. The next thing I knew, I was falling through space.

I've always read your life flashes before your eyes when faced with death. That wasn't the case for me. All I could think of were the people I cared about and would never again see. I was more frightened than I'd ever before been, knowing I had absolutely no control over the situation—and could very well become Timmy Tom's neighbor in an adjoining drawer at the morgue.

The elevator slammed into the ground, causing the

gate to fly open, as my knees buckled like a marionette's cut loose from its strings. A vacuum of silence embraced me, to be slowly replaced by a distant ringing in my ears. The chimes grew louder until my head was buzzing from the vibration. I felt something sticky against my cheek, and realized my face was plastered against the floor. I took a deep breath and every inch of my body ached.

"Holy shit! Are you okay?"

I nodded my head as Rage's face floated into view above me, like a pierced angel without any wings.

"Good thing there was only one level for the elevator to drop. Otherwise, I'd probably be scraping you off the floor," he added with a relieved grin.

How consoling. I glanced at him, wondering what made him think I *didn't* require the assistance of a spatula. Rage joined me on the floor as I checked to make sure nothing was broken, and then slowly sat up.

"This elevator really sucks. I've been afraid something like this would happen. That's why I always make Cassandra take the stairs."

"Good advice," I replied dryly, wishing he'd given me the same warning.

F.U., Jr. took hold of my elbow and helped me onto my feet. So much for my clean outfit. My shirt and pants had a new design—patchwork dust and dirt.

"You look pretty good for playing bungee jump without a cord," Rage remarked, helping to brush me off. "A little shook up but otherwise not a scratch on you."

Great. That meant the damage must be all internal. There went my excuse for plastic surgery.

"You sure you're okay? Maybe you should get some rest," Rage offered.

"I'm fine," I groaned and headed out the door toward my Ford. Everything hurt, making me feel as if I were ninety years old. I should have known the building was a deathtrap the moment I entered.

Opening the vehicle door, I pulled myself in with thoughts of lawsuits and landlords dancing in my head. That is, until I caught sight of the mess which awaited me. The glove compartment had been torn apart and the door pockets emptied, with papers and chocolate bars strewn all about. The only thing missing was a cow's head with a phone.

My assortment of aches and pains turned to fear as my teeth began to chatter. The point couldn't have been made any clearer. The plunge in the elevator had been no accident—I was lucky to be alive.

Eight

The clouds lay draped across the top of the Franklin Mountains, as thickly luxurious as a sleeping Persian cat. But I was barely aware of the surroundings as I drove. Two warnings so close together meant I had to be on the track of Tyler's killer. Now I just had to figure out what that track was. As for Rage, it was possible that he was just an overaged adolescent, bound and determined to screw with his father. It was clear neither he nor Lizzie liked one another, so maybe this was payback time for having been replaced in F.U.'s affections by a young and beautiful stepmother.

The other odd thing was this business with the Flying A ranch. It was possible Johnny Lambert had been kept on as manager by Southwest Heritage Trust. If so, they obviously hadn't bothered to check out his background. Even more peculiar was that Pierpont was allowed to maintain his lab there. Maybe a deal of some sort had been struck between F.U. and the Trust. Otherwise, a few of the Krabbs family members didn't appear to have their facts straight. My thoughts were interrupted by the ringing of my cell phone.

"Rach! It's me!" slurred a voice.

That helped a lot. With the country music blaring in

the background, I could be talking to Shania Twain, for all I knew.

"It's Lizzie!" the voice sobbed this time. "Don't you remember me anymore?"

Oh, oh. The new Mrs. Krabbs was sounding pretty plotzed.

"I'm at the Round-up. Can you come by? I really want to talk to you!" she shouted above the twang of a "my-wife-has-gone-and-left-me" guitar.

"You can talk to me anytime, darling," a male voice responded, sounding as if he were right next to her. That was followed by a deep grunt. I figured Lizzie had probably slugged the guy.

"Stay where you are! I'll be right over," I instructed, with visions of *Thelma and Louise* dancing in my head. The Round-up was a country-western bar known to get mighty rowdy—yet I was almost glad for the diversion.

I made my way to the run-down strip it was located on, and entered a joint where the Marlboro Man would have felt fully at home. Smoke curled like phantom lassoes roping the crowd closely together in a drunken reverie, where cowboy wannabes eyed eligible women as if they were picking out prize-winning heifers. I dosey-doed through the front door and headed directly toward the bar.

The good news was that Lizzie was easy to spot: she was the only cowgirl dressed head to toe in gold lame spandex with fringe. All except for her boots, which were missing. A couple of hotshot kids were drinking beer out of them. The bad news was that Lizzie was totally soused.

"Rach! You came!" she half-cried, and half-laughed. "Do you know you're the very best friend I've got in this whole, wide world?"

Lizzie tried to haphazardly sling an arm around my

shoulder but missed. I propped her back into place against the bar, then picked up her glass and took a whiff. The drink contained enough booze to knock me over with just a sniff.

"What have you been drinking? One-hundred-ninety-proof grain alcohol?" I asked.

Lizzie thought about it for a moment, and her brown eyes grew wide. "Jeez. How do you like that? I can't seem to remember. It could have been a tequila sunset. Or maybe it was a tequila sunrise." She laughed in surprise. "Oh, what the hell! Just as long as it does the job." Lizzie removed her gold cowboy hat, lifted it high in the air, and threw it at the bartender to get his attention. "Hey! Hot stuff! How about a coupla frozen Cuervo margaritas for me and my girlfriend over here?"

"Make that two ginger ales instead," I directed, before the bartender's palm hit the blender. I took the hat from his hand, and placed it back on Lizzie's head.

Then I tapped one of the kids drinking out of Lizzie's very expensive boots on the shoulder. "Finished with those yet?" I politely inquired.

"Why? You want to buy us another round?" challenged a kid with a chin full of peach fuzz.

"No. I want the boots back," I informed him. My mind was beginning to spin its own country western ballad: "Mothers, Don't Let Your Sons Grow Up To Be Morons."

"And why would we do that?" piped up his equally underaged companion.

"Because otherwise I intend to check your ID. And if I find that they're fake, not only will I slap you both with a fine, but give you a choice between community service or jail time."

I slammed my badge down on the bar hard enough to rattle all the glasses and bottles in the vicinity, then retrieved it quickly. With any luck, the two lunkheads would be too drunk to realize I was a wildlife agent.

The budding cretins instantly busied themselves wiping, drying, and finally buffing Lizzie's footwear.

"Thanks. By the way, do something about your breath. You boys could slay a dragon," I informed them, and took possession of the boots.

The bartender must also have caught a glimpse of my badge as I'd rolled out the gold. Two ginger ales promptly appeared on the counter.

"No charge," he muttered and walked away.

I steered Lizzie, her boots, and the two drinks past the heel-stomping dancers and grabbed one of the few spare tables. Lizzie sat with her shoulders slumped, looking like a tarnished statuette as she picked up the gingerale and took a sip. Then she burst into a torrent of tears. The fringe on her hermetically sealed outfit bobbed up and down in rhythm with the music. Even in her present state, Lizzie had what it took to pass as a Bond girl.

"What's the matter?" I asked. "Did you and F.U. have some sort of fight?"

Lizzie responded by crying even harder. I swiped the napkins from under some empty glasses at the next table and handed them to her. They were a little damp, but then so was she.

"Here. Blow your nose," I instructed.

Lizzie did as she was told.

"I feel horrible about the way I acted last night," she moaned.

"What are you talking about? You were fine," I assured her. All I could figure was that Pierpont must be miffed she'd told me about his project.

"You don't understand." Lizzie woozily shook her head. "I've been pretending to be happy, when the truth is that I'm totally miserable!" she confessed.

I wasn't all that surprised, considering the cast of characters she was dealing with.

"Even worse, I feel paralyzed. I know I need to make some kind of change, but I'm not sure what to do, Rach."

"You could always move in with me for a while. It's not a mansion on Crazy Cat Mountain, but Tia Marta and I will be there," I offered.

Lizzie had taken me under her wing and into her home after I'd received a little "housewarming" mailbomb from some Nevada homeboys, so the least I could do was the same for her.

"Are you saying I should leave F.U.?" Lizzie asked, tears welling up in her eyes once again.

"Well, it is one option," I suggested.

Lizzie despondently played with the diamond ring on her finger as she thought it over. "If I leave F.U., what have I got to look forward to? Another office job that I'll hate, as I watch my life and my dreams pass me by?"

As far as I could tell, that's exactly what she was doing now.

"What you love is dancing, Lizzie. Maybe it's time you get back to doing it," I advised. "You don't have to be in Vegas or treading the boards on Broadway. If you can spend millions on cloning Ten-Karat, why not start your own dance company right here in El Paso?"

"There's something else I haven't told you. I think F.U. is fooling around," Lizzie quietly said.

She was probably right. After all, the old coot had come on to me, not to mention whatever he had going with Velma.

"Do you still love him?" I asked gently.

"I'm not really sure anymore," Lizzie confided with

a sob. "Half the time, I'm wondering where he is. The rest of the time, I just want him out of the house. What I *can* tell you is that living with Crazy Krabbs doesn't make my life any easier."

Since Lizzie was asking for advice, I decided to give it to her. "You know what I really think you should do? Kick some butt, lay down the law, and get back to being who you were when F.U. first met you."

Lizzie blew her nose with newfound determination. "You're absolutely right, Rach. It's time I took charge of what's going on around me," she said decisively.

Hey, if I got canned from Fish and Wildlife, I could always go into counseling cowgirls who get the blues.

Suddenly I spotted close to four-hundred pounds in bib overalls on the other side of the room. It had to be Fat Boy. Even more intriguing was that he wasn't alone. By his side was none other than F.U.'s ranch hand, Dan Kitrell. This definitely called for some serious snooping around.

I turned back to Lizzie, whose head was now smack down on the table, and spent the next few minutes getting her outside into my Ford.

"Where to, Lizzie?" I inquired. "You know that you're more than welcome to stay with me."

Lizzie curled up and laid her head against the window. "That's sweet of you, Rach. But I really need to get home," she replied.

I drove her back up Crazy Cat Mountain, parked, and helped her inside the house. Then I got back in the Ford and followed the trail of stars home, my thoughts occupied with Timmy Tom, Fat Boy, and their odd assortment of business associates—and which of them might want me dead.

Nine

I woke to the sound of tapping on my window pane and glanced at the clock. Six A.M. I closed my eyes and Harrison Ford flashed a hot little smile, persuading me to pay no attention. But the rapping grew progressively louder. I rolled over to find out what all the ruckus was about, and discovered Sonny Harris at my open window.

"For chrissakes! Don't tell me you're into playing Peeping Tom these days," I chided, pulling the sheet tighter around me.

"If I were, I wouldn't be waking you up now, would I?" Sonny replied. "I'll let myself in the front door, so you don't think I'm peeking at whatever it is you've got that's so different from every other woman. In the meantime, stop dreaming about whoever's got you all riled up and stick some clothes on."

I shot him a glance, wondering how he knew about Harrison. By the time I'd thrown on jeans and a tee-shirt, Sonny was already heating his own pot of coffee. Literally. Harris refused to drink anyone's brew but his own.

"That's 'cause no one but a true cowboy knows how to make the real stuff," he'd once told me.

His beat-up aluminum kettle sat spitting and snorting on my stove like a bucking bronco, with good reason.

By his own account, Harris hadn't washed it in over ten years, claiming it was part of the "seasoning" process.

"Make yourself at home," I remarked, as he pulled out two mugs from my cupboard.

"I always do," Sonny responded in true buckaroo fashion, and handed me a cup. I took a sip. The brew was thick enough to float a horseshoe.

"This is the kind of stuff that'll put hair on your chest," Sonny boasted.

"That ought to be a real treat for some lucky guy one of these days," I retorted.

I knew something special had to be going on since Sonny was up so early. The second tip-off was the extra strong coffee. The third was the enormous black plastic bag which sat on the floor at his feet.

"Did you bring your own breakfast with you, as well? Or is there something else in that bag I should know about?" I inquired.

"It's an item I found out near your murder scene. I thought you might find it interesting," he informed me.

I untied the knot and took a peek. Inside lay a dead vulture. Maybe Sonny had just a little too much free time on his hands.

"Well? Aren't you going to take a better look than that? Or can't you be bothered checking something unless it jumps up and bites you on the nose?" Sonny reprimanded.

When he put it that way, there didn't seem to be much choice. I donned a pair of latex gloves and tried to weight-lift the creature out of the sack.

"Do you think you can help me with this thing?" I asked with a grunt.

Sonny broke into a guffaw. "Sure. I was just waiting until you asked."

Out came a turkey vulture, one of America's largest

birds of prey. Its unfeathered red head glared at me, pugnacious as a punch-drunk boxer. We spread open the vulture's seventy-two-inch wing span, then went to work giving it a preliminary exam.

No bullet wounds or other marks were to be found on the carcass. That ruled out foul play in my mind.

"So, what do you see?" Sonny prodded, impatiently waiting to hear what I came up with.

"Looks to me like you've got a dead bird here," I said with a shrug. As far as I could tell, the only difference between the vulture and Timmy Tom was that the bird didn't have a cell phone in its craw. "Perhaps it died of old age. Or maybe it got tired of living on the border and just gave up."

"You know, Porter, that's why I'm the master tracker and you're still the rookie when it comes to this stuff. Tracking is an art form—think of it the same as you would a fine painting. You can never catch everything there is to be seen the first time around. Why, I'll bet you haven't even been back to visit the crime scene, have you?"

I gave myself a mental kick in the ass. Apparently he'd unearthed information that I should have been out there digging up.

"Critters are always dying of natural causes out in the desert. What makes you think this bird is any different?" I quizzed.

"The spot where you found Tyler's body was marked off by the sheriff. This vulture was conked out a little too damn close for comfort."

"That's it?"

Sonny looked me square in the eye and gave a quick, firm nod. "Yup. That's it. Call it a gut feeling, but there's something about this vulture that just isn't right."

I sighed, wondering how I could send a dead turkey

vulture to the Fish and Wildlife National Forensic Lab to be autopsied with that flimsy explanation.

"I'll ship the bird off to our lab in Oregon, but it might take a while," I warned.

Sonny pulled on the brim of his hat, as though he'd already taken the problem into consideration. "I can speed up the process, if you like," he offered. "There's an old friend of mine who hasn't got much to do these days and could use some cheering up."

"So, you're going to give him a dead bird to play with?" Maybe what Sonny needed was a new set of friends.

"Yep," Sonny nodded. "Charlie used to work as a pathologist. But these days, he's just an old geezer like me, who could use a shot of excitement in his life."

I figured it would save me the trouble of sending off a bird that might only have died of heat stroke. Besides, it would be a gesture of goodwill on my part. Perhaps now was the time to ask Sonny for that new refrigerator I'd been longing for.

"Sure, go ahead."

"You're learning the ropes, Porter. But I'm still not buying you any new fridge," Sonny growled, as if knowing what I was up to all along. "What I will do is give you a piece of advice: listen to the wind speak, and maybe you'll hear some of the desert's secrets." Sonny picked up the vulture and stuffed it back inside the bag, tying the plastic closed with a double knot. "And if that bull dookey doesn't work, then just keep your nose to the ground, and don't squat with your spurs on."

I smiled to myself, having had an intriguing thought. Maybe if Miss Mae didn't work out, Mother Krabbs might prove more to Sonny's liking.

*   *   *

I decided that since I was already up, this might be a good time to make an early morning run and check out F.U.'s former New Mexico ranch. As I jumped in my pick-up, what little sunlight there was retreated, overtaken by an army of foreboding clouds. I headed off toward Mount Riley, a place not all that far from the Anapra Road. Thunder broke out in a symphony of biblical bellows, followed by a searing gust of hot wind which sliced through the air and spit out a torrent of rain. The drops danced a flamenco on the roof of my Ford.

My windshield wipers kept a steady beat as the rain poured down in sheets, evaporating in fingers of steam as they hit the ground. By the time I arrived at the Flying A Ranch, the pungent smell of wet earth hung heavy in the air.

The gate to the Flying A Ranch stood invitingly open, but a handwritten sign nailed to it cautioned otherwise: *Trespassers Will Be Shot. Survivors Will Be Shot Again. Live Through That, and We'll Try Hanging You.* An environmental group with a quirky sense of humor—how refreshing. I ignored the message and drove over a metal cattle guard, then proceeded through the open gate.

Thump, thump! went my tires as they rolled over the steel grating. *Crunch, crunch!* they sang as they hit the gravel road. The gravel slowly gave way to a rutted dirt path, causing my Ford to shake, rattle, and roll. I bounced along for another five miles before I reached a second gate, which was securely closed. If a padlock were the only obstacle, I'd have pulled out a pair of metal snips and cut through. But it held an alarm pad similar to those I'd seen installed at the Happy Hunting Ranch. In order to gain access, one had to know the code. I had little choice but to turn my pick-up around and head back the way I'd come.

Soon after, I heard a noise rapidly approaching from behind—the roar of a V-8 engine bearing down on my Ford. I assumed it would pass me, but as I glanced in the rear view mirror, a large black Suburban van locked on to my bumper. The next thing I knew, I was being pushed off the road!

I floored my F-150 for all it was worth, and as the rpms revved into gear, the Ford kicked up a shower of gravel and leapt away from the offending bumper. I leaned forward and gripped the steering wheel tight, watching the speedometer needle rise like a thermometer.

Fear noxiously mixed with anger in my stomach, as I remembered the warnings I'd received in the past few days. We clocked seventy, then eighty, then ninety, until my tires were spitting out stones and dust in a furious comet's tail. Still, I couldn't shake my pursuer, whose nose remained three inches from my bumper all the while.

Bang! The van rear-ended my Ford, causing my wheels to whine into a skid, and my pick-up threatened to turn over. I cursed, counter-steering to the left and then the right to guide the Ford back onto the road. All the while I pushed my foot down even harder, as ninety-two, ninety-four, ninety-five miles an hour flew by. The episode in the elevator now seemed like child's play, and this time my life did flash before my eyes. The Suburban easily kept pace, like a cheetah who knows it can catch up with its prey any time it wants. What kind of wacko environmentalist was this, anyway?

Thud! My body jerked forward as the van rear-ended me yet again. I swore that somehow I'd get revenge, and gave the pedal one last thrust to the floor. Ninety-seven, ninety-eight, one hundred. I was suddenly scared that I was truly going to die.

The pick-up hit a pot hole and the chassis shook with the fury of a gale force wind as I desperately fought to stay on the road. Then I saw the black top ahead. I sped out the gate and over the cattleguard so fast that my teeth rattled. I glanced back at the Suburban, but it was no longer on top of me. It had turned around just short of the gate, apparently believing I'd been taught a lesson.

My rage matched the roar of my pick-up's engine. *Oh, no you don't!* No anonymous menace was going to get the better of me. I slammed on the brakes and reversed direction as my Ford let out an astonished screech. Then my F-150 gleefully charged into action.

It wasn't long before I was on the Suburban's rear end. My Ford zipped in and out, taking calculated nips at his bumper, persistent as a mosquito drawing blood. I laughed as I caught sight of the sticker plastered on the tailgate: *Gun Control Means Using Both Hands*. Apparently I'd lassoed myself a real macho cowboy.

I kept up the role of tormentor, buzzing close behind, until the second gate came into sight. Only then did I finally slow down, knowing the Suburban would have to slam on its brakes and come to a halt.

I had a fast decision to make. I could pull my .38, or opt for something with more fire power. I swiftly reached back and slid the mini-14 rifle out of its case behind me. Then I stopped the pick-up and jumped out to stand in shooting position, the gun steady in both hands, my right arm locked and my index finger curled against the trigger. I decided my new friend was right: it really *is* best to practice gun control.

The Suburban's car door swung open and out sprang my assailant, with his own bolt action rifle.

"Stop where you are! I'm a federal agent." That little tidbit would either make him think twice, or shoot me on the spot.

My antagonist remained standing where he was, his rifle aimed at my heart. "Prove it," he tartly commanded.

"Lower your rifle and I'll get out my badge," I retorted.

"And let you take a shot at me? What do you think I am, some kind of fool?"

We continued to glare at each other in a wild West stand-off.

"Why don't we *both* lower our rifles for a moment?" I suggested.

Mr. Macho looked at me and cracked a "screw you" smile. "Okay. But we've gotta do it on the count of three."

Something told me this was the kind of guy that would cheat. I noticed his hands were quivering. In fact, so was his entire body. Either he was coming down off a fix, or had the shakes due to a drinking problem. Either way, he wasn't dealing with a full deck.

"Forget it. *You* were the one trying to kill *me*, remember? Put your rifle down right now, or I'll blow your damned head off."

My broken-down cowboy must have gathered I meant it. He hesitated only a second, then dropped the rifle to his side.

"All the way to the ground," I instructed, visibly tightening my grip on the trigger.

Mr. Macho did as he was told. Then I reached inside my pocket, pulled out my badge, and threw it to him.

"My, my, my," he chuckled and flashed a grin to reveal a set of dingy teeth. "You and me got something in common."

"Yeah? What's that?" I asked.

"I used to be with Fish and Wildlife, too," he responded.

I looked at the bonzai buckaroo. The man's body was

thin as a split rail fence. Bloodshot eyes stared out from beneath a beat-up cowboy hat. He reached in his shirt pocket, pulled out a ragged cigarette, and struck a match against the bottom of his boot. I put my rifle away, and retrieved my badge.

"Nice boots," I remarked. The leather was embellished with the initials, "J.L." "You wouldn't happen to be Johnny Lambert by any chance, would you?"

The guy took a drag on his cigarette. "How'd you know?" he asked, looking impressed.

"Let's just say your reputation precedes you," I responded.

"Oh, *that*," he remarked. "A guy's got to make a living. Besides, it was a set-up."

Why do the guilty always come up with the same excuse?

"Do you want to explain why you were trying to kill me?" I inquired.

"Oh, come on," Johnny chuckled. "That was just a little tickle-and-chase. You're not gonna hold that against me, are you?"

I was tempted to pull my .38 revolver and do a little tickle-and-chase of my own. "You haven't answered my question."

"I do believe there's a sign outside warning what happens to trespassers. Since you're on private property, maybe you'd like to explain what *you're* doing here," he retorted, his eyes suddenly hard.

Either Johnny Lambert was schizophrenic, or something had suddenly made him feel pretty sure of himself.

"F.U. Krabbs told me about the ranch, so I decided to come by and check it out," I answered.

"Oh, yeah? And did he know you were showing up here today?" Johnny Lambert demanded.

"Why should he care?" I parried. "After all, the ranch

is now owned by Southwest Heritage Trust."

Johnny Lambert stared blankly, as though I'd spoken gibberish.

"Or didn't you know that?" I challenged. "I assume they're the people issuing you a paycheck these days."

His complexion turned deep red. "Of course I know who they are," he blustered. "It's just that Mr. Krabbs still likes to come and visit the ranch from time to time. When you mentioned his name, I figured he must be meeting you here."

"Nope. But he did mention you'd be happy to show me around. So, how about it?" I bluffed.

"Mr. Krabbs told you that?" he asked suspiciously.

I nodded my head. "Why? Is there something wrong?"

"Yeah," Johnny Lambert retorted. "For one thing, he doesn't own the land anymore. Remember? I take my orders from other people these days."

"I understand that Southwest Heritage Trust is an environmental group. This *is* a land trust, isn't it?" I inquired.

"So what? They're still particular about who they allow on the Flying A."

"And why is that?" I shot back.

Johnny Lambert's cigarette had burned past the filter, and was now an angry stub in his fingertips. Either he was big into pain, or had weighty things on his mind. He finally reacted with a start, dropping the butt and grinding it beneath his heel. "It's 'cause folks in these parts aren't too crazy about conservation groups. You never know when some nut might decide to come out here and try something funny."

"That's true. Except I'm not just anyone: I'm a special agent with the U.S. Fish and Wildlife Service. You remember us; we're the good guys. Besides, you're the ranch manager here, aren't you? That should give you some clout."

Johnny Lambert flashed another *screw you* smile at me. "Fish and Wildlife must have been looking for a pushy bitch when they hired you."

"And they got what they wanted. So why don't you unlock the gate and take me for a tour of the grounds?" I suggested.

Johnny Lambert opened the passenger door of his Suburban and waved me inside, then walked over to the alarm pad and punched in the access code. The gate silently swung open and we drove on through.

The Flying A looked like every other ranch in New Mexico, pucker dry and bare. The only color came from a wiry stand of ocotillo. Tiny red blossoms covered the tips of the plant's long green stems, but the flowers weren't merely decorative. Their blooms cleverly camouflaged a series of prickly sharp spines running along the edge of each deadly stalk.

A gray loggerhead shrike flew down and gingerly perched on one of the plant's branches. It looked like a feathered bandito, with a wide slash of black covering its face. Tightly gripped in the marauder's sharply hooked beak lay a small brown mouse, its limbs quivering.

My head knows that nature is no sweet fantasy, but my soul still recoils when the natural order of things turns harsh.

My pulse pounded in rhythm with the rodent's rapidly beating heart as though I, too, felt a trap closing inexorably around me. The bird lifted its head high, as victorious as an Aztec warrior presenting a sacrificial offering to the gods. Then the shrike thrust down hard, brutally impaling its tiny victim on one of the plant's razor-edged spikes.

A premonitory tremor ran through me as I remembered the shrike's nickname: the butcher bird. I tore my eyes from the sight and focused on the motionless clouds whose bellies were tinged pink, reflecting the fiery desert floor. Cows lazily grazed on sparse clumps of grass, in sharp contrast to the violence only a moment before. I took a deep breath and slowly exhaled. The desert's exposed soul was not a romantic sight.

A large mesa loomed up ahead. The butte gleamed like a mirage in the hazy heat, its top as flat as a drill sergeant's closely cropped haircut. I caught sight of a pole barn butting up against its front as we drew close, along with a corral containing a goodly number of horses. We drove to the mesa's opposite end, where a large, circular water tank proved to be the major draw for the area's livestock. A green GMC pick-up was heading toward us.

"Is that Dr. Pierpont?" I asked, hoping to bump into my mystery man.

"Who?" Johnny Lambert responded, with all the guilelessness of a mangy coyote.

"You know, the scientist who's cloning the Krabbs dog here at the Flying A," I said, wishing I had an ocotillo plant handy to prod some sense into him.

"Oh. You know about that," Lambert responded with a chuckle. "Don't that beat all? Have you ever heard of such bullshit? Hell, when I think of what *I* could do with three million bucks." He shook his head in mournful contemplation.

I doubted that helping to save the world was at the top of his list.

"So, is that Pierpont?" I persisted. I rolled down the car window and was smacked in the face with a gust of hot air, followed by a light shake-and-bake coating of manure-tinged dust.

"No way," Johnny Lambert commented with a contemptuous sniff. "Pierpont doesn't believe in mixing with us common folk."

Lambert appeared to be right; the GMC that sidled up alongside us held a couple of cowboys.

"Who you got there with you, Johnny?" asked the driver.

He didn't appear to leave his pick-up very much; the man's clothes were as clean and freshly pressed as a city slicker's duds. His partner had a more rough and tumble look. A five o'clock shadow covered the lower portion of his face, though it was only seven o'clock in the morning.

"This here's the new Fish and Wildlife agent, Rachel Porter," Johnny replied. "She stopped by and wanted a quick look around, so I'm giving her the five-cent tour. That okay with you boys?"

"Sure. No problem," Mr. Clean responded with a disquieting smile. "It's just that you know we like to be kept informed of what's going on at all times." Though the words were softly spoken, there was no question that Johnny Lambert was being reprimanded.

The spic-and-span cowboy turned his attention to me. "We prefer visits to be by appointment only, ma'am."

"Actually, I'm a special agent. Not a ma'am, if you don't mind," I corrected him. "And why all the formality with appointments? Isn't that being just a bit paranoid?"

His partner opened his mouth to speak, but Mr. Clean held up a hand and stopped him. "I guess you haven't heard about the philosophical disagreement that's going on in these parts. There are a lot of development folks who'd rather be raking in big money by building second-home communities than leaving the range wild and free." Mr. Clean gazed out over the horizon, as if he were posing for a TV commercial. "But at Southwest

Heritage Trust, we're dedicated to making sure the land will be used in perpetuity for ranching. By placing the Flying A in our trust, Mr. Krabbs knows it will never be open to public use."

"I'm all for that. But what's the problem with my stopping by unannounced?" I questioned.

Mr. Clean appeared annoyed that I wasn't quite getting it. "A group of locals already suspect that we're taking over the land in a secret plot to do away with grazing. Having you show up here adds to the perception that we're trying to stop development because of some three-legged, six-eyed tadpole."

"So you think my presence will give the Trust a bad reputation?" I inquired dubiously.

"You got it," replied his partner in a voice as cold as a New England winter.

"I'd still like to finish my tour. Or should I find a reason to get a warrant in order to do that?" I pleasantly inquired.

"No, go right ahead, Agent Porter. Just be sure and call the next time you want to come by." Mr. Clean smiled and tipped the brim of his hat in farewell.

I caught sight of two Uzis hanging on the gun rack attached to the pick-up's rear window as it headed away from us. So much for tradition of Winchester rifles.

"I take it those were your employers?" I asked.

"Yeah. Two of 'em, anyway," Lambert drawled.

"How many people are involved with running the Trust?" I inquired.

"Who the hell knows?" he responded. "Too damn many of them. I miss the days when it was just F.U. and me out here on the range. Now, *there's* a guy who knows how to have fun."

I'm not sure Lizzie would have agreed with him.

The next highlight on our tour was a cluster of motor

homes, which gave the area the appearance of a trailer park.

"Are those Pierpont's quarters?" Maybe he lived in one and did his research in the others.

"No. That's housing supplied by Southwest Heritage for some of its workers," Johnny Lambert replied.

I counted twenty trailers in all. "Isn't it unusual for a ranch to house so many of its employees on the grounds?"

"Southwest likes to keep everyone happy," Lambert remarked.

Or keep them all close to the vest. "So, how many other scientists are working on this cloning project for F.U.?" I casually inquired.

He glanced at me out of the corner of his eye. "For a Fish and Wildlife agent, you sure have a hell of a lot of questions that have nothing to do with wildlife. If you want an answer to that one, why don't you go to the source and ask Pierpont?"

"Great idea," I agreed. "What say we head on over and see him. He told me to stop by whenever I was around."

Lambert responded with a chuckle. "Don't try to bullshit a bullshitter, Porter. I have specific instructions that he's not to be bothered by anyone."

"But we're good friends," I insisted. "I'm certain he wouldn't mind just this once."

"Maybe you don't care if my ass gets fried, but I sure as hell do. If you're so friendly with the guy, make your own arrangements to meet him. I plan to keep this job," Lambert firmly responded.

So far, my trip to the Flying A was turning out to be pretty much of a bust. That is, until I spotted a cherry red Jeep Cherokee bouncing along not far from us. I didn't need binoculars to identify its driver; the sun glinting off a copper colored Afro revealed that Pierpont was behind the wheel.

I hollered out, waving my arms like a shipwrecked sailor in the hope of getting his attention. But Pierpont wasn't letting on, if he noticed. I could stay sedately in my seat and let fate take its course, or grab hold of the steering wheel, plunk my foot down on top of Lambert's, and be captain of my own destiny. I figured it was a no-brainer.

"What the hell are you doing?" Johnny Lambert sputtered as I wrestled for control of the car.

"Sorry," I responded, veering the Suburban to the left, as I pushed hard on the accelerator. "You can blame it on Frank Sinatra."

"What the hell are you talking about?" Lambert fumed, trying to shove me away with his elbow.

I deflected the move and initiated my own elbow attack. "I've gotta do things my way," I retorted.

"Goddammit, Porter! You're out of your friggin' mind!"

Maybe so, but I was also getting what I wanted. My leg remained firmly planted though Johnny Lambert tried to shove me off. It must have looked to an outsider as if I were trying to hump the guy, and I was tempted to tell him to sit back and enjoy it.

I didn't remove my foot from off Lambert's boot until the Cherokee loomed dangerously close. Then I slammed on the brake and we screeched to a halt just inches away from the Jeep.

Pierpont calmly sat with that eternal smile, making it hard to tell if his nerves had been rattled. His prosthetic devices remained clamped to the steering wheel, glistening like two hot silver pokers.

"Well, Agent Porter. You certainly have a unique way of making yourself known," he remarked.

The fact that my antic hadn't fazed the man totally impressed me.

"I happened to be in the neighborhood when I saw you driving by, and thought this might be the perfect time for a visit. I know Lizzie would love for me to report back on how well your work is progressing," I suggested with a smile.

Evidently my wattage wasn't up to snuff. Pierpont's stare hardened behind his bottle lens glasses.

"I don't know how you found my lab, but as I told you, the work I do is very delicate. You'd be wise to stay out of my business." Pierpont's eyes next shifted to Johnny Lambert. "I'm afraid I'll have to report this to your superiors."

Pierpont took off, his Afro springing up and down like Ten-Karat with a bad perm.

"Yeah, I can see what good friends the two of you are," Johnny Lambert commented sourly.

"I must have caught him on a bad day," I absent-mindedly replied, wondering how F.U. could be so blind to the scam going on.

"You know what's scary about you, Porter?" Lambert asked, turning to drive back.

I shook my head, curious as to how a former agent would sum up my character.

"The fact that you honestly believe your mission is so important, you'll go to any lengths to do it."

I remained silent, knowing what he said was true. I waited until Lambert deposited me at my pick-up to ask him the question which had been preying on my mind ever since our chase.

"By the way, how is it that you know Timmy Tom Tyler?" I inquired.

Lambert stared off in the distance and cocked his head, as if waiting for the answer to be supplied by divine intervention. "Can't say I've ever heard that name before," he said diffidently.

"That seems rather odd, considering your name and number are listed in Tyler's cell phone directory. Any explanation for that?"

Lambert scratched his forehead, appearing to kill time until the answer was astrally forwarded to him.

"Nope," he finally said.

"Then you might want to consult with whatever spirits you're listening to and ask them to help jog your memory on this one. Timmy Tom was killed two days ago— and the police are searching for the murder suspect," I informed him.

I climbed into my pick-up and took off down the road.

Ten

I decided to take a quick break and check in on Lizzie. My suspicion was that she'd still be in bed, nursing a massive hangover. I stopped at the first convenience store I found, grabbed some nourishment in the form of soda and chocolate, then pulled out my cell phone.

Her groan filled me in on how she felt. "Thanks for coming to my rescue last night, Rach. I don't know what I was drinking, but I never want to have it again."

I could relate all too well to that.

"Listen, you might as well know I've been considering leaving F.U. for a while now. This is going to sound awful, but I'm just waiting until Martin successfully clones Ten-Karat."

"That's what I want to discuss with you." I wondered how to break it to her gently. "I found out Pierpont's lab is over at the Flying A, so I stopped by the ranch this morning. All I can say is, I've got a funny feeling about the place. Something's not right."

Lizzie gasped. "Oh, no, Rach! You didn't disturb him, did you?" she asked in horror. "You know how protective he is of his work!"

"Lizzie, my purpose in going there was to try and make sure Pierpont's doing what he claims, and isn't taking advantage of you."

"What makes you think he might be?" she asked after a moment.

"Nothing I can pinpoint yet. It's more of a gut feeling." God, I was beginning to sound like Sonny. "Believe me, Lizzie, I hope I'm wrong. I'd like nothing better than to discover Pierpont can clone Ten-Karat, and maybe help save other species."

My reply was met by silence and I began to worry that Lizzie was really upset.

"I'm afraid what you suspect might be true," she finally responded with a sniffle. "It always seemed strange that I wasn't allowed to visit his lab. I just didn't want to think about it before." She blew her nose and cleared her throat. "Okay. What can I do to help you find out what's really going on?"

I was relieved to hear a spark of my friend return to life. "I don't believe F.U. would fork over millions of dollars to Pierpont without having a dossier on the man. So what I need are any records pertaining to Pierpont's defunct company," I told her. "Also, any other files you can find that F.U. might've gathered on him."

"Hmmm. F.U. has a computer in his office here at home. If there's any information to be had, that's most likely where he's got it stashed. The only tricky part will be breaking the password in order to log on. But I've tackled harder assignments for you in the past. I can do it," she decided.

"There's one more thing," I added, enjoying hearing Lizzie become newly liberated. "Check and see if there's any information referring to Southwest Heritage Trust."

"They're the environmental group that F.U. gave the Flying A ranch to. Why should you care about them?" she asked in surprise.

"Because Pierpont has his lab there. That alone makes me curious. And since Southwest Heritage is a private company, there aren't any public records I can get hold of. It's just another angle to check out."

"I'll start in on F.U.'s computer tonight as soon as he falls asleep. Nobody's going to screw around with me or Ten-Karat and get away with it," Lizzie resolutely declared. "I have no intention of letting anyone take advantage of F.U. either, for that matter. Not as long as I'm still his wife."

We signed off and I headed out toward Little Chihuahua, fully fueled to take on Round Two with Fat Boy.

I parked in front of Juan's house and let myself in through the front gate. His home-made alarm must have been on the fritz: rather than being audibly attacked by a rabid Chihuahua, I was greeted by the slo-mo bark of what sounded like an intoxicated St. Bernard. I wove past his yard art and opened the door without bothering to knock. Inside, I found Fat Boy and one very annoyed capuchin monkey.

"Happy Trails to You" poured out of Juan's organ grinder as Lola sat fidgeting on his shoulder. Dressed to resemble a miniature version of Dale Evans, Lola pulled on her cowgirl hat, ripped strips of fringe off her skirt, and did her darndest to remove the toy gun glued in its holster. Finally she gave up, leaned over and champed down on Fat Boy's ear in frustration.

"Ouch!" Juan yelped in pain, and tried to pull her off. But Lola hung on until he dug a gummi bear out of his pocket.

Since Lola was dressed up as Dale Evans, I imagined Fat Boy was supposed to look like Roy Rogers. He was encased in a pair of fringed chaps large enough to cover a king-size bed, and an embroidered shirt whose fake mother-of-pearl snaps were ready to explode.

"Hi, Juan. How are you doing?" I asked, as Lola gummed her candy and gave me the eye.

"I got no time for your crap today, Porter," Fat Boy groused. "Lola and me are busy rehearsing."

"And I can see how well it's going," I retorted.

"Lola's being a little testy this morning, is all. But we got big plans. I got us booked for our world premiere tour of Texas. We're gonna be raking in the dough on the organ grinder circuit."

"That's great. How about taking a rehearsal break for lunch? You've got to keep up your energy. I'm buying," I offered, knowing Fat Boy would never turn down a free meal.

"Okay. But I gotta change first," Juan reluctantly agreed. "This costume cost me a bundle and I can't afford to get it dirty."

"No problem. I'll wait." I didn't bother to tell him Lola had already marked her territory on his shirt.

Fat Boy returned wearing a sleeveless white tee, and a pair of khaki shorts with an elastic waistband stretched to its limit. I stared at the angry red welts which covered his arms and legs.

"What happened to you?" I asked in alarm.

"Goddamn fire ants got me," Juan angrily rumbled.

Hmm. That meant he must have left the confines of El Paso within the past day to roam around the desert. That's where the insects build their mounds, from which they rush out to lock onto unsuspecting victims. Once attached, the beasties sting repeatedly. My bet was that Kitrell and Fat Boy had taken a desert sojourn last night after I'd spotted them at the Round-Up.

Juan wrestled Lola into her cage, then we went outside and climbed into my Ford F-150. The pick-up tilted precariously as Fat Boy sat down and unsuccessfully tried to buckle the seat belt.

"Where to?" I inquired, knowing he had a list of favorite eateries.

He pondered the choices. "I'm in the mood for protein today. Let's go to the Chicken Hut."

I headed down the strip to a neighborhood joint Ma Krabbs would have loved. The Chicken Hut's white-washed stucco exterior provided fertile ground for pornographic graffiti, while a mesh fence formed an enclosure at its rear.

Inside, the only available light was provided by a muted TV and a decrepit jukebox, whose rotating hues danced across the patrons' faces in an ever-changing rainbow of colors. The dive's mainly male clientele sat in booths drinking their booze, looking as if they'd not only been born in the place, but would die here. I slid into a seat as an ancient waitress with skin the texture of a worn out saddlebag made her way over to us.

"What'll it be?" she asked Juan.

"Give me four orders of the combo plate, and a side of chicken wings," Fat Boy responded without opening the menu. "Oh yeah. And a coupla cups of coffee."

"And for you, *gringo?*" she asked, not deigning to look me in the eye.

"I'll take the chile rellenos," I replied, refusing to rise to the bait.

Fat Boy snickered as she tottered away. "What she's telling you is you're not part of El Paso, no matter how hard you try."

"And why is that?" I inquired.

"Because you're not from here. You don't know this place—which is why you'll never stop the animal trade," he said, taking a sip of the coffee placed in front of him. "Dealing with smugglers around here is like trying to shoot coyotes. Hit one, and another always springs up to take its place. Also, everyone knows who you are.

That gives them the advantage. How many smugglers can you pick out of the crowd in here?" Juan asked, spooning four teaspoons of sugar into his cup.

I skimmed the sea of faces, and wondered if Fat Boy was right. There was no way to know how many of the men returning my stare were aware of who I was. Then I caught Juan's smirk.

"You're full of crap, Juan. The only thing anyone cares about is that I'm a gringo who's dared to come in here, whether I'm welcome or not."

Fat Boy's annoyance quickly faded as plates of food were set before him. He inhaled the first of his combo platters and instantly moved on to the next. "By the way, did you get that cell phone back for me yet?" he asked between bites.

I barely dodged the shower of refried beans which shot toward me. "What's the rush, Juan? Is there something on Timmy Tom's phone that you need?" I paused. "Or that you'd rather wasn't found?"

Fat Boy curled his upper lip, exposing a wad of chewed up food in his mouth. "Like I told you, it's got sentimental value."

He reached for a barbecued chicken wing and stuck the whole thing in his mouth. Next he grabbed a tortilla and began munching.

I made certain he'd had plenty of time to swallow, then asked, "You want to tell me what you were doing at The Round-Up with Dan Kitrell last night?"

Oops! I guess I was wrong. Fat Boy began to choke and pound on the table, but the tortilla remained stubbornly lodged in his throat. I knew I'd never get my arms around him to do the Heimlich, and the other patrons seemed to view Juan's plight as a form of entertainment.

I tried to shove him forward in the hope the table

ledge would work like a fist, but moving Juan proved as impossible as pulling Excalibur from its stone. Meanwhile, he was no longer coughing, but gasping for air and turning blue.

What I needed was leverage, and quickly. Sitting on top of the booth behind him, I drew in my knees and placed my feet squarely on Juan's back. Then I propelled him as hard as I could directly into the table. A lump of tortilla flew out of his mouth, and landed smack in my chile rellenos.

"Are you trying to kill me or something?" he gasped, glaring angrily at me.

"Kill you? You'd be dead if it weren't for the fact that I'm here!" And he could at least have had the courtesy to aim his tortilla somewhere other than in my lunch.

"I believe we were talking about your meeting with Dan Kitrell," I reminded him.

"Who?" Fat Boy asked, his left eye sliding like a Yankee toward home plate.

"You know: tall man, works at the Happy Hunting Ranch," I responded.

Juan continued to stare without saying a word. It was time to jerk his chain a bit.

"I'd hate to think something might happen to ruin your upcoming music tour," I remarked.

Fat Boy's eyes narrowed into two folds of fat. "What are you talking about? Like what?" he asked suspiciously.

I pushed my chile rellenos away. Fat Boy's fingers latched on to the platter and pulled it in his direction.

"Like my having to confiscate Lola on grounds that she was smuggled over the border."

"You can't prove that!" Fat Boy exploded.

"Sure I can," I confidently told him. "All I have to do

is go through your paperwork and see if she was brought in with any of the shipments marked for the One World Zoo. You remember that place—it's the one Timmy Tom was furnishing with huge shipments of monkeys. The facility without a phone number or address."

Fat Boy pushed the plate of chile rellenos back towards me. "I ain't hungry anymore. Thanks for spoiling my appetite, Porter."

The one thing I wasn't worried about was Fat Boy starving to death.

"Whadda ya want to know?" he sullenly inquired as his fingertips edged their way toward my plate once more.

"What were you doing with Kitrell?" I repeated my question.

"You'd really be mean enough to take my Lola away from me?" Fat Boy demanded.

"In a heartbeat," I assured him.

"And if I tell you what you want, you'll leave me and Lola alone?"

"Absolutely," I vowed, wondering how Timmy Tom would feel, knowing he'd been so quickly replaced in Juan's affections.

"What the hell. I don't owe Kitrell nothing anyway," he decided, and leaned in toward me. "Kitrell's been nosing around about chimps."

Like this was something I didn't already know. "Did he ask you to get any for him?" I inquired.

"Yeah—but there's a catch. He insists he's gotta see them first before he buys one. I guess he wants to make sure he bonds with it, or something." Fat Boy picked up a few remaining chicken wings and finished them off. "The problem is, I don't have a source for chimps. So I sent him over to see the Monkey Man."

My antennae immediately began to vibrate.

"Who's that?" I asked, hoping I sounded more blasé than I felt.

"You don't know who the Monkey Man is?" Fat Boy grinned. "Hell, I thought everyone knew about him. That's Admiral Maynard's nickname."

"You know that I'll nail you if you're lying to me about this," I warned.

Fat Boy stopped eating long enough to give me a solemn look. "When it comes to Lola, I don't fool around."

Odd as it seemed, I believed him.

"Okay. Then tell me how you know F.U. Krabbs."

Fat Boy snorted. "Who doesn't know him?"

"Nothing personal, Juan, but I don't see the two of you traveling in the same social circles," I replied.

He scowled as though I'd unnecessarily hurt his feelings. "Timmy Tom used to fill special orders for F.U. until the Admiral came along and wormed his way in. Then Timmy Tom was cut out and Maynard took over."

The connections were beginning to fall into place. Evidently Maynard was top dog for illegal animals these days.

"Are we done yet?" Fat Boy asked petulantly.

"Only one more question," I assured him. "What brought you into contact with Johnny Lambert?"

"Let's just say he was a very cooperative Fish and Wildlife agent," Fat Boy sneered. "Hell, Porter. You might find it pays to be a little more easygoing yourself, where us businessmen are concerned. Figure it this way: there's only one of you while there's a whole lot of us, which makes it open season for smuggling stuff in over the border."

Juan casually reached over and snatched a piece of

pie off a passing tray. "Just remember what I told you about shooting coyotes. You can never get rid of them."

Well, when it came to being wily, I was more than willing to go head to head with the best of them.

Eleven

I delivered Fat Boy back into Lola's capable hands and took off. It was time I made Admiral Maynard's acquaintance. Following Juan's directions, I headed southeast toward the town of Fort Hancock. Maynard's house wasn't visible from the road; a ten-foot-high chain link fence topped with barbed wire ringed the entire property. I pulled up to the gate at the stronghold's entrance, and pressed the buzzer on an intercom box.

"Who's there?" inquired a mechanical voice that could have passed for Robby the Robot.

"Rachel Porter, with the U.S. Fish and Wildlife Service."

The gate silently swung open. I drove through a grove of lush vegetation, so engrossed in the surrounding that I was caught off-guard when a sound reached my ears.

The haunting song of gibbons filled the air, as enchanting as sirens luring me into their lair. But the call I heard next sent a flurry of primeval shivers scurrying up my evolutionary spine.

whooo, whooO, whoOO, whOOO, wHOOO, WHOOO!

The hooting raced through the treetops and swung on the vines before swooping down to the ground. The cry was that of man's closest kin: Admiral Maynard had a colony of chimps on his land.

I was so enthralled that I nearly ran over the figure which unexpectedly stepped in my path. I slammed on the brakes to avoid hitting a rotund gentleman who stood beaming as though I were his long lost daughter.

Polyester royal blue pants were hiked high above his waist and held in place by red and white polka dot suspenders. Stretched across his barrel chest was a pink Banlon shirt, its hem creeping up to expose a strip of white belly. The man's green eyes twinkled from above a bulbous nose, and he wore a skipper's cap. His fingers scampered up to a small patch that covered the center of his throat.

"Whee dawgies, gal! It's about time you came by for a visit!"

I realized the tinny sound I'd heard over the intercom hadn't come from a recording, but from the admiral's implanted voice box.

"Come on in and take a load off," he cheerfully instructed.

I turned off the Ford's engine, feeling as if I'd landed in a strange new dimension. "I take it you're admiral Maynard," I said, and extended my hand toward him.

"Hot diggity, that's right! We haven't met before, have we? Don't ask me why, but I feel like I've known you for years, gal," he exuberantly informed me.

As we shook hands, I noticed the tips of two of his fingers were missing.

The admiral caught my glance and merrily wiggled all five of his digits. "Don't that beat all? Lucky Louie, one of my chimps, did that back in '94. He got a little too playful one day, and bit 'em off. But let's get out from under this hot Texas sun. Mother will be here in a minute with cold glasses of lemonade," he offered.

The admiral led the way up onto a screened-in porch, where we sat in the shade. He was right; it felt a good five degrees cooler here. The frenzied hooting which greeted my arrival had finally died down, replaced by the occasional chirp of a bird and the soft, muted cry of a gibbon.

I was about to ask the admiral about his collection of critters when a screen door emitted a high-pitched screech. A fanny, flat as the Texas panhandle, gave the door a hard push and a woman scooted out of the house.

She sauntered toward us, swinging a pair of bony hips. Her halter top held a pair of sixty-year-old breasts which seemed grateful for a place to rest, while her short shorts displayed the bottom halves of two saggy cheeks. A network of varicose veins ran through her legs. But it was the tinfoil dunce cap perched on her head that begged for my attention.

The woman approached with a cigarette holder clenched in her teeth, and carrying a tray bearing three glasses. She picked up one of the tumblers and held it toward me.

"Here you go, darlin'. A few telltale drips won't kill you."

The lemonade formed a random pattern of droplets on my pants, feeling cool against my skin. Then she removed the cigarette holder from her mouth, and blew a puff of smoke in the admiral's direction. He lifted his chin and sniffed the air in pure, exuberant bliss.

"I'm the admiral's wife, but you can just call me Loxie, sweetheart." She let out a deep groan as she sat down and kicked off her sandals. "I've been on my feet all morning, what with this menagerie we've got to take care of. My tootsies could use a good rest."

"Nice to meet you," I replied. "I'm Rachel Porter, the new Fish and Wildlife agent."

"Of course you are, dear," Loxie responded. "We just expected to see you around here sooner than this." Loxie clamped the cigarette holder back in her mouth in such a way that she resembled a mutant version of FDR.

"Why, is there some sort of problem?" I took a sip of the lemonade and nearly choked as a mouthful of syrupy liquid went down my throat.

"Nope. So far, so good on this end. Which is how we're hoping to keep it." Loxie smiled and blew another cloud of smoke towards the admiral.

He closed his eyes and inhaled deeply. "Now, Mother, there's plenty of time for that. Why don't you have Mr. Max bring out some cookies and introduce himself?" he suggested.

"Show time, Max! Come on out with the treats!" Loxie called with a tilt of her head.

The screen door burst open, and out flew a young chimp precariously balanced on a pair of roller skates. He was dressed pretty much the same as the admiral, and carried a tray holding cookies and a can of soda. Loxie casually snagged the tray from his grasp as the chimp continued to roll past, screeching at the top of his lungs. The admiral reached out and locked onto the chimp's waist right before Mr. Max went crashing through the screened-in porch.

"It's a new trick we're teaching him," the admiral explained. "He hasn't learned how to stop on these things yet. But we figure as soon as he does, he'll be a big hit at parties. You know, like at kids' birthdays and stuff. He'll come skating out carrying a cake with candles, and the little bastards will go crazy. What do you think?" the admiral asked, obviously waiting for approval.

Mr. Max gave his own opinion on the matter by reaching over and attempting to rip the patch off the admiral's throat. A wrestling match ensued between Maynard and the chimp, who could easily have passed as a hairy, out-of-control kid.

"Here you go, Father. Let Mr. Max have his soda. That'll help calm him down," Loxie suggested, and held out a can of Dr. Pepper.

Mr. Max instantly lunged for the soda, grabbing the can from her grip. Then he turned back around and gave the admiral a juicy Bronx cheer.

"Soda for a chimp?" I questioned. "Do you think that's really a good idea?"

"Sure. Why not?" Loxie replied, crossing her legs. The skin around her ankles sagged like a pair of loose sweat socks. "Chimps love sweet stuff, just like kids. In fact, you'd better nurse that lemonade as long as you can. I'd offer you more, but Mr. Max here already polished off what was left in the pitcher."

I was about to respond, when Mr. Max skated over and unexpectedly scrambled into my lap. A hairy arm curled around my neck as he squirmed to find a comfortable position. Then he wrapped a lanky finger under the pull tab, popped open the soda can, and extended his long, leathery lips to take small, delicate sips. I gently put my arms around him and sat there for a moment, amazed and delighted.

"Just push him off if he's bothering you," Loxie advised.

That was the last thing I wanted to do. I was feeling as protective as a new, doting mother. Without asking permission I reached down and untied Mr. Max's boots, pulling them off to free his feet from the oppressive skates. Mr. Max responded by looking at me with a pair of soft brown eyes which floated into my heart. I stared back at him, overcome by the strangest emotion. I could have sworn it wasn't a chimp's eyes gazing at me, but those of another person. More than anything, I wondered what he was thinking about. He answered my question by offering me a drink of his soda.

"No, that's okay. You finish it," I responded, never doubting that he understood.

Though I barely knew Mr. Max, I was already sick at the thought of his fate. He'd most likely end up the same as many other chimps who start out as pets or work in the entertainment trade.

Primates don't stay cute and cuddly forever, but inevitably grow large as they mature, acting like children who don't know their own strength. By the age of six, Mr. Max would weigh one hundred fifty pounds, prove hard to control, and easily be able to tear a man apart. Once that happens, these former "pets" are either quietly killed or furtively sold off to labs, where they spend the remainder of their days as subjects for painful experimental research.

Max pulled my head down and, puckering his lips, gave me a kiss on the cheek.

"That's just how he started with me," Loxie nodded knowingly.

"How's that?" I asked, having no idea what she was talking about.

"He began by offering his soda. Then he tried to bribe me with Happy Meals. Finally, he was even willing to give me some of his booze. The problem came when I took him up on the offer and drank a shot of his scotch. The next thing I knew, I'd been knocked face down on the floor and he was climbing on top of me. That's when I told Father only one of us was going to continue living in the house, and he'd better make up his mind which one of us it was going to be," Loxie said smartly.

"Who did he choose?" I asked, noticing Mr. Max was looking a little googly-eyed in my direction.

"That's a good one, Mother. You hear that?" the admiral asked, with a slap of his knee. "I picked Mother, of course. But sometimes I still wonder if I made the right decision." Maynard broke into a laugh which sounded like a gag machine from a novelty store.

Enough chit chat; it was time to get moving. "I'd like to have a look around your facility, if you don't mind," I said, planning to do that whether they liked it or not.

"Of course," the admiral's mechanical voice squawked in agreement. "I was going to suggest it myself." He gave me a wink.

"I'm staying here. I already see more of the damned place than I need to." Loxie placed her bunioned feet on a chair.

As I followed the admiral, Mr. Max ran alongside me, broadly swinging his hips in a comic blend of Marilyn Monroe and Popeye. The chimp slipped his hand into mine, and a lump rose in my throat as I glanced down to where our palms pressed together. I was startled at how very similar our fingers, flesh, and nails looked.

Maynard led me to an area filled with cages containing South American spider monkeys, ring-tailed lemurs, African greens, and Rhesus macaques. There were even a couple of baboons the size of large dogs. One bent to moon me, exposing a bright hairless rump. Mr. Max grimaced and let loose a wheezing laugh.

"Do you sell all the monkeys as pets?" I asked, knowing nobody would buy a baboon to keep around the house.

"Most of them. But not all, of course. Some I rent when they're making a movie in town. Others I keep just 'cause they're kind of nice to have around," the admiral cordially explained.

"I take it that your facility is regularly inspected?" I questioned. Captive bred animals aren't under Fish and

Wildlife's domain, but rather that of the U.S. Department of Agriculture.

"Of course! Matter of fact, the USDA has given me their full blessing," the admiral beamed. "Anything else I can show you before we head back?"

I looked at him in surprise. "Yes. I'd like to see where you keep the chimps." What did the guy think, that I hadn't heard their racket upon my entrance?

"Chimps? What do you mean?" Admiral Maynard asked. Then he broke into a round of canned laughter. "I gotcha good on that one, didn't I? I bet you figured I was gonna try to get away without showing them to you. Of course we're gonna see the chimps! Those are my babies you're talking about!"

Maynard took one of my arms while Mr. Max held onto the other, as if I were Dorothy about to enter the land of Oz.

The chimps caught our scent, and the hooting began to build before they even saw us. They rattled the steel fencing of their pen as if planning a massive break-out. I walked into a clearing to find a chain link enclosure containing at least a dozen chimps, whose pandemonium erupted into a full blown frenzy.

One of the primates picked up a handful of feces and threw it in my direction. I ducked just in the nick of time, while Mr. Max shrieked in delight—until another chimp nailed him head-on with a mouthful of water. Then Max hooted in rage, first rushing at the fence, then running back to hide behind my legs. Still another adolescent leaped off his perch and charged, while pounding on the floor of the cage.

"They're just showing off," the admiral chuckled. "Displaying to let you know you're on their territory. Don't worry, they'll quiet down."

Soon, all we heard was the *slap, slap, slap* of their

limbs on concrete. I couldn't help but wonder how many of these chimps had ever climbed a tree, or felt the cool, silky texture of grass beneath their feet. My reverie was interrupted as a stream of water shot out of nowhere, hitting me smack in the face. I jumped backwards to a barrage of side-splitting hoots, howls, and shrieks. I wiped my face and joined the chimps in their laughter.

Then, I walked over to where a baby with sparkling eyes and oversized milk chocolate ears poked a hand out through the fencing toward me. I gently touched each tiny finger, while looking around for his mother.

"Do you rent the chimps out, as well?" I asked the admiral, who was casually scratching his belly.

"Sure. 'Course, they're also in big demand for shows in Vegas. Why, a circus even comes by and picks up a couple every now and then. They're popular animals—did you know some TV station's got itself a show called the Chimp Channel?"

"How about as pets?" I inquired. "You ever sell them for that market?"

The admiral shook his head and wrinkled his nose. "Nah. They're too expensive for most people."

"Hey, this is Texas," I parried. "You mean nobody around here has the money to buy one?"

The admiral's cheerful mask remained in place. "Tell you what: you find me a buyer, and I'll be glad to cut you in on a percentage of the sale price. How's that for an offer?"

I began to count the number of females. There were only three, not one of which was breeding age. Yet I'd spotted a half dozen babies.

"I see plenty of adolescents and baby chimps in here. Where are your adults?" I questioned.

The admiral pulled on his suspenders before answering. "Well, it's like I was telling you. I recently rented a bunch of 'em to a production company in Hollywood for a film they're doing. Something with Clint Eastwood." Maynard leaned in toward me. "You know, he's got a thing for apes in his films. And a few of the others are taking it easy in the Caribbean shooting a commercial. That's the life. Now, don't you wish you were one of my chimps?" he teased.

"You mean you send the mothers away from their babies?" I was appalled.

"It's no problem as long as they've finished nursing," the admiral answered defensively.

Nursing or not, most of these babies should still have been with their mothers. One of the adolescents pressed his back against the cage, and I reached in and absentmindedly scratched it.

"Why don't you hold on there, and I'll get some bananas you can feed them," the admiral offered in a show of goodwill.

I waited until he'd disappeared, then walked over to a shed which stood at the far end of the clearing. Color me curious and call me nosy, but I've never been able to stop myself from snooping. I opened the shed door and peered inside, where a jumble of tools were piled high next to a wheelbarrow. Other than that, there wasn't anything of much interest. Closing the door, I was about to return to the chimps when I spied some plywood crates peeking around the rear corner. I took a quick look to make sure the admiral hadn't reappeared, then headed to investigate.

Lying on the ground were four crates of half inch plywood, each the size of a small cage. Three of the boxes were pockmarked with irregular holes. I ran my fingers over the rough edges, and discovered no tool had created the punctures. Teethmarks confirmed that the wood had been chewed clear through.

"You get tired of playing with the chimps already?"

The admiral's metallic voice cut through the air, as steely cold as a knife. I turned to find him standing behind me with a bunch of bananas in his hand.

"No, I just decided to take a walk around the area when I came upon these boxes." How long had he been there? "I could use something like these for transporting injured critters that I sometimes find. Any idea where I might be able to get hold of a couple of them?"

The admiral slowly shook his head. "Can't say that I do. I get chickens delivered in those every once in a while."

Chickens, huh? They must have had beaks as strong as pick axes to have broken through the wooden crates.

"I guess you've got yourself a farm as well as a zoo, then. So why don't I see any chickens running around?" I guilelessly questioned.

The admiral smiled ominously at me. "That's because Mother has killed them already. We buy them for eating. But Mother gets a real kick out of wringing their necks—she says that's the way to be sure they're fresh."

Goosebumps broke out on my flesh.

Maynard threw the bananas to the caged chimps as we walked back to the house, prompting Mr. Max to fly into a rage. Loxie was still seated in her chair, trying her darndest to manipulate a cigarette into the end of the holder clamped in her mouth. Her eyes squinted as it kept missing its mark, as if she were trying to thread a needle.

"God dawgy, Mother! How many times do I have to tell you to take that damn thing out of your mouth and just stick the cigarette in it!" the admiral instructed peevishly.

I figured he was probably overdue for his nicotine hit.

"I know what I'm doing. Just leave me be," Loxie stubbornly retorted.

The screen door slammed open and a pregnant teen-aged girl appeared. She sullenly waddled past without uttering a word.

"Helen May! Where are your manners? You just stop where you are and say hello," Loxie demanded.

Helen May kept right on walking.

Loxie frustratedly drew in on her cigarette, then blew the smoke at the admiral. Maynard took a series of quick gasps as he struggled to inhale all the vapors.

"That's our daughter. She's not usually impolite; it's just that she's in a bad way these days," Loxie informed me with a note of resignation. "She hasn't been able to contact the child's father to let him know she's pregnant."

"Is he out of town?" I asked sympathetically. The admiral shook his head in disdain and disappeared inside the house.

"Yeah. Way out of town," Loxie remarked sarcastically.

I looked at her questioningly.

"Like on another planet. He's an alien," Loxie replied.

I cracked a smile. "That's a joke. Right?"

She shook her head indignantly, and the foil cap began to teeter. She reached up and braced it. "I'd never pull your leg about something like that. It's the reason I'm wearing this thing."

"To not get pregnant?" I skeptically asked.

"Of course not!" Loxie tartly retorted. "That was the reason twenty years ago. Now my eggs are too old, so the bastards are trying to suck out my brains!"

I remained silent as Mr. Max climbed once again into my lap. He started to pull at the neck of my tee-shirt, forcing me to take hold of his hands and stop him.

"It's a curse the women in our family have had to bear. I was just lucky that it skipped my generation," Loxie remarked.

I remembered the paintings at F.U., Jr's. place that were done by his girlfriend. Maybe this helped explain them.

"What about your other daughter, Cassandra? Does she have the same problem?" I asked, deciding to play along. Mr. Max pulled his hands out of my grip and headed for the button on my pants.

"Max! Stop that! Just control yourself!" Loxie barked and handed him a cookie. "Cassandra? Who the hell's that?" Then she nodded, having suddenly remembered. "Oh, you mean Virginia May. I keep forgetting that she uses a different name these days. Where did you meet her?"

"We haven't actually met. I heard that she's F.U., Jr.'s girlfriend," I replied.

Loxie scrunched up her face. "Virginia May would be better off if she *were* involved with an alien. Have you seen all those flypaper strips that boy keeps inside his place?" Loxie shuddered with disgust. "I can't tell you how much he's hurt his poor father. It's something awful, what with F.U., Jr. being his only son and all."

"Cassandra must see something worthwhile in him," I offered.

"Yeah! Money, most likely," Loxie snorted. "I keep telling her that you don't need a rich man. All you need is one with good credit."

"Tell Rachel the other piece of advice you give the girls," the admiral prodded, walking back out on the porch. "You might find this useful," he added with a wink.

"It's something my mother passed on to me, and damned if she wasn't right," Loxie drawled. "Men are like linoleum: lay them just right, and you can walk on 'em for years."

Ooookay. I turned my attention back to the admiral. "Speaking of the Krabbs, I understand you supply some of the animals for the Happy Hunting Ranch."

Maynard nodded his head. "That's right. I fill special orders. All through the proper channels, of course," he hastened to add. Maynard reached for a cookie and Max let out a reproachful shriek. The admiral swiftly pulled back his hand. "I never had any problems when Johnny Lambert had your job. He was a very understanding man."

I silently wondered how much that had cost the admiral.

"And I'm hoping we can work something out which will likewise prove mutually beneficial," Maynard said with a smile.

"Such as?" I mildly inquired.

"Well, I guess I'd leave that up to your discretion," the admiral replied, tiptoeing around the subject.

"I don't intend to give you any trouble at all," I said.

The admiral sighed.

"Just as long as you don't furnish the Happy Hunting Ranch with anything illegal. Like a black rhino, for instance."

Maynard's beam quickly lost its radiance.

I lifted Mr. Max off my lap and stood up to take my leave. "By the way, I imagine you've already heard that Timmy Tom Tyler was murdered."

The admiral's expression turned into a perfectly blank slate. "Can't say that I have. Why? Is he someone I should know?"

I would think so," I replied, used to this response by now. "Tyler was the animal dealer Krabbs worked with before he switched to you."

Maynard remained silent, as did Loxie. Only Mr. Max made any noise, greedily munching on the cookies.

"In fact, Tyler's partner recently sent someone over to see you about buying a chimp. A guy by the name of Dan Kitrell," I pressed.

The admiral shrugged. "Sorry, but it doesn't ring a bell," his electronic voice croaked.

It was amazing how bad everyone's memory was. Either I'd hit yet another sensitive topic, or the alien brain-sucking phenomenon was a real problem out here.

Twelve

There was no doubt in my mind that primates were being laundered at Maynard's place. The problem would be trying to prove it.

Once numbering close to a million in population, there are now only around a hundred thousand wild chimps left. This is partly due to habitat destruction. The rest of the blame lies with the voracious demand from circuses, roadside zoos, the entertainment industry, illicit research facilities, and the exotic pet trade.

The capture of a baby chimp is a quick, easy way for a poacher to make cash. However, the infant is never their only victim. An entire family always comes to the baby's defense, and inevitably winds up being mercilessly slaughtered. That translates into ten to twenty deaths for every baby chimp that's abducted.

I wished a mothership of aliens would beam up every poacher and smuggler around, including Loxie and her husband. This seemed the perfect time to pop in for a visit with F.U. to pump him for additional information.

I reached the ranch and was about to turn in, only to be stopped by a pair of prostrate bodies. F.U., Jr. and a young woman had secured themselves to the entrance gate with bicycle chains and locks.

"Ooowww!" F.U., Jr. howled in greeting.

The girl joined him in the call of the wild.

"Are you out catching a few rays of sun? Or should I take it that this is some kind of protest?" I inquired.

Rage removed his ever-so-cool wraparound shades and cocked a pierced eyebrow in my direction. I noticed there was a sterling silver fly perched on one of the hoops. "We've decided to up the pressure on this place," he informed me.

I observed the cans of red paint by his side and didn't have to guess what they were for.

"What are *you* doing here? Come to mingle with the enemy?" he demanded.

"I need to talk to your father," I replied.

"Cool. You gonna bust him?" F.U., Jr. asked, with a note of hopeful expectation.

"Not today. I just have a couple of questions for him."

The girl lying next to Rage was a young, updated version of Morticia Adams, with a stud in her brow and a ring in her nose.

"I take it that you're Cassandra," I said, not waiting for anything as bourgeois as an introduction.

The girl looked at me with a bored expression. "Yeah."

Lucky me. I got to see that a stud pierced her tongue as well.

"I saw your paintings at Rage's loft the other day. They're interesting," I remarked, hoping that might help loosen her up.

"Hey, if Georgia O'Keefe could get away with all her crap about vaginas looking like flowers, I can do whatever the hell I want with dicks!"

She seemed a tad sensitive about her work.

"Listen, I don't mean to break up your party, but I need to get into the ranch," I said to end the small talk.

F.U., Jr. pulled his shades back on. "Sorry, but you're

going to have to skip the visit with Big Daddy today. We didn't bring the keys for the chains."

I pulled out my trusty Leatherman, flicked it open, and jimmied each of the locks on their necks. Sometimes you just had to wonder why life wasn't always this simple.

"Say, where did you learn to do that?" F.U., Jr. asked eagerly.

"It's a secret they teach you when you become a law enforcement officer."

Then I jumped back in my pick-up and drove through the gate. I parked next to the motorized herd of snoozing zebras, bounded up the steps, and entered the lodge. I hurried through the gallery of decapitated heads, and strode into F.U.'s outer office.

Velma naturally manned the entrance to Krabbs' inner sanctum. Today she was attired in a lovely chartreuse jumpsuit, doodadded up with garish black and white bejeweled zebra stripes. Someone needed to take this gal in hand and tell her that horizontal lines were not the way to go.

"Well, lookee here. If it isn't little Miss Fish and Wildlife, herself. If you think you can just sashay in and disturb Mr. Krabbs' schedule, I'm here to tell you that you're one-hundred-percent dead wrong," she sneered.

"Don't even think of trying to stop me," I snarled. "This hasn't been one of my better days, plus my PMS is acting up and I'm just itching for an excuse to kick some butt. So get out of my way, or I'll cite you for hindering a federal officer!"

Velma reluctantly moved out of my path. "You just better make sure all your ducks are lined up before you try pulling anything funny," she hissed.

"Don't worry, Velma. I plan to have my ducks and

whatever else it takes geared up, ready to aim, fire, and hit a perfect bulls-eye."

Let her chew on that for a while. Heck, even *I* hadn't figured out what I was up to yet. I entered F.U.'s office.

Talk about being transported to la la land: this was a hunter's paradise. Zebras, cheetahs, and emus gathered about, mingling with panthers, leopards, and lions. Each critter had been tenderly taxidermied in tribute to F.U.'s heartfelt affection for them.

"Cupcake! What a surprise!" the well-aged bourbon voice drifted toward me.

My Western-fried colonel sat behind a massive, semi-circular desk with amber push buttons lining a built-in panel. He came over to greet me. Grabbing my hands, he held them against his chest. His Elvis pompadour never swayed, giving the impression it had been molded from plaster of Paris. He lifted my hands to his lips and eagerly tried to kiss them as I pulled away.

"Oh, oh. You're angry with ol' F.U., aren't you?" Krabbs asked, slipping a sad expression on his face. "I know I promised to call, but things have been pretty hectic around here the past few days. Tell you what: let me make it up to you. You got a hankering to shoot anything today? 'Cause you know I can have it arranged."

If he'd known what I was gunning for, he might have thought twice before asking.

F.U. tried to grab my hands again, but I held them firmly behind my back, so he went for my waist.

"I gotta be honest with you, Cupcake. There's a little problem, what with you being my wife's best friend, and all." His voice dropped to a husky whisper, and he gave my midriff a squeeze. "But I'm also finding this whole thing pretty damned exciting."

I pushed his forearms away. "You're right; there is a

problem. I don't like the way Lizzie's being treated."

"Okay. We'll play it your way for now." F.U. ambled back to his desk, where he gave me a sly smile. "You're one smart gal. You know us men always enjoy a good chase."

This seemed to be especially true in F.U.'s case, so I decided to play along, certain I'd get a whole lot further.

"This is quite the office," I flattered him.

"You like it? I did it myself," F.U. said proudly. "Come here and I'll show you how my toys work."

I had to admit I was curious. Besides all the buttons, his desk had an assortment of high-tech gadgets, making it look like a space shuttle cockpit. James Bond could have died and gone to heaven in this place. F.U. waited until I was standing beside him, then pressed a button. Two wall panels off to the right whipped around, producing a wet bar.

"Pretty fancy, huh?" he eagerly asked. "Just wait till you see this."

F.U. pushed another button and other panels spun open to reveal a large TV monitor. I remembered the camera mounted near the ranch entrance, and sure enough, there were F.U., Jr. and his girlfriend with their necks once again padlocked to the front gate. Somehow they knew they were being watched; they simultaneously turned and shot the camera the finger.

"Children can be a joy in your life, but they can also be a major pain in the ass," F.U. conceded. "Still, we all need to do our part by propagating if we want to ensure the continuation of our species."

"Why, do you think that's going to be a problem in the future?" The animals in this room were closer to extinction than the human population.

"Hell, yes!" Krabbs said with conviction. "It's gonna be harder than ever to survive, what with all those itty bitty countries whose names nobody ever remembers, always declaring some sort of war. Never mind the damned, crazy terrorists running helter skelter all over the world."

Whadda ya know? F.U. Krabbs actually thought about something other than shooting animals.

"So, how about it? Don't you think about having a coupla little ones galloping around your skirts?" He flirtatiously slid his fingers up my arm.

I swatted his hand away as if it were an annoying fly.

"I can see 'em now. Maybe a boy and a girl with your curly red hair, and my baby blue eyes. Hell, I could even teach them to shoot good," he coyly added.

"I believe you have a wife to help you in that department," I responded repressively.

"Well, me and Lizzie haven't been getting along all that well these days. She doesn't really understand me," he confided.

Now, *there* was an original line.

"Besides, you look to me like a filly with good genes. And since the Krabbs family lineage speaks for itself, I'd be more than willing to offer my services," he generously proposed.

"Thanks, but I'm not in the market," I replied, taken aback. It was bad enough being viewed as a sperm bank recipient, but F.U. apparently believed he was the best I could do. How did Lizzie ever hook up with this guy?

"Let me be blunt and quit beating about the bush," F.U. continued with a lascivious gleam in his eye. "I'm proposing to set you up in style somewhere close by. What's more, I'm willing to give my personal guarantee that you and our little darlins will always be safely out of harm's way."

"Safe from what?" I asked skeptically.

"Oooh, let's just say anything and everything," he answered with an enigmatic smile.

At the moment, the only thing I needed protection from was him.

"To sweeten the proposal, I'll provide you with a large enough monthly allowance that you'll never have to work again," F.U. magnanimously offered.

No wonder Ma Krabbs was worried about her money.

"I happen to like my work. Why would I want to stop?" I asked, giving him enough rope to hang himself.

"Hell, working for the government can't be any picnic. What you enjoy is saving animals," Krabbs shrewdly replied. "Why, I can set you up with your own zoo. Just think about it a minute." He drew a step closer, and his breathing grew heavier. "I'll get you whatever critters you want. We'll have two of everything so they can spend their time breeding like bunnies, while you and me are busy doing our thing in the bedroom. What say we consummate the deal right here and now, on the couch?"

The thought was nearly enough to make me lose my lunch.

"It's tempting. But it's not that easy setting up a zoo. There are all sorts of paperwork and regulations to follow. I'm afraid you'd find it difficult," I wistfully remarked.

His caresses became bolder. "Leave that part to me, Cupcake. There are always ways around those things." He punctuated his point with a vigorous wink as he led me toward the couch.

"Like the One World Zoo?" I asked, with feigned naiveté.

"Exactly!" he agreed, only to realize his blunder. His hands shot up to his ears and began to fiddle with his hearing aids faster than you could say "monthly allowance." "Sorry, Cupcake. What was that you said again? Darn these things! I don't believe I heard you properly."

I gave his auditory range a boost by turning the volume higher. "We were talking about the One World Zoo,"

F.U.'s hand dropped and nervously hit a button on the side of the couch. A video camera popped out of the ceiling, aimed directly down at the sofa. I shot him a dirty look, but Krabbs' attention was focused on other matters.

F.U. shook his head, and cleared his throat. "Can't say I ever heard of the place."

I now suspected that One World and the Happy Hunting Ranch were one and the same—which zoomed Krabbs onto my A-list of suspects for the murder of Tyler. Maybe Timmy Tom had been blackmailing Krabbs by threatening to turn over information.

I decided to play out my hunch. "Tyler told me that you dropped him and moved on to Maynard when he couldn't get hold of the animals you wanted."

"Let me tell you something about Tyler, sugarplum." Krabbs voice was tinged with a menacing edge. "He was a no-good scoundrel who didn't care a fig about anything other than himself. Never mind your precious wildlife."

"And Admiral Maynard is a man of such upstanding character?"

"Maynard's a man of his word, and that's all I'm gonna say on that subject." F.U. fixed me with a hard stare. "Now, let's get down to business. I hope you haven't got it in your head to try and shut down my ranch. Because I'd hate to start cutting back on your future allowance already."

"Well then, I guess that all depends on how much

you're willing to cooperate," I sweetly responded. "Who came up with the One World Zoo scam?"

F.U. clucked his tongue and sadly shook his head. "This is all because I didn't call you sooner, isn't it?" he asked dolefully.

I wondered how the man could be so blasted conceited. "Believe me, one thing has nothing to do with the other," I assured him. "Just answer the question."

"Well then, I guess I gotta tell you, don't I? It was all Tyler's idea. I told him I wanted nothing to do with it. That's why I started using the admiral," he said, flashing a sly smile.

I leveled Krabbs with my best dubious glare. "Funny about that. Timmy Tom told me the zoo was *your* idea."

F.U. shrugged good-naturedly. "Well, being that Timmy Tom is lying dead on a slab, I guess you're gonna have to take my word on it."

"Okay. In that case, I want to see the paperwork on all the animals that Timmy Tom had shipped to you."

"That wouldn't be a problem if it were up to me, Cupcake. But Tyler kept all those records. Maybe that boyfriend of his can get 'em for you," he cordially responded.

"Then I'll settle for the paperwork on all the shipments that were arranged by the admiral. Or did those happen to burn up in some fire?" I asked snidely.

F.U.'s face immediately lit up. "Why, heck! How'd you know about that? Now, there's a truly sad story." He shook his head despondently. "Just like you said, the admiral up and had a fire at his place a while back, and every single one of his records went right up in flames."

"How convenient for him."

"This isn't gonna cause any hard feelings between us, I hope," F.U. added.

"Not at all. But I can tell you here and now that I

intend to watch every single move that you make. I'm going to be closer to you than your underwear," I warned, having always wanted to use that expression. Unfortunately, it didn't get the response I'd been hoping for.

"Has anyone ever told you that you're a damn tease, Cupcake?" F.U. asked. "But that's fine by me, 'cause I'm planning to hunt you down and get you in the end, no matter what it takes."

What a delightful vision.

I glumly left, ignoring Velma's murderous glare.

I drove off knowing that whatever F.U. had been involved in wasn't over yet. I pondered the problem all the way back to the entrance gate, where I again jimmied the locks around F.U., Jr. and Cassandra's necks.

"So, how'd you make out?" Rage inquired.

"I suspect your father's involved in something illegal, but it's going to be difficult to prove," I responded, having turned my back to the camera.

"What I'm about to tell you has nothing to do with the fact that you like my artwork. It's because Rage says you can be trusted," Cassandra said with a toss of her long black locks, displaying a pair of penis-shaped earrings.

"Fair enough," I replied, wondering if it was too late to take Charlie Hickok up on his offer. Rednecks were beginning to same pretty normal compared to the folks out West.

"Because I don't give a shit whether you really like it or not," Cassandra emphasized with a stomp of her studded black boot.

Enough, already! Just get on with it!

Cassandra apparently received my nonverbal message. "Okay. Just as long as you know. I found out this morning that there's going to be a delivery."

"Of what?" I inquired.

"I don't know. But I'll bet it's gonna be something good, 'cause my father was all excited."

"And when is this delivery supposed to take place?" I wasn't sure if Cassandra was all that reliable a source.

"Tonight," she confided in a whisper.

I paused, then plunged ahead. "Sorry, but your father isn't a stupid man. I find it hard to believe he'd talk freely about something like that when you're hanging around the house."

Cassandra smiled. The girl was quite pretty when she wasn't snarling. "You're right; that's why I don't get information by eavesdropping on my father. My sister Helen May gives it to me."

"And why would she do that?" I inquired. The very pregnant Helen May hadn't appeared to be big on communicating.

"Let's just say my sister and I came to an agreement," Cassandra smirked. "It wasn't an alien that knocked Helen May up, but Billy Bob Holder next door. My parents would kill her if they ever found out."

Now, *this* was something that finally made sense.

"The delivery is supposed to take place at the border around midnight, somewhere along the Anapra Road," Cassandra revealed.

I had a pretty good idea of the exact spot—and I planned to be there.

Thirteen

Maybe there would be an illegal shipment tonight. Then again, maybe there would not. In either case, I had plenty of time to kill. I decided to make the most of it by moseying around to the back of the ranch and sneaking onto Happy Hunting's property. With any luck, I'd be able to spot an illegal critter and slap Krabbs with a violation.

I drove past land so still that it seemed to exist merely to hold the surrounding mountains apart. It's at times like this that my mind is set free to wander. My thoughts were instinctively drawn to Jake Santou like a magnet pulled by a stronger source. We hadn't been in touch since our break-up in Miami and I'd told myself that was it; our relationship was finished. Still, something inside refused to let go, giving me hope that it wasn't yet over.

Since there was no star to wish upon, I silently said a prayer. I know it sounds silly, but I've always been one who searches for a sign that my request will be answered. Being that no wishbone was handy, I looked outside for some sort of clue. Glancing upward, I slammed on my brakes to witness an event I'd only heard about before.

Flying overhead was a majestic pair of bald eagles in

the midst of an aerial courtship. Interlocking their talons, the birds became united as one, swirling in a revolving whirligig of feathers. Caught up in the voyeuristic vision, my blood pulsated in union with their undulating rhythm as their powerful wings beat rapidly, causing the very air to throb around them.

Then the eagles suddenly plunged, locked in a downward death spiral. I held my breath and watched as the birds nearly crashed to the ground, breaking apart only at the very last second. Then with a quick flap of their wings, each flew off in a separate direction.

I finally remembered to inhale, and the air seared my lungs. If I'd been looking for answers, I realized there were none. I would have to let nature take its own course in working things out. I put all thoughts of Santou away for the moment.

I drove on, and soon reached the far end of F.U. Krabbs' ranch. It was time to begin my own hunt. I parked, grabbed a pair of heavy work gloves, and stood on the pick-up's hood. From there, I was able to reach the top of the wooden fence encircling all of Happy Hunting's fifteen thousand acres. I climbed over and leapt down to discover there was still one obstacle left: a barbed wire fence that gleamed bright as a rapier's edge, daring me to get through. I only hoped F.U. hadn't had it electrified.

I pulled on my gloves, walked over to a mesquite tree, and cut off one of its branches. Then I spread two strands of the barbed wire fence apart by using the stick as a wedge. After that, I tested the brace, reminded of an old cowboy saying.

There are three kinds of men. Those who learn by reading. The few who learn by observation. And the rest, who pee on an electric fence before they finally get it.

I wiggled through, determined not to become one of

the barbecued, and made it onto the Happy Hunting Ranch without injuring myself.

Walking along the fence line seemed like a good place to start until I felt sure of my bearings. Soon a mound of loose dirt caught my eye. Part of the ground had been dug up under the fence, creating a hole for a coyote to slip through. If that weren't proof enough, I caught sight of the critter's four-toed track. I cut off another mesquite branch, sharpened its end, and poked around the area.

Snap!

A jarring crunch severed the heavy branch neatly in two. Hidden beneath the dirt lay a steel-jawed leghold trap.

The mechanism resembles a medieval torture device, which aptly describes how it works. Its bone-crushing jaws bite painfully deep into the animal's flesh. Once the critter is caught, it suffers until a trapper eventually shows up to slay and claim his prey. There was no doubt that where one leghold trap had been set, others were also planted. Envisioning myself as yet another captured varmint, I left the fence line and headed into Happy Hunting's interior.

It wasn't until I heard the muffled rumble of a man's voice that I came to a halt. Sonny had taught me to track in grassland as well as in desert sand, tiptoeing as stealthily as a stalker. I began now, quietly treading toe-heel, toe-heel, until I drew close enough to catch a glimpse of the man. The large, hulking form clued me in that it was none other than Happy Hunting's own Grizzly Adams, Dan Kitrell.

I froze, afraid he would hear me, but he remained focused in the opposite direction. With any luck, I'd be able to turn and backtrack without being detected. I started toe-heeling away, when the snarl of an animal in pain stopped me in my tracks.

A young buff-gray coyote stood in front of Kitrell with its lips pulled back and its teeth bared. Another snarl emerged from deep within the critter's gut. Bile rose in my throat as I saw that the coyote's leg was painfully pinned inside a leghold trap.

More than anything, I wanted to stop Kitrell from killing the critter. The problem was that I had no legal means to do so. I couldn't run for my truck and just leave; if I did, I'd be haunted for the rest of my days. If I stayed and intervened, I'd end up being hauled into court on trespassing charges. The only other option was to stand my ground and watch how the scene played out.

I decided to slam, bam and ram through door number two, solving things my own way. I reached for my revolver, determined to stop Kitrell and damn the ensuing consequences, as he began to make his way toward the animal. But to my surprise, instead of moving in for the kill, Kitrell's steps were slow and his voice was soft. I remained where I was, wondering what he was up to.

The coyote violently lunged toward the man, only to be sharply jerked back by the trap. However, that didn't stop it from fighting. The critter charged forward again, bringing Grizzly to a halt. All the while, Kitrell never stopped talking. The hypnotic timbre of his voice wound through the air, his tone as soothing as being wrapped in a stole of luxurious velvet. Either he was the most sadistic trapper alive, or he was up to something highly unusual.

Kitrell kept up the melodious patter until the coyote finally stopped struggling. I didn't know if it had become mesmerized by the man's voice or was just completely exhausted. Grizzly drifted forward once more, taking one half-step, and then another. The coyote never took its eyes off the man but listened to the sing-song words with its ears raptly pricked in attention.

I remained glued where I stood, not daring to twitch a muscle. Kitrell sank down next to the trap as he pulled a knife from its sheath. I tightened my fingers on my revolver, unsure of his intent. But rather than lean in to slice the coyote's throat, Grizzly tried to jimmy the steel jaws of the trap.

I looked on in disbelief as Kitrell worked his knife back and forth, as if prying open a clamshell. But the trap's main spring remained invincible. Grizzly wiped the sweat from his face with his forearm and, dropping the knife, sat back on his heels. One look at the coyote was all it took to know the critter understood the situation. He pathetically sat awaiting his fate, and a cry throbbed against the back of my throat.

Don't stop now! I silently urged, not knowing what else Kitrell could do.

Grizzly cautiously crept closer. The coyote pulled back and then stopped, allowing Kitrell to reach out and lift the trap in his hands. The muscles in the man's back visibly strained as his fingers painstakingly worked their way between steel teeth and mangled fur. He briefly stopped and my stomach flip flopped, afraid he'd given up. But Grizzly made one last valiant effort, applying brute strength against the contraption with a roar as loud as thunder. The trap's spring gave way, and the contraption miraculously sprang open.

I covered my mouth to keep from breaking out in a victorious cheer. The last thing I wanted to do was rupture the bond between animal and man. The coyote faced Kitrell in a moment of silent communion, then backed away and silently took off.

Its long, yellowish legs trotted away until even the black tip of its bushy tail disappeared from sight. Then I realized my plight: now *I* was the prey left standing there. The magic moment dissolved, and I imagined an alternate view of what had taken place.

I was alone with a man who liked to ambush and torture his quarry. Only after the animal's spirit had been broken did he release the injured critter back into the wild to possibly die. Maybe he considered it a form of sport, in which he was the ultimate conqueror.

Whatever the case, I felt sure Kitrell wouldn't be happy should he discover an uninvited observer. Especially one who could talk.

I began to back off, but my skills were nowhere near as good as the coyote's. A twig crunched underfoot, taking perverse pleasure in giving me away. Kitrell reflexively grabbed his knife and turned in one fluid motion, ready for action even before having sighted the prey.

I didn't wait to see what would happen but spun around and ran, my feet pounding against the unyielding ground. There was no sound of Kitrell behind me, but I probably wouldn't have heard a Mack truck. My breath roared in my ears, throwing a blanket of silence on everything around. I was certain I'd eluded my pursuer until the Mack truck I hadn't heard pulled alongside me.

Swinging around, I flung my fist in an attempt to nail Kitrell in the kisser. But the man crouched low, anticipating my move. Using my own momentum, he flung me face down on the ground with a resounding thud. I squirmed, trying to shake the refrigerator-size man off, but Kitrell easily pinned my arms behind my back and removed the revolver from the waistband of my pants. In his other hand was his knife.

"I'll let you roll over if you promise not to try anything funny," he rumbled in a take-no-prisoners tone.

"All right," I promised.

Kitrell raised his body and I quickly rolled over to thank him with a knee in his groin, but my aim was off.

Kitrell held my wrists tighter and sat on me like a human Rock of Gibraltar. The one good thing was that he'd put away his knife.

"I thought we had an understanding," he said calmly.

I screamed at the top of my lungs, and immediately found myself rolled back onto my stomach, my face in the dirt, breathing in Happy Hunting's down-home aroma.

"We don't have to do this, you know. I'm not planning to hurt you. I just want you to remain quiet and listen to what I have to say. Otherwise, you're going to be here the rest of the day."

It felt as if I were being pinned down by Godzilla.

"Now, what do I have to do to make you behave?" Kitrell asked ominously.

"Maybe you should try using the same tone as you did with that coyote. It seemed to work wonders with him."

"You're fast with the snappy remarks," Grizzly commented. "I noticed that the last time we met."

"I always like to make a good first impression."

Kitrell rolled me onto my back and I looked up at a pair of fiery eyes. "You need to understand that I'm not who you think I am. I conned Krabbs into hiring me under false pretenses, but there's a good reason why I'm working at this ranch," Grizzly said.

"Oh, yeah? And why is that?" I asked to humor him. As far as I was concerned, he was just another wacko. Unfortunately, he happened to be the wacko who was sitting on top of me at the moment.

Kitrell gaze bored into mine. "Because I'm looking for a particular animal."

Well, aren't we all. Mine just happened to be a homicide detective who was probably right now dining on oysters while listening to jazz down in the Big Easy.

"So who does that make you? Captain Ahab, or are you tracking Bigfoot?" I inquired. A pebble began to bite into my back. At least that's what I thought it was, until the damn thing started moving.

"How about we call a truce? What say you cool it with the wise cracks and listen?" Kitrell offered.

I saw a spider crawl by and nearly passed out. God, I hated creepy-crawlies! "Deal," I agreed faintly.

Grizzly remained looking down at me, giving me a lovely view up his nose.

"Cross my heart. Just let me get up, already!" I pleaded.

Kitrell shifted his weight and I scrambled to my feet, brushing off anything that hadn't previously been on my body.

"For chrissake, what did you think I was going to do, anyway? I'd no more hurt you than I would an animal," Kitrell grumbled.

I shot him a dubious look. "That's pretty funny, coming from someone who's employed on a hunting ranch."

"I told you, I'm only working here as a cover. I followed a lead to this place," Grizzly retorted.

"So, what are you, some kind of cop?" I asked skeptically.

"I could be," he said brusquely.

Yeah, and I was Goldilocks. "Why don't you just fill me in on this mystery animal you're searching for," I responded. "I'd also appreciate it if you gave me my gun back."

Kitrell studied me for a moment. "I'm looking for a chimpanzee," he replied and handed over my .38.

"Try checking out Admiral Maynard's place. He seems to have plenty of them," I suggested.

"I didn't say *any* chimp; I'm trying to track down a *particular* one. Besides, Maynard is as dirty as Krabbs when it comes to the animal trade." Kitrell glanced around the area. "Look, it's a long story which I'll be happy to tell you—but this isn't the place to do it. If Krabbs spots us out here, we'll both be in trouble."

He was right. And if he'd planned to hurt me, he'd have done so by now. I thought back to how he'd opened the steel-jaw trap with his bare hands. Maybe he was the genuine article, after all.

"Okay. What do you suggest?"

"Since it's quitting time, I'll check out for the day. Where are you parked?"

I pointed to the direction from which I'd entered.

Grizzly shook his shaggy head in disbelief. "In that case, I'll walk you back first. That's the last area with traps that I haven't gotten around to tripping yet."

I wasn't about to argue after having found one, my-self. "You mean, you go around planting traps only to sabotage them?"

Kitrell gave the slightest hint of a nod. "F.U. pays me to plant the things, and that's what I do. I can't help it if there happen to be a lot of wily coyotes running around."

"How about releasing coyotes once they're trapped? Is there anything regarding that in your contract?" I questioned.

Grizzly abruptly grabbed my arm and pulled me to-ward him. "There's a trap right where you're headed."

Picking up a stick, he dug around until the trap sprang closed. I suddenly realized how lucky I was that he'd come with me. We reached the patch of barbed wire fence lodged open by my mesquite branch.

"Very clever." Kitrell nodded approvingly.

I carefully slid through the opening, then found my-self facing the high wooden enclosure. Only this time, I didn't have the hood of my Ford to clamber up on.

"Tell me. Just how were you planning to manage this part by yourself?" Kitrell inquired.

All right, so there was one minor item I hadn't taken into consideration.

Grizzly made it through the barbed wire without coming into contact with either strand, then he boosted all one hundred thirty pounds of me up and over the wall.

"Stay there. I'll meet you in a few minutes," he said and headed back.

Fourteen

I was daydreaming about clever critters catching Happy Hunting's clientele in traps of their own, when Dan Kitrell pulled beside me in a battered Toyota Land Cruiser.

"Ever been to an area called Hueco Tanks?" he asked. "It's only about twenty minutes from here, and private enough that we can talk."

About thirty miles east of El Paso, Hueco Tanks is a state park known for its Native American pictographs. In addition, it's a mecca for rock climbers and sun-baked desert rats. There was no doubt it met the standard as a secluded place; it also provided an excellent locale in which to knock me off.

Kitrell noticed my hesitancy. "Well, well. You really are afraid of me, aren't you?" He laughed.

If his objective was to get me there, he'd just succeeded.

"You lead, I'll follow." I'd be damned if some human Smokey the Bear was going to scare me.

I knew we'd arrived when I caught sight of three enormous red rock outcroppings eerily rising out of the desert. Kitrell pulled alongside one, and I parked next to him.

"Let me know if you need any help," he offered, and clambered up the rocks with the skill of a billy goat.

I hate it when someone older than me is much more agile. I pulled myself up by grabbing onto the *huecos*, or basins, in the boulders, then placed each foot in the indentations as though I were climbing a ladder.

I'd spent my formative years riding elevators up and down skyscrapers without ever giving it a second thought. Yet stick me on the side of a rocky precipice, clinging on for dear life, and I suddenly discovered I had a nauseating fear of heights. I tried to ignore that by concentrating on the pictographs carved into the rocks around me. I passed men riding noble stallions, dancing torsos, and writhing snakes. Then the stony gaze of a mythological figure nearly caused me to lose my balance. He had the horns of a devil and a bird's large hooked beak, and wore an amulet for protection and strength around his neck. Three concentric rings formed each eye, which locked onto mine, refusing to let me pass. It was almost as if the warrior had sprung to life, his mission to scare the hell out of me.

You don't belong here. Tempt fate and the price is your life.

I dug my heels in, gritted my teeth, and continued to climb. Kitrell was enjoying the view by the time I reached the summit, panting like an out-of-shape poodle. It really was time to dig out the Richard Simmons exercise tape and do more than just watch it.

"Congratulations. You made it to the top," Grizzly said, and threw me a Power Bar.

I ripped open the wrapper and took a bite. Boy, he had no idea of how to reward a gal. The very least I deserved was some chocolate.

"Look over there."

I followed the direction of Grizzly's finger, grateful that I hadn't been asked to speak yet.

"That's where Hueco backs onto Fort Bliss. Come up

here on the right night, and you get a free fireworks show compliments of the military. It's one of the little known bonuses that comes with being a resident of this place. You get to kick back and celebrate the Fourth of July a lot more than once a year."

"You live here?" I asked in surprise.

"Yep. That's home, sweet home right down there," he replied, pointing to one of the many broken down trailers in the area.

Interesting as this was, it wasn't what I was here for. "I believe you have a story to tell me," I reminded him.

Grizzly looked at me for a moment before he spoke. "I checked you out, you know. Just to make sure you're honest. That's the only reason you're here."

This was a new twist; I was used to it being the other way around. "And how did you do that?" I inquired.

"It was easy," Kitrell replied with a smile tugging at his lips. "I asked Juan Hernandez if you were somebody I could do business with. He thinks I want to buy a black market chimp."

So, Fat Boy hadn't been lying to me when he'd passed on that information.

"Why would Juan think you're shopping around for a primate?" I pounced.

"Because I told him so. I *am* looking for a chimp— but one that was stolen, not smuggled," Grizzly replied.

"So what did Juan say about me?"

"He said you were a real pain-in-the-ass. That's how I knew you could be trusted." Kitrell smiled.

Then he looked out over the horizon and his entire demeanor changed. He exuded the intensity of a fiery prophet consumed with a burning passion. "Have you heard of a project that teaches chimps to use American Sign Language to communicate with humans?"

An unexplained chill tickled my neck, though the temperature hadn't budged below a torrid ninety degrees.

"That's what I used to do," he disclosed. "I worked as a behavioral scientist at a university center for primate behavioral awareness. We started with the concept that it could be physical rather than mental differences which kept chimps from forming spoken words. In which case, they should be able to correspond with us through sign language."

"I remember hearing something about it when I was a student. But I thought that research was over and done with years ago. I had no idea it was still going on," I responded.

Kitrell gathered the loose strands of his hair and pulled them back into a ponytail as a drop of sweat rolled down his cheek and got lost in his beard. "Well, it is. Studies like this tend to go on for the lifetime of a chimp, so we're talking up to sixty years. I spent nine years of my life doing that research." Kitrell's voice grew thick with emotion and caught in his throat.

I silently waited.

"My job was to do hands-on training with a group of six chimps. The way it worked was that I signed to them, and observed their signings back to me. And you know what I learned, Porter?"

"What's that?" I asked, my own voice a whisper.

"The line that divides humans from chimps is a whole lot slimmer than anyone can imagine."

I shivered, thinking of the chimps at Maynard's place.

"There were no random signings, or monkey-see, monkey-do imitations. These chimps formed complete sentences on their own. They were fully able to communicate their wants and needs and feelings to me. Granted, it wasn't the same level on which you and I are talking. But the seven of us broke through the language barrier that divides us as species. Within the first five years, most of the chimps were using a good one-hundred thirty signs, and were able to understand hundreds of others. We actually *spoke* to one another. The feeling was something I can't even begin to describe." Kitrell turned away, his eyes filled with tears.

"It's obvious you loved your work," I said sympathetically. "So why did you leave it?"

Kitrell's mouth compressed into a hard, thin line. "I'd never have voluntarily left those chimps for anything in the world. Our funding dried up, and the university threatened to shut down the center. I pleaded my case by pointing out how prestigious the project was for the university's reputation, and was finally told that there was only one way we could continue to operate. Cutbacks had to be instituted."

"Don't tell me they fired you?"

Grizzly shook his shaggy head. "No, the university wanted me to stay, but my efforts were to go into other areas of primate research. They decided to get rid of my chimps."

Kitrell's body slumped at the memory. "Obviously, I turned the board down. There was no way I could ever desert the chimps I'd raised and with whom I'd spent so much time. They were no longer just research subjects; they'd become friends who had entrusted their lives to me."

"So, what happened?" I was dying to find out.

A derogatory grunt escaped the man's lips. "The university promised I'd be allowed time to raise the money to move the chimps someplace safe, where I'd be able to continue my work. While I was off on my first fundraising trip, word leaked out about the situation. A number of people immediately expressed an interest in the chimps and offered the university a decent price for them."

"Then someone else is working with them now?" I hazarded a guess.

Kitrell caught my gaze and held it prisoner in an invisible vise. "They wanted the chimps for biomedical research."

I stared at Kitrell in stunned silence.

"You have to understand, I'd raised these chimps by hand, as one would a child. They slept in their own beds, and had their own special toys. Their daily routine was to laugh and play games as they learned and ran around outside. Suddenly, not only do I disappear, but they're torn from the only home they've ever known, and thrown into isolated cells without even a blanket on the floor. Now tell me, how would you have reacted to that?" he demanded.

"How did you find out?" I wanted to know every detail.

"Someone at the university tipped me off, but by the time I returned, the chimps were already gone. Even worse, the university refused to tell me where they'd been shipped to." Grizzly snorted. "They were afraid I'd go after the new owners and make trouble—which is exactly what I would have done. So, there I was. The most important beings in my life had been snatched away because I wasn't there to protect them."

This time I was the one brushing away tears. "But the board gave you their word!" I futilely protested. As a federal employee, I already knew how much that was worth.

"Yeah. Isn't that great? Welcome to the backstabbing world of academia."

"How long ago did this happen?" I was already trying to figure out if there was any way to rectify the situation.

"It's been three years. Needless to say, I immediately resigned from the center—after vowing to castrate every member on the board. I hear they still wear athletic cups at all times." He grinned. "Anyway, I swore to devote the rest of my life to tracking down the chimps and freeing them, no matter how long it took."

Kitrell scratched his beard, and I almost expected him to let out a chimp-like hoot. "Oh, yeah. I should mention that there actually is a good part to the story."

"Which is?" I anxiously prompted.

"I managed to obtain a list of all the scientists' names who'd expressed interest in acquiring the chimps."

"Great! So, did you track them down, then?" I wanted to hear that the story had a fairytale ending in which each creature lived happily ever after.

"I did manage to track down most of them. Three of the chimpanzees had been sold to a biomedical lab in Maryland. I found another two locked away in stainless steel boxes in a research facility in Pennsylvania."

I had a whole new set of questions, but Kitrell cut me off with a warning glance.

"It took a good deal of threatening, but I finally managed to convince both labs that the press would have a field day if they happened to get their hands on the story. Especially since I'd be more than willing to give my own heart-rendering version of what had actually taken place," he continued. "By the time I was through, the labs couldn't hand the chimps back to me fast enough."

"Where are they now?" I inquired, wondering if they were holed up in his trailer below.

A bittersweet smile flitted across Kitrell's face. "After all they'd been through, I felt they deserved to spend the rest of their days in a place where they could live as naturally as possible. So I managed to relocate them to a sanctuary specifically designed for primates."

"That still leaves one chimp unaccounted for," I said, figuring out loud.

"That's right," Kitrell somberly verified. "And this last one, Gracie, is truly special to me. Not only was she the first primate I ever worked with, but we had the strongest bond. Gracie was the most loving of chimpanzees, along with being the brightest of the entire bunch."

"But you said your chimps were sold to research labs." I was still trying to make sense of it all. "If that's the case, why would either Maynard or F.U. have anything to do with the chimp you're looking for?"

"They don't. They're just conduits leading to the man I believe is really holding Gracie captive," Kitrell grimly informed me.

My adrenaline began to accelerate. "And who would that be?"

"Dr. Martin Pierpont." Grizzly announced in a voice of doom.

Dr. Scissorhands? What would he want with a chimp? "If you're really convinced Pierpont has Gracie, why haven't you approached him directly about it?"

Purple shadows had begun to glide in, draping themselves heavily over the mountains like a dark, funereal shroud, the air palpably thick with a sense of mystery.

"I tried contacting Pierpont in the past, but he always let me know through others that he was resistant to being approached. I nearly tracked him down once before; the next thing I knew, he'd packed up and disappeared. I can't take a chance on that happening again. Not when I've finally gotten this close." The intensity in Kitrell's voice slashed through the canvas of dusk.

Maybe I was being dense, but I still had a problem understanding what this hide-and-seek game was all about. "Granted, Pierpont is strange. But what makes you think he's the one who has Gracie? After all, he's making plenty of money off F.U. with his claim of being able to clone Lizzie Krabbs' dog."

Kitrell's eyes blazed like twin meteors set on a crash course. "There's one other contact we had in common which you don't know about. You weren't the only one Tyler was spilling his guts to," Grizzly revealed. "He'd heard I was nosing around for a chimp and went out of his way to get in touch with me. Tyler said he didn't have any chimps on hand at the moment, but planned on getting a shipment in soon.

"I mentioned that I'd heard there was a scientist working for Krabbs who had a chimp, and asked Tyler if he knew anything about it. He said Pierpont had purchased some primates from the admiral. I offered to pay for any information he could dig up on one chimp in particular, one that hadn't been obtained from Maynard. I told Tyler that Gracie had been stolen from me."

"Was Timmy Tom able to get the information for you?" I asked, wishing he would hurry up.

Grizzly scratched his beard, as if the answer lay hidden inside his forest of facial hair. "That's the strange part. Tyler left a message a few days ago saying he had evidence that Gracie was here. He'd even come up with a way for me to steal her back. The catch was that he wanted more money. That was no big deal; I'd have been willing to negotiate. I've sworn to bring Gracie home no matter what."

Kitrell's words floated on the mantle of twilight which swiftly began to descend. "But there was no answer when I tried to return his call. It turns out Tyler phoned me right before you found him dead."

A cold chill settled on my shoulder, and began to nibble at my ear. I tried to brush it away, but the incubus clung on, softly laughing at my fears.

"Say all this is true—that Pierpont has your chimp. What type of research do you think he's doing?"

Kitrell shook his head, his profile softened by the

dwindling light. "Whatever he's up to, Pierpont's doing his best to make sure nobody knows about it. That alone puts me on guard."

He leaned forward with his shoulders hunched and his hands tightly clenched into fists. "What you've got to remember is that the difference between humans and chimps is merely a matter of degree. We share 98.6% of the very same genetic material, which is why they're considered the perfect test specimens. Chimps are the best thing scientists can experiment on, next to human beings."

Dan rhythmically thrust his fists together and pulled them apart, like a boxer caught in a private prayer. "But chimps are intelligent beings who possess the ability to reason and communicate. They deserve to be considered more than test tubes with a pulse."

I reached inside my pocket and pulled out the papers I'd taken off Timmy Tom's corpse. Then I handed Panfauna's business card to Kitrell. Even the fading light couldn't conceal the expression which swept over the man's face.

"You know something about this company!" I pounced.

But, Grizzly shook his head as he continued to stare at the card. "No. But look at the name. What does it say?"

I wasn't in the mood for guessing games. "Exactly what's there: Panfauna Associates. Or is something written in invisible ink that I'm supposed to be seeing?"

"Let me try to make it clearer for you," Grizzly retorted. "You do know that pan troglodyte is the scientific term for chimpanzee, right? Well, fauna means animals of a specific region."

My head felt as it if had been whacked by a hammer as the significance began to sink in.

"Oh, my God," The words left my mouth before I even knew I had uttered them. "It sounds like a company that's smuggling chimps in from the wild."

I handed Kitrell the second piece of paper. He unfolded the note as if it were a map of buried treasure. For a moment I thought that's exactly what it was, as his eyes scrutinized it.

"I've found her!" Kitrell finally exclaimed in a trembling voice. "Tyler was right; Gracie *is* here. Pierpont has her."

"How do you know?" I asked, caught up in the excitement.

His finger stabbed at the paper. "One set of these numbers is the identification tattoo Gracie was given at the university."

Maybe this was crucial information for Kitrell—but how did I fit into the picture? Tyler wouldn't have called me that morning unless there was something he'd wanted me to know, as well. My old boss Charlie Hickok's words came back to haunt me.

You gotta learn to look at every nitty gritty detail if you're gonna solve a case, Bronx. Otherwise you're just an agent sitting on your ass, wasting valuable time. The piece you don't look hard enough at is usually the one that's gonna solve the puzzle. It may take a few whacks in the face with a skunk, but eventually you'll find the clue to the case is sitting right there in front of you.

I tried looking at the whole picture now, but Pierpont's face kept looming before me.

"Pierpont used to work for the government. Do you think that could play into this?" I asked, attempting to jiggle the pieces together.

"No. This isn't *The X-Files*, if that's what you're getting at. Pierpont was the head of an upstart biotechnology company when he came to check out my chimps at the university. I'm sure the research he's doing isn't funded by federal grants. As for cloning the Krabbs dog, that sounds like nothing but pure bunk to me."

"Okay. Then let's figure out what it could possibly be," I suggested. "Aren't lab chimps basically just research subjects for HIV testing these days?"

"You've got to be kidding," Kitrell retorted in amazement. "There are scientists who plan to use chimps not only as living blood and organ banks, but for invasive studies for spinal injury. Chimps are already guinea pigs for respiratory diseases, malaria, and parasite research. That's aside from all those who've been infected with hepatitis C, in the hope of finding a cure."

I felt as if I were being bombarded with too much information. "Hold on a second! What I'm trying to figure out is if Pierpont could possibly be hooked up with Panfauna Associates, and if so, why. From what I understand, there's an overabundance of chimps in research labs these days. Isn't that correct?" I inquired.

Kitrell nodded his head vigorously. "Uh huh. But the labs *you're* referring to are those overseen by government agencies, where rules and regulations apply. All research conducted at universities and facilities which receive federal or state government grants has a large degree of transparency. The Freedom of Information Act allows us, as taxpayers, to see what testing our money is funding. The problem lies with private biotech companies. There's no way for us to know what kind of secret research is going on inside those places. It's these upstart companies that have trouble getting hold of chimps."

Kitrell had now gone over my head, and was soaring into the proverbial stratosphere.

"If you expect me to follow along, you're going to have to explain this a little better," I told him.

"Here's the problem in a nutshell: there's a moral dilemma in this country as to whether chimps should be used for medical experimentation. Because of this, labs funded by the government are under strict supervision regarding what kind of research can and cannot be performed. However, if one of these private companies decides to do some sort of secret testing, there's no public watchdog to oversee what's going on. But they still face one enormous obstacle: no legitimate lab will rent, or sell, their chimps to a facility without knowing what type of experiments will be done. So, these private companies have to hunt around to get hold of their own personal supply of primates. And that's where the trouble begins."

Grizzly held up a finger the size of a small tree root. "First off, chimps cost between thirty-five to forty grand apiece. So a private company has to come up with mucho moolah to establish even a small colony of research chimps. They might be lucky enough to grab one or two primates from a university that's lost its funding. Other than that, what do you suppose is the best way around the problem?"

I promptly supplied the most logical answer. "To buy smuggled chimps, of course."

Kitrell flashed a stern smile, his teeth gleaming in the last of the brooding light. "You betcha. Probably with the help of some little mom and pop operation situated along the Tex–Mex border. Maybe one that does a quick turnover, laundering their primates with the claim that they're being leased to the entertainment trade." Dan held up a second stocky finger. "In addition, there's a shortage of young chimps who aren't infected with some disease as a result of testing done at a very young age. By smuggling chimps in, unscrupulous labs get their primates cheap and clean, all in one fell swoop."

"And that's where Panfauna Associates comes in," I murmured, my thoughts clicking together in mental Morse code. "Panfauna's probably pipelining chimpanzees from Africa into Spain, and then flying them into Juarez, Mexico. After that, they're trucked in along the border, all at a bargain price. What do you think?" My pulse pounded to the beat of a van's tires transporting living cargo more precious than gold.

Kitrell no longer looked like an angry prophet, but a man rip-roaring and ready for the adventure of a lifetime. "What I think is, if this isn't a smoking gun, we have one hell of a hot pistol."

Another piece of the puzzle fell into place as my memory pulled the handle on my mental slot machine. *Click, click, click!* Three cherries gaily lined up to reward me with a jackpot.

"That's it! This is what Cassandra was talking about!" I howled in elation.

Grizzly swiftly grabbed my shoulders to stop me from falling off the rocks. "For chrissakes, Porter! Nobody's asking you to sacrifice yourself to the gods over this. Keep your butt in place and your mind on where you are, or we'll never get through this thing in one piece," he gruffly admonished.

He was right. I looked down at the sharp boulders below and my fear of heights came roaring up like a bullet train filled with screaming banshees. I quickly wriggled back until my rear-end hit a rock wall.

"Don't worry; you're safe. And I think that's about as far as you can go unless you plan to burrow into the next stone," Kitrell teased. "Now, what were you babbling about before you almost pulled a Humpty Dumpty on me?"

"Admiral Maynard is supposed to be receiving some sort of delivery late tonight along the border," I revealed.

"Where'd you hear this?" Kitrell asked.

"I guess I've still got some contacts that you haven't yet discovered," I responded loftily.

Grizzly pulled out a dust-bitten, wrinkled excuse for a handkerchief and waved it in surrender. Knowing the state of his laundry was worse than my own made me feel even better.

"I've been getting information from F.U., Jr. and his girlfriend," I disclosed.

"Ah! The Texas Romeo and Juliet. Rebellious kids— don't you just love 'em?" Kitrell gleefully rubbed his hands together. "She didn't happen to tell you where this is supposed to be going down, did she?"

"Somewhere along the Anapra Road. My guess is that delivery always takes place around the area where Timmy Tom was murdered, so we'll have to arrive early and stake it out. That is, if you're interested in coming along."

"Just try keeping me away." Then Grizzly took a look around. "Unless you plan to descend in total darkness, I suggest we climb off this outcrop now. We can go to my trailer and have some dinner. By then, it should be time to head out." He stood up, ready to take off. "And you'll find it's easier going down if you think of climbing as dancing to music. Just go with the flow."

That was a big help. I started to clamber down the rugged rock face, choosing a different route this time. Its trail was longer and more circuitous than the one I'd climbed up, but it pretty much guaranteed I'd arrive at my destination all in one piece. Even better, I found that Grizzly was right. I didn't opt for a rhumba or fox trot, but came up with my very own form of break-dancing, sliding down on my fanny. Kitrell watched in amusement as I touched ground.

"Here. Take this to remember your climb." He held

out a sharp, pyramid-shaped piece of granite.

I had the feeling I'd be reminded of my adventure every time I sat down for the next week, but I took the proffered souvenir and stuck it in my pocket.

Kitrell led the way to his trailer. Inside, he pulled out a match and lit a couple of kerosene lamps. He must have picked up on my sense of wariness. "Calm down, Porter. I'm not putting the moves on you with mood lighting. The place doesn't have any electricity."

That was okay by me. Especially since I felt certain I wasn't looking my best after hauling up and down that rock pile.

Kitrell began to rummage through a lopsided aluminum kitchen cabinet. "Lucky thing I just stocked up. You've got yourself a real gourmet choice tonight: I can either fry us up some slices of Spam, or heat a can of franks 'n' beans."

His pantry was obviously no better supplied than my own. I selected the franks 'n' beans and Grizzly dumped the contents into a pot. When he headed outside to heat dinner over a campfire, I began to nose around.

Besides an unmade bed and a threadbare couch, the only personal touches were framed photos scattered on every available surface. In one, Grizzly and a chimp intently signed to each other. Another showed a primate with long limbs loosely wrapped around Kitrell's neck. I leaned in close to view a third picture, but the light was too dim. Picking up the photo, I walked over to a kerosene lantern. The lights danced along a black and white portrait of a younger Grizzly with a small chimpanzee. The infant could easily have passed as one of my childhood toys, with its jug-handle ears and flat, tiny nose. Instead, it was a living creature who gazed at Kitrell adoringly. The moment had been eternally captured as the two lightly touched lips and kissed.

"That was Gracie as a baby."

Kitrell took the photo from my hands and gently gazed at it, then put it down and walked back outside. I followed and sat by the campfire as he dished up two plates.

"By now Gracie's twelve years old, her hormones have kicked in, and she's probably a hell-raising teenager." The corners of Kitrell's eyes crinkled in a smile, until he remembered where the chimp might be. "So what about you, Porter? Do you have any ties that bind?"

Santou's face flickered before me in the bonfire. I imagined I could feel his touch and my skin grew warm, as I momentarily surrendered to my own inner conflagration.

"There was a man I planned to marry. But that changed," I said quietly.

"What happened?" Kitrell asked in the soft tone he'd used on the coyote.

I shrugged. "Things didn't work out. Sometimes life takes funny twists and turns."

Grizzly gave a knowing nod. "Let me guess: your job got in the way."

I looked at him in surprise. "What makes you say that?"

"Why do you think I'm alone? We're kindred souls, you and I. We're both consumed by our work."

Santou's face began to fade from the firelight. "I'm not so sure that's something I want anymore," I wistfully replied.

"I don't think people like us have a choice." Grizzly's voice curled around me. "It's not only what we do; it's who we are. That's something that can never be compromised. Without your dreams, your spirit will shrivel up and die."

Kitrell was depressing the hell out of me. My dreams included having Santou back in my life.

"Don't worry, Porter. Your Prince Charming will come by some day," he said consolingly.

"I just hope I haven't been knocked out cold by a smuggler at the time, so that Prince Charming doesn't see me and passes right by," I said morosely.

"I can do you one better. Always make sure your cell phone is safely locked away in your glove compartment when hanging out with a questionable crowd," Kitrell joked.

The franks 'n' beans turned into a hard lump in the pit of my stomach. The fact that the cell phone had been shoved down Tyler's throat hadn't been made public yet.

"How did you know about that little detail?" I asked.

Grizzly's eyes were as intense as those of the warrior whose image I'd seen on the rocks. "Juan told me about it. How else would I know?"

I wordlessly nodded, reprimanding myself. Of course Fat Boy would have told him. What was wrong with me, anyway?

"What about you? What do you dream of?" I asked in an attempt to thrust the warrior's image from my mind.

"My dream is to make sure that wild things stay wild. I don't want to live in a world where we're faced with one doomed species after another," Grizzly said ardently.

He looked up at the star-filled sky, and I followed his gaze, picking out one to wish upon.

"Wild chimps have been on this planet a hell of a lot longer than man, and I'll be damned if they're going to go the way of the dodo or carrier pigeon as long as I'm around."

I heard the hoot of a great horned owl, and the night

turned a little colder. Kitrell instinctively picked up on my reaction.

"The problem is that people have become too separate from nature. Hell, even you're not totally comfortable out here," he snorted.

"Of course I am!" I responded defensively, silently wondering what had been the giveaway.

"Then what is it that you're afraid of? Bogeymen in the dark?"

The fire had begun to bank, casting menacing shadows all around. A hand clutched my arm, and I instinctively jumped.

Grizzly let loose a low laugh. "Relax, Porter. We're the only monsters out here. Not the animals."

It wasn't the animals I feared.

"You know what my dream is, Porter?" His words floated toward me on a wisp of smoke. "That someday soon people will stop experimenting on chimps, and let them have the life they were put on earth to live."

Fifteen

The waning moon was high, its silver crescent spilling milky beams onto the rugged land below. My Ford crept along until I spotted a good-sized patch of foliage. I signaled to Kitrell, and we nosed our vehicles into the shrubs alongside the road. Neither of us spoke as we hiked in, edging tantalizingly close to the battered barbed wire that marked the New Mexico–Mexican border. I angled my watch to catch the glint of the moon. It was nearly midnight—the smuggling hour.

I looked up from the path for a second and tripped across something lodged in the sandy track. As the ground rose up Grizzly pulled me back, helping to break my fall. I shot him a grateful glance, then looked to see what I'd tripped on. It appeared to be the body of a corpse, and it took all the self-control I had not to leap onto the man next to me. Kitrell would truly believe I was afraid of my own shadow, then.

Get a grip! I scolded myself, and moved in for a closer gander. It was just a gnarled piece of juniper wood, its form contorted by the elements. I'd swear I heard the moonlight giggle.

We continued on in silence. Finally, we hid in a dry-wash camouflaged by a veil of creosote branches, through which there was a good view. The snap of the desert wind sent a clump of tumbleweed rolling across the slashed barbed wire that lay in the dirt around us. The area was just one of many uncontrolled crossings along the 1,943-mile border. My gaze fell upon a single path leading from Mexico to the trampled wire. From there, it extended into the United States to intersect with a network of dirt roads. The trails ran across the tabletop of barren land before disappearing in different directions, as did the couriers who used them. El Pasoans claim that Mexico is creeping north. In truth, it's more of a steady gallop.

Having picked our spot, there was nothing to do now but wait. Over the years, I've come to notice that silence appears in different strengths. Tonight, the absence of noise in the desert was dense enough to be absolutely spooky. The quiet was so deep I could hear the *beat, beat, beat* of Kitrell's heart. I had an insane urge to leap up and break the stillness with a deafening shout. The odor of meat cooking on the Mexican side of the border kept me from doing so. Most likely, the smell was coming from a smuggler's camp.

As the temperature began to lower my eyelids fluttered closed, and my limbs became as heavy as stone. Soon I was leaning back against Grizzly without giving it a second thought. Kitrell responded as if I were one of his chimps, and wrapped a protective arm around my chest. I allowed myself to be swallowed up, my senses drowning in the warmth that embraced me. It had been so long since I'd been held that I'd forgotten how good it felt.

Perhaps there wouldn't be any delivery tonight, after all. I might very well be the butt of another joke—an elaborate hoax planned by Cassandra and the admiral, along with Juan and Mother Krabbs. My mind wandered as I lightly dozed, my subconscious taking me far away.

I thought of Mr. Max and Gracie, and wondered if they ever dreamt of nestling in their mothers' arms, at peace in the place from which they'd been snatched.

I'd nearly fallen asleep when the chilling sound of nails ripping across a hard surface jerked me out of my dreams, dragging me fully awake. I felt Kitrell's body grow tense. The cry wailed through the night like a ghost come to life—a high-pitched shriek which reeked of terror. It was followed by the sound of tires crunching over the ground. I peeked through the creosote to discover the howl had been produced by slender branches of mesquite, shrilly keening where they scratched against metal. The oncoming headlights of a vehicle twitched in the night, as if caught in an epileptic seizure. A Suburban van bounced over the bumpy terrain, headed for a rutted dirt section of the Anapra Road.

The van slowly pulled up, parking almost too close for comfort. Then the engine shut off, and the headlights were doused. All remained black and quiet. I began to think maybe the admiral had also been duped. Possibly all three of us were sitting here in the middle of the night, being played for fools while waiting for nothing.

Then a pair of headlights blinked from out of the void in Mexico, stretching across the gaping darkness. The Suburban acknowledged the wink by flashing its own peepers. Then the rumble of a motor gradually grew closer as the second vehicle lumbered toward us from across the border.

The Suburban suddenly started its engine and began to pull away, only to maneuver into position so that its rear lights now faced the border. Then the doors flew open, and a mini-explosion of fireworks tingled through my veins. Not only did Admiral Maynard step out of the van, but so did my tickle-and-chase pal, Johnny Lambert.

The moonlight transformed them into pale marble statues as they stood side by side, waiting in the dark of night. Lambert and Maynard moved only when the approaching Mexican van came to a stop at the barbed wire fence. This vehicle had likewise turned and backed up, so that the rears of both vans now faced one another. The front doors of the Mexican van opened with a sharp metallic crack, then two men hopped out and silently began to unload their cargo.

A wooden crate appeared, carefully carried by the *hombres*. It quickly disappeared into the Suburban's bowels. My breath floated in and out, on a magic carpet of tiny, quick puffs. I could hear the crunch of the men's boots and their grunts as they worked. I began to fear they could hear me, as well. I must have imagined a little too hard; the next second, my pager went off.

My lips flew open in an involuntary gasp and Kitrell's hand covered my mouth. The pager continued to quiver against my hip, and I was grateful it was in vibration mode. Even so, every nerve ending in my body fluttered as fast as a frightened bird. Grizzly's arms pulled me tight to his chest, as if he feared I might fly off the ground. I reached up and removed his hand from my mouth. We hadn't made a sound.

Maynard and Johnny Lambert finished up, and finally all the men returned to their vans. Both motors roared to life and their headlights turned into four balls of fire. The mating ritual over, the vehicles pulled apart and headed in opposite directions.

My eyes followed the Suburban's lights, which bounced over the terrain before finally hitting the pavement. Then it took off like a homing pigeon, leaving no doubt in my mind as to where it was headed. Mount Riley loomed like a beacon, even in the dead of night: the Flying A ranch was the van's destination.

"I believe what we just witnessed was Panfauna Associates' delivery service in action," Kitrell remarked, his voice cleaving the stillness.

"How can you be sure?" I asked, even now wondering if someone might be hidden close by, listening to our conversation.

Kitrell's eyes gleamed. "By the size of the crates. Each was exactly large enough to hold a juvenile chimp."

"In that case, you might be right about Pierpont. Maynard and Johnny Lambert are headed toward the Flying A ranch, which happens to be where the good doctor is based."

"Then I guess Gracie will be joined by a few others of her own kind tonight," Kitrell grimly replied.

The idea of trailing Maynard and Lambert back to the ranch in the dark was more than ludicrous, it was potentially suicidal. Our headlights would be a dead give-away, setting us up to be knocked off as easily as sitting ducks. As for hiking in on foot, we'd be forced to climb over security gates while tracking across land neither of us knew. The logical choice was to wait until just before daybreak to make our move. At least then, we'd stand a shot.

We headed back to where we had parked, having agreed to meet at my place before sunrise.

"We can't fuck this up, Porter. I don't want to have to worry about something happening to you," were Grizzly's parting words.

"Screwing things up is not what I do. You watch your back. I can take care of my own," I retorted, and drove off.

Sixteen

When I arrived home, Sonny's collection of animal skulls leeringly greeted me. All in all, it seemed the appropriate way to end my day. I wandered into the kitchen to find a surprise: Tia Marta had hung a colorful strand of dried red chiles on the wall. But that wasn't the only thing she'd left for me. Sitting on my kitchen table was a small pouch attached to a leather thong and a hand-written note. I opened the fridge and grabbed a can of soda, then read the message.

> *I made this amulet especially for you. It includes all the right herbs to help keep you safe. But remember, it won't do any good unless you wear it! Something is causing bad spirits to hover around the house. I'll be over first thing in the morning to give you another cleansing.*

I picked up the leather pouch, opened it a crack, and took a whiff. *Whew!* It contained enough vile herbs to drive away a legion of werewolves. I threw the amulet on the table and began to walk out of the room, only to be stopped cold by my incessant Jewish guilt. If Tia Marta arrived before I woke up and found the pouch lying there, her feelings would be hurt. Besides, it wasn't as if I was bunking down with some hunky male who'd be offended by the smell. I backtracked and slipped the thong around my neck. Harrison was the kind of man who'd understand. Anyway, I had the advantage: I controlled his sleeping habits.

My pager went off again. It had driven me crazy the entire drive home, and I hoped the vibrating action had at least firmed my left hip a bit. I planned to wear the gadget on my right hip all day tomorrow. I slipped it off my belt, secretly hoping it was Prince Charming, desperate to get my attention. But wouldn't you know, Fat Boy was trying to reach me.

First things first. I strode into the living room, removed my .38, and bent over to slip it in the desk drawer. Something sharp jabbed my thigh, and I reached down to discover Kitrell's granite souvenir. I pulled the stone out of my pocket and threw it on the desktop, then headed into the bedroom to return Fat Boy's call.

Juan picked up before the phone barely had a chance to ring. "Where the hell have you been, Porter?" he demanded. "Haven't you heard me paging you all night?"

"I just got back from a cruise in the Caribbean," I wisecracked, wishing there was a pina colada in my hand. "What do you want?"

"What I want is protection!" he screamed. Lola jabbered furiously in the background. "Someone is out to get me and it's all because of you! You must have told people that you've been talking to me!"

I clicked back through my memory bank. The only person aware of my connection to Juan was Kitrell. I shelved any doubts on that subject, and took another approach.

"I haven't spoken to anyone," I told him. Maybe we'd been spotted at the Chicken Hut together. "Why? What happened?"

"Oh, nothing much," Fat Boy retorted sarcastically. "Besides someone sneaking into my yard and destroying my entire statue collection. They lopped off the heads of all Seven Dwarfs, and buried Jack and Jill up to their necks in sand. Mother Goose was cut into eight different pieces and strewn about. It's too disgusting to even tell you what they did to Mary and her little lamb!"

I knew how much the yard art meant to Juan, and made a note to pick him up a couple of new statues. "I'm sorry it happened. But it sounds like the work of mischievous kids."

"Oh, yeah?" Fat Boy spat. "Then what do you call the fact that someone broke into my house and threw everything around? The place is a total wreck!"

"Lola trying her hand at housecleaning?"

"Very funny, Porter. You won't think it's so amusing when you learn that whoever was here also took all of Timmy Tom's business papers!" Fat Boy exploded.

He was right; suddenly the events took on a whole new meaning.

"Poor little Lola was so scared, I couldn't find her for hours. I almost keeled over, thinking someone had stolen her from me." Lola added her own two cents by grabbing the phone out of Fat Boy's hands, continuing to chatter like a lunatic. "Lola! Give me the phone back, dammit!"

"Juan! Are you still there?" I yelled, trying to be heard above the ruckus.

"Lola's very upset and is probably going to need a sedative just to go to sleep," Juan sullenly responded.

I could relate to that. "I want you and Lola to take a few days off, and get out of town. Go tour the clubs where you're going to be playing. Or head down the coastline and kick back for a while," I suggested.

"No way!" Fat Boy protested. "This is a critical time

for us. I've still got a bunch of costumes to make, and Lola's not totally confident about the act yet. We've got to work out the glitches before we hit the road, or we'll never get a recording contract!"

"Look, what I'm trying to say is that I'm a little worried," I admitted, not wanting to frighten Juan any more than necessary. But I'd seen this pattern before: people who cross my path during an investigation too often end up in trouble.

"Yeah, well, I'm a little worried too." Fat Boy snorted. "Why the hell else do you think I'm calling? But as for leaving town, you can forget about it. Lola and me have too much to do. I just want to make sure that whatever you've got going doesn't get us killed! Comprende?"

Juan hung up without waiting for my answer. The problem was, I still wasn't sure what I'd become involved in. I needed to figure out not only why someone would nab Timmy Tom's files, but how the admiral and Pierpont fit into the picture. And I feared whoever had killed Timmy Tom was now after Fat Boy.

The phone rang again and I swiftly picked up, for once hoping it was Juan on the line.

"I'm glad you called back! Just say the world and I'll have you out of town by tomorrow," I instantly offered.

"Rach? It's me, Lizzie. Is everything all right?"

The voice floating through the phone wire was barely a whisper. Either we had a bad connection, or something was wrong. I glanced at the clock. Three fifteen A.M. Prickly needles of concern pierced my skin, sharp as a porcupine's quills.

"I'm fine. What are *you* doing up so late?" I asked apprehensively.

"I've found something I think you should know about."

"Is it safe for you to be on the phone?"

"I think so," Lizzie responded in a voice taut as a bowstring. "Anyway, I'm too wired to sleep after what I discovered."

She instantly had my full attention. "What did you learn?"

"I found out that Martin was the former head of a biotechnology firm called Alphagen," she said in an excited whisper.

Other than the name, this was already old news to me. "Did you trip across anything indicating what kind of research Pierpont planned to do?"

"Yes, I scribbled down a few quick notes." She rustled through some papers. "They were developing a new drug delivery technique—which sounds pretty boring. But they also had plans to experiment on nonhuman primate models. Some kind of study was to be done to determine the effectiveness of a specific antibody injected in chimps," Lizzie responded. "I figured you'd be interested in that."

It suddenly felt as if all the oxygen had been sucked out of the room. This was exactly what Kitrell was talking about! Alphagen must have been one of those private labs trying to get chimps in order to conduct secret medical experiments.

"Except testing was never done because Alphagen ran out of money," Lizzie read from her notes. "But you know what's interesting?"

"What's that?"

"Alphagen formally shut its doors the same day Martin arrived in Texas to begin work for us on cloning Ten-Karat. I remember the exact date because I was so excited."

That *did* seem like a funny coincidence. "Was there any mention as to whether Alphagen was bought by another firm? Or did the company simply file in bank-ruptcy court and close its doors?"

"Alphagen was taken over, all right. But not by your normal, everyday company," Lizzie said, stringing out the suspense.

"Then by what?" I asked, wishing I could reach through the phone and grab the information.

Lizzie remained silent for a moment, making me won-der if she was still there, or if F.U. had snuck up from behind and grabbed her. "Lizzie?" I asked worriedly.

"Sorry, Rach. It's just that I'm having a hard time understanding this whole thing myself. It seems Al-phagen was purchased by a private conglomerate of wealthy business associates."

I tried to figure out where all this was headed, but couldn't.

"It gets even weirder, Rach. I checked out the envi-ronmental group which took over the Flying A ranch, and guess what? Not only is the Flying A the only land-holding that Southwest Heritage Trust ever acquired—but their board of directors are the same people who purchased Alphagen from Martin Pierpont!" Lizzie hes-itated, letting me know there was still more to be dis-closed. "To top it off, you'll never guess who the CEO of Southwest Heritage Trust is—my soon-to-be-former louse of a husband, F.U. Krabbs!" she proclaimed, re-leasing her bombshell.

"What!" My mind raced to catch up with the infor-mation. "Are you telling me F.U. is secretly running the very environmental group that he gave the Flying A ranch to? And that this group owns Alphagen?"

"Exactly!" Lizzie responded. "What a scumbucket! I still can't believe he'd do something like that."

Passing the ranch off as a landtrust was probably the least of F.U.'s chicanery. Southwest Heritage was obviously nothing more than some sort of front. The question was why a conglomerate of businessmen would pose as an environmental group to hide the acquisition of a biotech company? I now understood why Johnny Lambert had been so determined to run me off the property.

"I also found an odd set of numbers in one file. I wrote them down just in case you might want them," she offered.

A set of numbers, huh? Now, *that* had a familiar ring to it. I copied them down and stashed the paper in my pocket. With any luck, they'd prove to be the phone number for Panfauna Associates.

A wave of exhaustion hit me like a tsunami, telling my brain it was time to close down for the night. Then I remembered there was one more thing I'd asked Lizzie to check.

"Did you find any mention of what Pierpont did when he worked for the government?" I reminded her.

"Darn it! I knew I forgot something. That's okay; I'm still sitting at F.U.'s desk. I'll just boot his computer back up."

"Lizzie, please be careful!" I warned.

"Yeah, yeah. Don't worry. I've got F.U.'s hearing aids right here in my pocket. He can't hear a thing," she replied.

A moment later, a series of high-tech beeps told me F.U.'s computer had thrummed to life.

"By the way, how did you figure out his password for the computer?"

"Oh, that was easy," Lizzie remarked. "All I did was type in his favorite expression."

"What's that?" I asked, trying to calm my frazzled nerves.

"Cupcake. It's what he calls every woman he wants to sleep with," Lizzie informed me.

So much for any illusion that I was special.

"Hurry up, Lizzie," I urged.

Pierpont and F.U. had gone to great lengths to hide whatever they were up to, and my stomach clenched tighter as I realized the danger in which I'd placed my friend. I was about to tell her to forget the whole thing when Lizzie emitted a low laugh.

"Here we are! I think I've found something," Lizzie's voice throbbed with excitement. "Martin worked on a military project identifying the genes special to humans, by sequencing the full DNA of chimps and then comparing the two. Does that make any sense to you?"

All I knew was that I didn't like the sound of it. "Thanks, Lizzie. Now get off the computer, and destroy any notes you've got," I cautioned.

"Rach, is this beginning to frighten you as much as it is me?" she asked anxiously.

Probably even more. I just didn't want to tell her.

After I hung up, I noticed the red light flashing on my answering machine.

"I gotta hand it to ya. You're a real firecracker, Porter," Sonny's voice rumbled. "My friend finished his autopsy on that vulture. I think you'll find the results real interesting. Give me a call soon as you get in and I'll hop on over."

It was 3:33 A.M., far too late to call. Besides, I needed to catch a few hours sleep before dawn. I crawled into bed, too exhausted to replay Lizzie's conversation in my mind.

Soon I was no longer in the room, but back clambering over the rocks at Hueco Tanks. I climbed towards the sky when my fingers brushed the pictograph of a deer, and the creature sprang to life. It turned its head in my direction, and I fell into two pools of liquid light. I ascended the boulders once more, only to discover that instead of two legs, I now had four. So *this* was how it felt to be a doe! I reveled in my new-found freedom.

My hooves leaped over crags and stones. I pranced onto escarpments and passed bleached bones, until I saw the rock painting of the warrior adorned with a bird's hooked beak and a pair of devil's horns. My heart beat to the sound of invisible drums jostling the air with the *rat-a-tat-tat* of a dead man's bones. The warrior locked onto my eyes and I began to run so fast that my hooves didn't touch the ground. But my warrior easily glided along. Extracting an arrow from its sheath, he placed it in his bow, pulled back, and fired. The steel point ripped through my sinew, muscle, and bone. But rather than the rush of pain, there was only the distant, eerie tinkling of chimes as the warrior's stare bore into my eyes.

This is what happens when you choose to dance with the devil.

I bolted upright in bed to the sound of chimes jangling louder, as my blood shot through my veins with the speed of a train, carrying me from the Land of Nod into reality. I took a deep breath and stale air rushed into my lungs.

Then I heard the tinkling again. It took a moment before I realized it came from the windchimes dancing outside my bedroom window. I lay back, lulled by their song until it suddenly hit me that there wasn't enough breeze to rock them. The sound was some kind of warning. I knew enough not to question what was happening, but to get up, run for the door, and head for my revolver.

I swung my feet onto the floor, when a hard blow rapped me on the back of the neck. My legs gave way and the room began to spin as my knees hit the ground with a heavy thud. I tried to grab onto the bedpost with my palms, knowing I had to keep moving or my life would be over.

Scrambling past the bed, I headed for the door. Someone grabbed my hair, nearly pulling me down to the floor. I stumbled back against pointy boots of cold, scaly leather. A second hand grabbed at my chest, and a tremor of revulsion rushed through me. My fear turned to anger, and my survival instinct kicked in.

Drawing my arm forward, I rammed it back with all my might, transforming my elbow into a one-woman pile driver. I heard a grunt, followed by a groan, as my assailant's grip loosened. Spinning around, I slammed the side of his head with my fist. He fell to the ground, and I ran for the door.

Lurching out of the bedroom, I headed for the living room desk. I was nearly there when the heavy clomp of boots came behind me, guided by a faint beam of moonlight.

I tried to lunge for the drawer, only to be roughly jerked back as pain ripped at my throat, taking my breath away. My attacker had grabbed hold of the leather thong which lay around my neck, and proceeded to strangle me with Tia Marta's amulet.

I struggled to breathe as my limbs thrashed and my eyes filled with tears. All the while, I tried wedging my hand between the cord and my throat, but the leather fought back, biting deep into my fingertips. I reached once more for the drawer, and my hand fell upon something sharp with a triangular point—the granite chunk from Hueco Tanks. My fingers wrapped around the rock.

My assailant responded by twisting the cord even tighter. Spots of bright light danced before my eyes as I frantically lodged the rock's razor sharp point between the thong and my throat and sawed at the leather cord with my last ounce of strength.

The next moment, I heard the cold, silken swish of a blade being drawn from its sheath. The rock nipped my skin in a foretaste of what was nearly upon me, then the leather cord finally broke.

I fell forward on the floor, and a gust of air rushed down my lungs. Then I quickly rolled on to my back to confront my attacker. The gleam of steel obscured his face. I pulled my knees into my chest and violently lashed out, ramming my feet into him.

His body hurtled backward against the wall, where his head collided with Sonny's black buck antelope skull. Both the skull and the man fell to the ground as I pulled my gun from the drawer, then grabbed his knife off the floor. But there was no need to hurry. My unwanted visitor was soundly knocked out.

I started to shake uncontrollably. One more of my lives was gone, forcing me to wonder how many I had left. My hand slid along my throat, its skin marked by a prior close encounter in the Louisiana bayou.

Tempt fate and pay with your life, snickered a ghostly voice.

I lobbed a loud *NO!* back into the darkness. Then I walked to the switch and turned on the light.

The intruder was none other than Johnny Lambert. If this was his latest version of tickle-and-chase, I didn't want to play another round. I headed into the kitchen and dug out some rope.

I was in the midst of trussing Lambert up like a roaster chicken when the front door suddenly burst open. I grabbed my .38 and took aim from where I was straddled across Lambert's back. Sonny Harris came to a dead halt, his mustache twitching like a drunk with the jitters. He took in the scene and tugged on the brim of his ten-gallon hat.

"Just tell me this isn't one of those sadomasochistic sex things," he muttered.

Leave it to a man to come up with that.

"Yeah. That's why he's trying to fit one of your skulls on his head," I retorted.

Sonny grunted. "Sorry to barge in unannounced. But I was up and saw your lights on and it struck me as kinda odd at this hour."

"Then why the hell didn't you come sooner?" I demanded.

Sonny took over tying Lambert up. "It's like I said. Who knows what sort of kinky things you young folks are into these days?"

Sonny had cleverly used the magic word 'young,' knowing I'd forgive him almost anything.

"Who've you got here, anyway?" he asked. "Some guy who wouldn't take no for an answer?"

My social life should have been half as exciting as Sonny liked to imagine.

"This is former U.S. Fish and Wildlife agent Johnny Lambert. I was staking out the Anapra Road at midnight and saw him taking possession of smuggled cargo. My guess is that there were illegal critters inside the crates," I informed Harris. "I just don't know how he got wind of what I was up to."

Sonny gave a shrug. "Maybe he didn't. Could be you gave someone else reason to be suspicious, and they decided to nip any trouble in the bud." He lifted his hat, and patted the thinning hair on his pate. "I suppose what you're telling me is the truth. Otherwise, you've gone to one helluva lotta trouble just to get a skull off the wall."

"Actually, I'm beginning to grow fond of the things," I reluctantly conceded. "One of them saved my life tonight."

Sonny looked down at Lambert. "Well, we're gonna have to figure out what to do with your friend here. Or are you planning to keep him as some sort of trophy?"

"Not unless I can have him stuffed, mounted, and hung on the Happy Hunting Ranch's wall." I grinned, having just noticed Sonny was still in his striped pajamas.

"In that case, I guess we better call the police and have him taken away."

"You can't do that!" I cried.

"And why not?" Sonny stared at me incredulously. "You claim this guy attacked you, so why don't you want him behind bars? Unless there's other stuff you're not telling me."

"Look, I'm on to something big," I admitted. "If I reveal my hand now, the other players will be tipped off, and the case could vanish. Besides, you know how the local police feel about us wildlife agents and retired trackers," I brazenly added, going for the "us-versus-them" approach. "They'll horn in and close me out without giving it a second thought."

Sonny pulled the bandanna off his neck and used it to gag Lambert. I sighed in relief, and Harris nailed me with a warning shot.

"Don't go getting any ideas, Porter. I'm not siding with you on this thing yet. I just want to make sure he remains quiet while you fill me in on what's really going down," he responded.

I headed straight for the heart of the matter. "Okay. F.U. Krabbs is apparently running a hell of a lot more than the Happy Hunting Ranch. He's also heading up a group of wealthy individuals posing as environmentalists. This group, Southwest Heritage, is using F.U.'s other place, the Flying A ranch, as a front, claiming to have turned it into a land trust. But in reality, the group is a private conglomerate conducting some sort of illegal biotech research. Whatever they're working on involves the use of chimps smuggled in from the wild. The Flying A is where Johnny Lambert took those crates tonight."

Harris wasn't blinking an eye.

"I need time to head over there and discover what's going on. Otherwise the group will get wind that Lambert's been arrested, and the entire operation will only go deeper underground." I hoped Sonny believed me.

"You on some kind of drugs?" he snorted.

"I know it sounds crazy, but I swear it's true. Just give me a day to find some evidence to nail them," I pleaded. "I have to get onto the Flying A ranch and nose around."

Harris cocked an eyebrow in my direction. "Yeah? You and who else? General Custer? Or are you planning this attack all on your own?"

"No. Someone's going with me. In fact, he should be arriving any moment," I added, with a glance at the early morning sky.

"No way am I gonna keep a former government agent hog-tied up here all day, Porter. Hell! Do you want me to lose my retirement pay?"

"Give me eight hours, then," I bargained.

"One hour," Harris retorted.

"Oh, come on!" I howled. "That'll barely get me inside the gate! How about seven?" I countered.

Sonny tugged on his hat. "Goddammit, Porter. Tell you what I'll do. I'll meet you halfway: you get three and a half hours, and that's the end of it. After that, I have your friend here picked up."

"It's a deal," I quickly agreed. "Do you mind keeping an eye on him for me? I've got to rush and get dressed before my ride gets here."

"What the hell else do you think I'm gonna be doing

for the next three and a half hours?" Sonny sourly remarked. "Who's this fellow that you're meeting, anyway?"

"Some guy looking for his monkey." I headed into the bedroom.

"Now, *there's* a pick-up line if I ever heard one," Sonny replied caustically.

Come to think of it, he was right. It had certainly worked on me. I jumped in the shower, then threw on a tee-shirt and jeans. I was pulling my curls back into a loose mop when I remembered Sonny had some information for me. I walked back into the living room while sticking my .38 into the waistband of my pants.

"I forgot to ask. What did you find out about that vulture you had autopsied?"

"Seems the bird fell victim to a ring of death," Harris replied, taking a seat on Johnny Lambert's back.

The expression generally referred to poisons that ranchers illegally plant in baited meat, hoping to kill off predators who attack their cattle and sheep. The problem is that the poison doesn't just knock off the critter taking the bait, but also those that dine on the predator's carcass. Not to mention all the other wildlife which dies as a result of eating the poison's secondary victims. And so the ring of death continues.

"Are you telling me that the vulture ate tainted meat?" I asked, wondering if Sonny had just stumbled upon my next case.

"You could say it was something like that," Harris philosophized. "Hell, poison is poison and meat is meat. Ain't that right?"

Sometimes there was no way to respond to cowboy logic other than to simply nod your head.

"Did your pathologist friend say what kind of poison the bird died from?" I asked, laying the groundwork while I still had a few minutes to kill. With any luck, it would turn out to be a compound banned by the Environmental Protection Agency years ago.

"As a matter of fact, he did. Seems the bird was done in by a drug normally used by anesthesiologists. Frank said there's only trouble if it's given in too large a dose. Then the patient becomes paralyzed, and winds up suffocating to death," Sonny explained.

"You wouldn't happen to recollect what this drug is called, would you?"

"There ain't no way in tarnation I can pronounce the darn thing." Sonny chuckled as he caught sight of my disappointed expression. "Come on, Porter. I *did* have enough brains to catch over a thousand men. Whadda ya think, that I lost 'em when I retired? Here. I wrote the name down for you."

He handed me a piece of paper. The name of the drug was succinylcholine.

"How do you suppose a vulture would end up ingesting something like that?" I mused aloud. I thought back to the morning I'd found Timmy Tom dead, and mentally walked through the scene again.

I remembered the sunrise that had welcomed the day as I sped down the road in my Ford. There was the *Driving Aerobics* infomercial I'd concocted in my eternal quest to resemble Sharon Stone. Then the buzzards flying overhead, which had led me to Tyler's corpse. I'd phoned the police, and after that, fought off a vulture which had begun munching on Timmy Tom's arm.

Ohmigod! My mind whirled at the realization. The vulture must have been the same bird that Sonny later found. However, there was still something more which nagged at my memory. A tiny detail as annoying as the buzzing of a gnat. It pricked and teased, daring me to remember. I refused to give up, fully determined to re-call every minuscule item and fact.

A freshly imprinted heelmark lay hidden beneath a creosote bush, along with the striated pattern zigzagging through the sand. Timmy Tom's money belt had coughed up Panfauna's business card. The only other thing left was what the killer had used to camouflage his tracks—a mesquite branch with thorns sharp as a honey bee's stinger.

That's when I collided head-on with that irritating lit-tle detail. A red bump, tiny as a pinprick, had been on Tyler's arm next to where the vulture fed. I walked over and checked the bottom of Johnny Lambert's boot, won-dering if he could have been Timmy Tom's killer. Damn! No five-pointed star in the center.

"Do you think succinylcholine could be injected into a person?" I asked.

"I don't see why not. Animal or human, what's the difference?" Harris replied.

"What do you mean?" I jumped on the remark. "How would it be used on an animal?"

Sonny softly clucked to himself as he shook his head. "Hell, Porter. I can understand why *I* wouldn't know, but you work with wildlife every single day. Don't you think that's something you'd be aware of?"

I knew Sonny was making me eat crow for having implied he couldn't remember the drug the vulture had ingested.

"Okay, Yoda. I apologize for ever doubting your memory. *I'm* the one that's forgetful. Now, would you please just tell me?"

Sonny gave a nod to let me know my apology had been accepted. "Frank said it's one of the medications veterinarians and ranchers use in dart guns to tranquilize wildlife. Only in small doses, of course."

You fool! my brain screamed. Images furiously flashed through my mind.

After finding Timmy Tom I'd headed straight for the Happy Hunting Ranch. My memory cranked out the succession of events like frames in a movie. I was riding in a jeep with F.U. when I'd spotted deadly razor wire wrapped around a black buck's neck. Minutes later, a second vehicle sped into view. My mind's eye zoomed in on the door where Kitrell popped out with a dart gun in his hand.

How could I have been so blind? Hadn't I learned anything yet?

My intuition had warned me something wasn't right about Kitrell from the very first second we'd met. Why hadn't I listened to myself back then? Hell! I'd even given the man every hard-earned scrap of my information.

Suddenly the puzzle was neat, the pieces beginning to fit, leading straight to tonight's attack. It had to be Kitrell who'd tipped off Johnny Lambert. The only question I had was, why?

The beaked warrior sprang to life, dancing inside my head. Getting me out of the way must have been the price Kitrell agreed to pay in order to get Gracie back. I began to suspect Kitrell never even intended to show up here this morning. Probably the plan was to have Johnny Lambert knock me off, after which Kitrell would receive his chimp, and business would go on as usual.

It was the low growl of Kitrell's Toyota chugging through the pre-dawn air which broke the spell. I pulled my revolver as the Land Cruiser came to a halt and parked in front of my house.

"What the hell's going on?" Sonny asked in surprise.

"You're about to meet the man who set me up," I tersely responded.

"But I thought this guy was gonna help you get on the Flying A ranch," Harris replied with a puzzled expression.

"Up until a few minutes ago, so did I," I told him.

Kitrell walked in the door to find my revolver pointed straight at his heart. His eyes flew from my .38, to Johnny Lambert on the floor, to Sonny Harris, then back to me.

"What's all this about?" Dan quietly asked. But his hands curled into fists the size of grizzly bear paws.

"That's exactly what I'm trying to find out," I firmly responded. "Slowly remove your boots and slide them over to me."

Kitrell's eyes began to smolder. "I don't appreciate the prank," his deep bass ominously rumbled.

"Do it now!" I brusquely ordered. I backed up my command by cocking the .38's trigger, so there'd be no mistaking that I was serious.

"I'd listen to her if I were you," Sonny advised him. "Trust me on this. She can be a mean sonuvabitch."

No wonder I was so fond of the man. He deserved at least a couple of extra beers at the bar tonight.

Kitrell held off, as if still expecting to hear this was some sort of joke.

"You have exactly two seconds before you join your friend on the floor," I informed him.

Kitrell's eyes never left mine as he proceeded to kick off his boots.

"Very good. Now slide them over to me," I instructed.

He did as he was told. I picked up first one boot, and then the other, carefully scrutinizing each of its heels. Neither bore the imprint I was looking for. A hint of doubt began to eat at me, but Kitrell was a clever man. Most likely, he'd been smart enough to change his footwear.

"Let me take a gander at those," Harris offered.

I kicked the boots over to Sonny, who began his own meticulous examination.

"Tell me, Kitrell. What kind of tranquilizer do you use to immobilize critters?" I asked.

"Why should you care about something like that?"

"Just answer the question, or I'll tie you up for the sheer fun of it," I warned.

"It's called Sucostrin," he cautiously replied. "Why? What does that have to do with anything?"

"I believe Sucostrin is a form of succinylcholine," I bluffed, not having the slightest idea.

Kitrell warily nodded his head. "That's right. It's liquid succinylcholine chloride. So what? Almost every veterinarian uses the stuff."

"Yeah. But I don't know of many veterinarians who might have wanted to kill Timmy Tom Tyler," I informed him. "And had enough succinylcholine on hand with which to do it."

"*That's* how he died?" Kitrell was silent for a moment before snapping out of his reverie. "Is that what this nonsense is about? You think that *I* murdered him?" He looked at me in astonishment. "What the hell would I go and do something like that for? Tyler had the information I wanted! Only part of which you were able to give me last night. Remember?"

"And what information were you going to get from Timmy Tom that I didn't supply you with?" I asked testily.

"How to get Gracie out of that damned place!" Dan snapped. "For God's sakes! Tyler was my one and only lifeline!"

"It's okay, Rachel," Sonny interjected before I could respond. "This isn't the guy who killed Tyler."

"How can you be so certain?" I asked skeptically.

"He's just wearing a different pair of boots than the ones he had on when he murdered Timmy Tom."

"I'm certain because I found another footprint with a five-pointed star that you missed. The man you're looking for is smaller." He threw the boots back to Dan.

"He still could have set me up for the attack," I stubbornly insisted, angry that I'd missed yet another piece of evidence. "He had plenty of time to call Johnny Lambert after we parted earlier."

"I see you've got this whole thing figured out," Kitrell retorted. "So I expect you must also know why I'd do such a thing. How about letting me in on it?"

"You betrayed me in exchange for Gracie," I said angrily, even as I wondered if I might be wrong.

"Then just what the hell am I doing here now? Can you answer me that?" Kitrell irately demanded. "According to your scenario, I should already have Gracie and be long gone."

Sonny came over to my side. "He didn't do it, Rachel. He didn't kill Tyler, and he didn't set you up. You know I wouldn't say that if I weren't absolutely sure."

I looked at Harris and knew he was right. I nodded my head, and lowered the revolver.

"That's more like it," Kitrell said huffily, pulling his boots on. "Now what happened here? Did this goon break in and attack you?"

"No. I dragged him home with me for a good time," I retorted.

"Porter!" both men cried in unison.

"All right!" I silently ordered myself to behave. "Juan called last night after I came home. It seems someone broke into his place and absconded with all of Timmy Tom's business papers. But I didn't realize how truly serious the situation was until I received a call from Lizzie Krabbs soon afterward."

"F.U.'s wife?" Kitrell asked incredulously.

"An old friend—long story," I offered, by way of explanation. "She hacked into F.U.'s computer, where she discovered that Southwest Heritage isn't an environmental group, but a front, headed by F.U., comprised of wealthy business associates."

"Sonuvabitch! I knew it!" Kitrell pounded his fists together. "There's no way a man like Krabbs would give up all that valuable acreage to a land trust."

"It gets even better. Southwest Heritage bought Pierpont's biotech company when it went bankrupt. Pierpont now works for them as some sort of subcontractor."

Grizzly stood stock still and stared. "You know what this means, don't you?"

I silently shook my head, not prepared to hazard a guess.

"Pierpont has to be working on something that F.U. and his cronies are betting will bring in one hell of a huge profit. Otherwise they'd never fund such a venture. It also must be highly illegal, which is why it's being kept secret."

"Maybe Krabbs and his friends just want to keep whatever it is all for themselves. Could be it's some superduper new form of Viagra," Sonny suggested.

"Nonetheless, their product must nearly be ready for market," Dan speculated.

"Why is that?" I asked.

"I'm sure what we saw coming in last night were juvenile chimps," he said. "Pierpont would use less expensive, more expendable monkeys for the initial creation of a product and all the way up to its final stage of development. He wouldn't risk losing a valuable primate like a chimp until his mystery drug was finally ready for a clinical trial run. So he must be at that point now."

"What kind of primates would Pierpont have worked with before this?" I questioned.

"Probably something cheap and easy to get hold of, like Rhesus macaques or African greens," Kitrell replied.

A goodly number of both species had been at Admiral Maynard's place. "How about squirrel or spider monkeys?" I persisted. "Would those be used as well?"

Dan grimly nodded. "Sure. Researchers test with them all the time."

It now made sense why Timmy Tom had brought in such large shipments of spider and squirrel monkeys for the One World Zoo. Then he must have lost his contract when Pierpont no longer required those, but wanted something more special, which Timmy Tom was unable obtain. Say, smuggled chimps. Evidently that was the admiral's forte.

I remembered Lizzie's bombshell and every nerve in my body began to tingle. "One more thing. I told you Pierpont used to work for the government. But what I didn't fill you in on was the project. He was involved with DNA analysis."

"Well, he'd have to be if he were trying to clone a dog, wouldn't he?" Grizzly replied, with a note of condescension.

If this was a game of one-upmanship, I intended to rise to the top with the ease of a trapeze artist. "That's true," I retorted. "Except his work involved the dissection of chimpanzee DNA."

Grizzly's face abruptly turned pale at that bombshell. "Dear God! We've got to get out there right now! I only hope Pierpont's not involved in what I'm afraid he's doing."

Grizzly's reaction transformed the butterflies in my stomach into an angry nest of hornets. "Which is?" I questioned, half afraid to know the answer.

"There's no time to explain—but it's something involving Gracie." Kitrell headed for the door. "We've got a ranch to invade. Let's get moving."

I followed, wondering if Pierpont was cloning a factory line of little Gracies.

"Hold on there a second!" Sonny called out. He pulled Johnny Lambert's battered cowboy hat off the unconscious man's head, and threw it to Grizzly. "Put that on, along with a pair of sunglasses," he instructed.

"What for?" Kitrell asked, momentarily perplexed.

"So that whoever catches sight of you from a distance will think you're Johnny Lambert. You're also gonna want to take his vehicle in place of your own."

"Who are you two, anyway? Cagney and Lacey?" Grizzly inquired with a grin.

"Personally, I see us more as Starsky and Hutch," Sonny retorted without missing a beat. "Just remember, I'm giving you just three and a half hours!"

"What's he talking about?" Dan asked as we stepped outside.

"Nothing we need to be concerned with," I responded, hoping I was right.

Johnny Lambert's black Suburban sat alongside my house. Kitrell opened the cargo doors to find the van still contained one of the crates from the night before. He pulled out the box and replaced it with wire cages from inside his own vehicle.

"What are those for?" I asked, the prickles multiplying to cover my entire body.

"For Gracie," Kitrell replied with stone cold determination. "And whatever else we might find."

Seventeen

The sky was beginning to marbleize with color, its soft pastel hues ready for baking in the morning sun's kiln. I could almost feel the pull of Mount Riley drawing me, as strongly as a magnetic force, even before it came into view.

We arrived to find the gate snugly secured by a padlock. I rustled through the bag of goodies I'd transferred from my Ford and produced a pair of large metal snips.

"Let me do the honors," Grizzly snarled, taking them from my hand. "I'm in the mood for tearing into something, and this will do for starters."

Kitrell surgically dismembered the lock and then gleefully threw the gate wide open.

I hopped out after we'd driven through and closed the gate behind us.

"I'm sorry about this morning," I offered, as we drove down the gravel road.

"It's okay, Porter. I understand. Sometimes it's hard to know who you can trust. That's why the two of us are loners," he said with a shrug.

There was no need to say any more. Soon we reached the ranch house, along with our first hurdle—the alarm pad controlling the gate to the main body of land.

"No sweat. It's probably the same code we use on the

Happy Hunting Ranch," Kitrell assured me.

His fingers reached outside and entered a series of numbers. But the gate adamantly refused to budge.

"Shit! Wouldn't you know that crazy old coot would use a different code here?" Grizzly complained.

A thought hit me like a cattle prod. "Hand me that slip of paper I gave you last night with all the numbers!"

Grizzly poked in his pockets to produce the wrinkled slip of paper.

"Try punching in that first series and let's see what we get," I suggested, hoping my hunch proved correct.

Kitrell took another few stabs at the alarm, eventually entering three sets of the numbers. However, the alarm's grip remained tighter than Ma Krabbs' hold on her money.

"Goddammit to hell!" he furiously hissed. Then he punched in the last set—Gracie's ID number—and the gate effortlessly flew open.

We drove through and the gate automatically closed behind us.

"Okay. Take a look around, and tell me what you remember from when you were here," Kitrell said.

"I recall some motor homes, and a pole barn situated against a mesa, as well as livestock drinking from a water tank. Oh, I also spotted Pierpont driving by and chased him down," I added as an afterthought. "He paused long enough to warn me to stay out of his way."

"Well, you're doing one hell of a job on that front," Grizzly remarked.

"Thanks," I responded, keeping an eye out for landmarks. "I think we should head over here."

I pointed off to my left. Grizzly followed my finger as if it were a compass, and it wasn't long before a distant mesa floated in to view.

"That's the area Johnny Lambert and I drove through."

Kitrell pressed on the Suburban's accelerator, but slowed down as we passed the metal pole barn with its corral.

"What is it that we're looking for, anyway?" I restlessly asked, checking my watch. An hour and fifteen minutes had already elapsed since we'd left the house.

"I'll let you know when I figure it out," Kitrell distractedly replied.

We'd nearly reached the end of the mesa when Grizzly slammed on the brakes and turned off the engine.

"Why are we stopping here?" I asked in alarm.

Dan had his head cocked to one side, with his eyes closed, as if listening to a desert rhapsody. He placed a finger to his lips.

"Shhh. Don't say a word," he whispered. "Just sit and listen."

All I heard at first was the murmur of tumbleweed keening a lonely Western tune. Then the whir of locusts broke through the silence—except their chatter held a mechanical edge. The humming originated from somewhere near the water tank.

"What do you think that sound is?" I asked, my voice soft as a puff of smoke.

Kitrell shook his head, continuing to listen. "I have absolutely no idea. What say we go and find out?"

It wasn't until we'd parked next to the metal container that I realized how enormous it was.

"I've never seen a water tank this size before. How big do you think it is?" I asked.

"Taking a guess, I'd say around fifty feet in diameter," Grizzly replied, checking the rearview mirror. "Nobody seems to be in the area. Let's step outside and poke around a little."

The whirring sound was now a good deal louder, and appeared to originate from deep within the tank itself.

We walked over to the four-foot high metal wall, and looked down to see that the water was contained in a donut-shaped trough. This moat cleverly masked what lay in the vat's center: a separate, roofless container. The sound seemed like the buzz of giant fans, but we couldn't see beyond the moat from where we were standing.

I turned to find Kitrell scrambling onto the Suburban's roof, where he stood silhouetted against the sun. He let loose a low whistle.

"Come up here. You've got to get a load of this," he said quietly.

I made my way on to the vehicle's hood, and Kitrell grabbed my hand to pull me up beside him.

Rising up from the ground were five silver pipes evenly spaced within the center—and large, industrial sized fans were mounted on their tops.

"Very clever," Kitrell acknowledged. "Whoever designed this facility took the time to plan it out well."

I gazed around, wondering what Grizzly was talking about. All I could see was miles of endless desert.

"Exactly what is it that we're looking at?" I asked, feeling left out.

"While anyone passing by will see cattle drinking and be faked out, the container's real purpose is right there in the middle," Dan said, directing my gaze to the tank's center.

"Which is?" I repeated in exasperation.

"Those tall silver shafts are intake pipes for a ventilation system," he explained.

"What's being ventilated? There isn't anything out here besides some lonely looking cows," I stubbornly responded.

"Sure there is," Kitrell softly replied. "Take another look around."

I gazed at the barren land until my eyes fell on what lay directly in front of me—the protruding mesa which thrust up out of the ground like an enormous coffin.

"That?" I asked, pointing to the tabletop mountain.

"Exactly!" Grizzly exclaimed. "What you're looking at is the perfect camouflage for a secret underground facility. It's being supplied with air from those pipes. And that tells me Pierpont doesn't want any recirculation, but only one-hundred percent passed-through air."

"Why would he want that?" I asked, trying to understand.

"Probably because whatever he's working on needs to be contained. Do you understand what I'm saying?" he asked grimly.

I nodded, not having the slightest idea what he was talking about.

"How do you suppose we break into this thing?" I asked, glancing at my watch again. Time was ticking away, and I had yet to spot an arrow pointing to a sign that said, *Entrance.*

"There must be a door disguised as something else," Grizzly replied, looking about.

Ha! I realized where the entrance into the plateau had to be. "The way inside is through the pole barn."

Grizzly's face lit up. "You're right! The cover couldn't be more perfect!"

I was just feeling like a Grade A student when Kitrell abruptly turned toward me.

"This is something I have to do, Porter. If you're smart, you'll stay the hell out of it," he sternly advised.

"If I were smart, I'd never have gotten myself exiled to Texas to begin with. Why should I change my track record now?" I retorted. "There's no way you're leaving me behind. Don't even try!"

Grizzly's eyes crinkled in a smile. "If we make it through this, I'll teach you how to free coyotes," he promised.

"It's a deal," I agreed.

We scrambled off the truck roof and into the vehicle, backtracking to the pole barn. Guarding its entrance were large double doors, along with another touchpad alarm.

"Let's drag out those damn numbers again," Grizzly grumbled. "You keep an eye open and make sure no one sneaks up on us."

Kitrell tapped in Gracie's ID number again and the doors obediently pivoted open.

We drove inside the empty shell of a building, where a road sloped downward into darkness. Kitrell stopped at a post which held a solitary red button.

"Okay, Miss Genius. What do you suppose this is?" he asked, with a nod.

"It better be for closing the doors, or else we're in trouble," I responded. "It won't take long for someone to notice the barn is wide open."

Kitrell quickly punched the button, and the doors closed, sealing us inside.

I stared into the dark abyss as a growing sense of foreboding embraced me. "What do you suppose Pierpont's doing down there?" I whispered.

"Something that he shouldn't be." Kitrell glowered.

We turned on the van's headlights, and followed our fate down the road. The path led directly to a small lot where just one SUV sat parked. I breathed a sigh of relief, secretly glad to discover no cherry red Jeep. In front of us was an elevator, whose door smoothly slid open. We left our vehicle and walked toward it.

"After you," said Dan, with a cordial wave of his hand.

Great. I got to play guinea pig. Inside were three buttons to choose from, offering to take us to Lower Level 2 or 3.

"Okay, what does your womanly instinct suggest?" Dan queried.

My instinct was to call in the Desert Storm troops and get ourselves some back-up.

"Let's start at Level 3, and work our way up," I proposed.

Dan's finger hit the button.

The elevator glided down and noiselessly came to a halt, opening to a hall of concrete covered in sterile whitewash. The pervasive hush was heavy as a cemetery's at midnight. Dan took my hand silently and we headed for the first closed door. Kitrell tapped lightly. Receiving no response, we slipped into the room to find stacks of paper clothes neatly folded in piles.

"Put these on," Kitrell commanded, handing me a pair of coveralls.

After that came booties, followed by paper hats, until we resembled two fast order cooks at McDonald's.

"This is a good sign," Dan remarked, while cuffing up my pants. "If the chimps were infected with some sort of contagious disease, the clothing would be far more protective."

He fastened a cloth mask around my nose and mouth, and I did the same for him. Then we headed back out into the hall, fully cloaked in our disguises.

Swish, swish, swish, whispered our paper-clad feet, sounding like dust mops waltzing down the corridor. Kitrell cracked open the door to each room, followed by a shake of his head, after which we moved on. Soon a musky aroma snuck beneath our masks: the odor of chimps. Our steps grew faster.

We didn't stop to check each room; that was no longer necessary as faint whimpers reached our ears. We raced toward the sound and, without stopping, flung open the door and entered.

Four tiny chimps sat locked in small prisons. They stared back at us, probably wondering what was going to happen to them next. Two of them had most likely been part of the smuggled cargo last night. Perhaps Timmy Tom had stumbled upon the delivery of the other pair, which was why he'd been murdered.

"It's all right. You're safe now," I softly reassured my new-found charges.

Two diminutive arms stretched toward me, begging to be comforted. That was all the prompting I needed. I was ready to rip apart each wire cage. I heard the door open behind me and whirled to catch Kitrell heading out.

"Where are you going? We can't just leave them here!" I exploded.

"We'll come back. But first I have to find Gracie," Kitrell tensely informed me.

I took one last look at the young chimps and promised to return, then slipped away. Kitrell was already tearing down the hall, opening doors. Then he stepped inside a room and disappeared. For a moment, I feared that he'd been caught and all was lost. Until I heard the soft cry "*Gracie!*," and knew Kitrell had found what he'd been searching for.

I walked in on a reunion I'd never forget. Kitrell knelt beside a cage that was clearly a cell. Inside sat its gloomy prisoner with her back to the wall. Dan slowly pulled down his mask and gently asked, *"Do you remember me, Gracie?"* in a trembling voice. All the while, his fingers carefully formed each precious word.

The chimp gazed at Dan and then at his hands, which quickly repeated their message. The melancholy clouding her eyes visibly began to brighten. A series of soft pant-hoots left her lips as she tentatively approached him. Gracie hooted once more, and then eagerly signed back, the flood gate of pent-up emotions opened. They focused on each other as if they were the only two beings on the planet, their fingers dancing in a language I couldn't speak, exchanging secrets I wasn't privy to.

"What's she saying?" I asked, clamoring to be included.

Dan laughed and tell-tale tears escaped his eyes. "Gracie knows me! She even remembers my nickname!"

"What is it?" I asked, dealing with my own case of sniffles.

"Gracie would pick flowers, which she called 'pretty,' and weave them in my beard," Dan replied, his fingers still moving in a private conversation. "One day she linked the two activities together and came up with the nickname 'Pretty Beard.' That's what she's calling me now. It's the reason I never shaved this thing—I was afraid that if I did, when I finally found Gracie, she wouldn't know who I was." Kitrell's voice caught in his throat. "But Gracie didn't forget me."

Gracie abruptly stopped and stared at him, causing my heart to flutter. Then, slipping her hand between the metal bars, she extended a slender finger and began to wipe away his tears.

My vision blurred as Dan caught Gracie's hand in his own and brought it to his lips, where he lightly kissed her fingertips. The bittersweet moment came to an end when Kitrell began to sign to once again. Suddenly, both pairs of hands flew in fast and furious motion.

Magical as it was, I knew the longer we stayed here, the greater the risk. "You've found Gracie. Now let's free the other chimps and get going," I reminded Kitrell. A growing sense of urgency was beginning to nip at me with sharp teeth.

Dan's expression had turned to sheer exasperation. "That's what I've been trying to tell Gracie. But she insists I have to find something before we can leave."

"Whatever it is can't be that important," I impatiently insisted, the nipping now keener and more persistent. "Let's just open this cage and get her out of here." I pulled out my Leatherman and went to work.

However, Gracie's behavior grew increasingly agitated. She soon stopped communicating altogether, and banged at the bars in a fit of rage. Finally, she folded her arms against her chest as if she were holding a bundle and rocked back and forth.

The catch popped open. "Grab her and let's go," I instructed, not in the mood for dealing with a temper tantrum.

Kitrell placed a hand on my arm. "Wait a minute. Gracie's trying to tell me that she has a baby," he disclosed.

What? I nearly screamed in frustration. "But wouldn't the baby still be with her, if that were true?"

"Yes. Infants generally aren't taken away, unless the mother's a bad parent. And I don't believe that would be the case with Gracie." Kitrell watched as the chimp repeated the sign once more. "Maybe she's got it confused. She always loved to cuddle small things, from dolls to kittens. It must be something like that."

There was still another floor to be checked for primates; we needed to wrap this up. I was prepared to drag Gracie out by force if necessary, when my eyes fell upon a peek-a-boo line that ran across the width of her lower belly. A fine layer of newly grown hair barely camouflaged the pink scar which peeped through.

"Oh, my God." My finger drew Kitrell's attention to the spot.

"Maybe she's telling the truth after all," he responded, staring at the incision.

Then he turned to me with an expression far more fierce than that of any Old Testament prophet. Cecil B. DeMille would have killed to cast this guy in *The Ten Commandments*.

"That could be due to a cesarean," he said somberly.

It had been my immediate guess, as well. Still, I'd never known of a chimp to need such a procedure. "Even if Gracie had a baby, why would Pierpont perform a C-section?"

Kitrell opened his mouth to speak, but nothing came out, as if he didn't dare voice what he feared. He turned and dashed from the room as fast as if hounds of hell were after him. This wasn't the time for Kitrell to lose his cool—not if we planned to get the chimps and ourselves out of here, all in one piece. I closed Gracie in her cage and followed Kitrell to the very last door, its entrance guarded by one of F.U. Krabbs' pain-in-the-ass alarms.

Kitrell banged the wall hard with his fist, and then clamped onto my shoulders.

"Okay, Houdini. I've already tried Gracie's ID, along with the other numbers on that piece of paper, and none of them work. You figured out the other alarms. Now I need you to come through for me on this one." His fingers dug into my flesh. "I've got to find out if Pierpont's done what I suspect—so I need to get inside this room."

This guy was getting to know me all too well. There was no way I could turn down such a challenge. Especially since I was hell bent on discovering what was going on, myself.

"Okay. Let me think, let me think, let me think," I

muttered, hoping the words would help kickstart my brain. Sometimes it pays to let your mind wander. Mine was tap dancing away, which made me think of Lizzie and last night's conversation.

Yes! The code had to be the series of numbers Lizzie had copied off F.U.'s computer!

The best thing about wearing the same clothes every day is that everything is always right there in your pockets. My fingers trembled as I pulled out the note and punched in one set of numbers after another. But the door remained as maddeningly stubborn as Gracie.

It was then that I stopped thinking about codes, and began to study the hardware before me. For the first time, I realized the numbers were arranged like those on a push-button phone, with corresponding letters of the alphabet.

Screw this! I thought, deciding upon a totally different tack. I crumpled the paper and punched in the letters for F.U.'s favorite word: *Cupcake.* The lock opened with a sharp, metallic click. Dan placed his hand on the knob, took a deep breath, and entered.

The room gleamed with spic-n-span polish. On a stainless steel counter sat a sparkling array of stainless steel containers and surgical instruments.

My eyes were drawn to a metal box mounted on four sturdy legs. It contained a door with a plexi-glass window mounted in its center, and was as enticing as having stumbled upon an early Christmas present. Especially since the receptacle was angled just enough to block my view inside. I headed straight for the box, bursting with the need to know exactly what Dr. Scissorhands was up to. As I got closer, I realized it was some sort of high-tech incubator, with a tube attached to the back providing the air supply.

I was certain it wouldn't contain a mini-replica of

Lizzie's barking darling, Ten-Karat. My curiosity pounded as I cautiously peered inside, only to be held captive by what I saw. Reality had suddenly taken on a whole new dimension.

Looking back at me lay an infant with ten perfect fingers, and ten tiny toes. Her round little skull held a pair of pink lips, and a cute little button nose. A set of bright eyes gazed into mine, filled with a growing sense of wonder. Their color was cornflower blue, leaving no doubt as to the identity of the father. The only other eyes I'd ever seen in that shade belonged to that bonzai buckaroo, F.U. However, that's where all similarity between father and daughter ended. The rest of the gene pool belonged solely to the child's mother.

The baby's face wasn't tucked beneath the brain case like a normal child's, but projected beyond it. Her ears were the shape of miniature jug-handles, and her jaw jutted strongly forward. A soft coat of dark, downy hair covered her head and continued down to the tips of her toes. I stared at an infant not quite human, yet not totally chimpanzee. The baby was an entity entirely of Pierpont's warped creation.

"It's happened."

Kitrell's whisper resounded in my brain.

"The bastard's actually gone and done it."

The infant whimpered and moved its lips as if it were trying to speak. Scrunching its reddened face, it clenched its hands into puckered fists, and all too-human tears rolled down its plump little cheeks. The cry which emerged was totally unlike any other—yet even this cry needed no translation: the baby wanted its mother.

"Tell me what I'm looking at." The words rang strangely in my ears, leaving me unsure I'd even spoken them.

"That DNA analysis that Pierpont was involved in when he worked for the government?" Kitrell's voice sounded equally distorted. "Do you know any more about it than you've already told me?"

The conversation with Lizzie felt as though it had taken place a lifetime ago. I forced myself to concentrate on it as I shifted my gaze around the room, wanting to focus anywhere except on what lay before me. But there was no escaping the magnetic pull emanating from inside the metal box. I looked down, and the little girl's eyes locked onto mine. That's when Lizzie's words came flooding back to haunt me with their meaning.

"Oh, my God—that's it. Pierpont was identifying those genes specific to humans by sequencing the full DNA of chimps and comparing the two."

"There's your answer." Dan tilted his chin in the baby's direction. "Pierpont went the extra step—one that he was probably never supposed to take. He created a hybrid by inserting those genes special only to humans inside an ape."

I looked at the baby again, and could have sworn F.U. was staring back at me.

"But how?" I asked, unable to pry my gaze away.

"Through genetic engineering." Kitrell's voice trembled. "Pierpont took a female chimp's egg, a human male sperm, made those additions to their DNA, and combined them. Then he popped the fertilized egg back into the female's womb. And just like that, you've got yourself a brand new species. I knew something like this could be engineered through cutting-edge science; I just never imagined anyone would be crazy enough to try it." Kitrell's jaw tightened as he stared at the baby. "But that's exactly what Pierpont's done, using Gracie as both mother and incubator."

I was still trying to comprehend why F.U. was involved.

"All right. So Pierpont gets his kicks out of screwing around with evolution and playing God. But what's in it for Pierpont's financial backers?" The urgency I'd felt earlier warned me to get moving.

Dan lowered his chin and ran a hand through his shaggy hair, as though confounded by the very same question. When he looked back up, his face was flushed with excitement.

"Of course! What the hell have I been thinking? This all makes perfectly insane sense!"

Kitrell began to pace back and forth. "Scientists claim their quest to produce better vaccines and antidotes is hampered because they can't test on human beings from start to finish."

"So what are you getting at?" I impatiently prodded, knowing there was no time to waste. The longer we were here, the more likely we'd be caught.

Dan's pace grew faster. "A drug which works on a mouse can be a dud when finally tested on humans, after years of research and millions of dollars. The creation of a hybrid would provide them with something much closer to man to test on, but there's always been a silent agreement that such a deed would be horrific. Now this bastard has thrown all ethics to the wind and done it!"

A further implication suddenly hit me like a battering ram. "Oh, God! There's even more to it than that. Pierpont's engineered an entirely new species. Do you know what that means?"

Kitrell stopped pacing and looked at me blankly.

"A hybrid doesn't fall under the Endangered Species Act."

Dan's gaze revealed he still didn't understand.

My words began to fly fast and furious, aware that

time was slipping past. "There's no protection in place for Gracie's baby! Pierpont could raise an entire colony of these hybrids for gruesome tests, or even use them as slave labor. And until a law is enacted to regulate the trade, every hybrid like this will be at Alphagen's mercy. Pierpont's opened up a Pandora's box with mind-boggling implications!"

Kitrell's thoughts flew as swiftly as my own. "That's not all—you can bet Pierpont plans to impregnate this baby when she comes of age. That way, her offspring will be even genetically closer to man. Once he finally creates the ideal hybrid for optimum testing, he'll then clone the creature."

"And since they aren't listed as endangered species, the critters can be shipped to research labs all over the world. Pierpont's a Dr. Frankenstein!" My internal clock screamed that time was running out. We had to get out of here now.

The baby cried again inside its crib, wanting what every infant craves. To lay fast asleep in her mother's arms, being loved and held and protected. She was no more aware of what awaited her than any other newborn babe.

"We can't leave her here," I firmly stated.

"I never intended to," Dan agreed. "That's Gracie's baby. I'm taking her with me."

I still wanted to check the second floor and make sure Pierpont didn't have anything else locked away, but a glance at my watch told me that Sonny would be calling the police any minute. We needed to be off the Flying A ranch before they arrived and stumbled upon our discovery. Once news of Gracie's baby spread, she'd never escape probing scientists and the freak show circuit. We had to keep her existence a secret.

"We're going to have to split up in order to finish," I told Kitrell.

He quickly agreed. "You check the other floor while I load all the chimps into the van."

I turned to head out, only to feel Dan's fingers wrap around my arm like a tourniquet.

"Be careful, Porter," he warned. "If either of us if found, it's all over. Pierpont's not about to let us leave after what we've seen."

Kitrell wasn't telling me anything I didn't already know.

Eighteen

My paper slippers brushed along the floor toward the elevator as if of their own accord. Stepping inside, I pressed the button for Level 2. I arrived all too quickly, causing my heart to divide and multiply. Thousands of miniature tickers flew into my veins, pumping blood in my ears and in my throat. It drummed in each finger and in between my toes. In contrast, a heavy web of silence loomed outside, waiting to pounce on me.

I left the safety of my mechanical cocoon and approached the first room. I listened to make sure no one was there, peeked inside, then slipped through the door.

The small office looked ordinary at first, with a miniature replica of Rodin's "The Thinker" on the desktop. Then I noticed that in place of a man's head was that of an ape. The desk was pristinely neat, and a mini stainless steel refrigerator stood nearby. The room was as sterile as the mausoleum I'd just left.

I sat down and flicked on the computer. A prompt appeared, demanding the password. *No problemo*, I smugly thought, and typed in *Cupcake*.

An animated prosthetic hook emerged on each side of the screen and they scuttled toward one another in a mating dance, only to devour the word *Cupcake*. The two claws next formed a pair of crossbones, and underneath appeared the message, *Entrance Denied.* Call it a lucky guess, but I was willing to bet this was Martin Pierpont's office.

Since the computer wouldn't cooperate, I decided to try the desk. I dragged out my pocket-tool, and jimmied open the drawer.

Inside lay a thin stack of papers begging to be examined. I quickly rifled through them, and the logo for Panfauna Associates caught my eye. In my grip was the delivery receipt for four juvenile chimpanzees shipped to Mexico from Burundi. A notation on the bottom stated the arrival of several more chimps could be expected shortly.

I scurried deeper inside the drawer, and my fingers hit upon several square pieces of hard plastic. I'd discovered four zip disks, labeled "Hybrid Experiment," "Antidotes," "Viruses," and "Clones." This was the mother of all motherlodes.

I scooped up all four disks along with Panfauna's receipt, and next checked out Pierpont's mini-fridge. Inside were a few sealed jars containing what appeared to be a milkshake. Pierpont's version of a protein drink? I walked back to the door, peered into the hall, then stepped outside. I'd take a quick look around the rest of the floor, then double-time it out of here.

I was halfway down the corridor when I heard the sound of someone approaching around the corner. Dashing for the nearest room, I ducked inside, and held my breath as the footsteps drew steadily closer. Only when they receded did I crack the door and peek. A balding man in a lab coat had passed by. *Shush, shush, shush.* The harsh cotton of his coat seemed to scold like a stern librarian. The warning was clear: employees were beginning to show up for work.

The room I'd taken refuge in was the size of a large

walk-in closet. On second thought, what it really resembled was a bunker. Along with some empty lockers, there were six rows of metal shelves. Those held lightweight tangerine Tyvek suits, double-layered latex gloves, rubber boots, and goggles. Next to the shelves was a sign instructing that all clothing must be removed before putting on protective garments.

Nearby hung two varieties of masks. One was a transparent, full face respirator complete with two purple virus filters. The other, a flexible Racal hood, slipped over one's head and shoulders to snap snugly inside the suit. Next to it was a respirator pack that was to be attached to the Tyvek suit.

Shivers marched up my spine like an invading unit of soldiers as I realized the bunker was actually a foyer, with a thick metal door standing guard at the other end of the room. And on that door was a warning: *Caution— Respirators must be worn beyond this point at all times.*

Pierpont was up to something even more menacing than what we'd already uncovered. I glanced back at the Tyvek suits, the gloves and the masks. Now I knew why ventilation pipes had been hidden inside a water tank: it was to conceal a Biosafety Level Four Hot Lab.

There are some diseases so horrific that no cure has yet been found for them—ebola, hemorraghic fever, and Marburg disease, to name but a few. Then there are viruses which are further engineered to produce lethal genies in bottles. The disks burned in the palm of my hand as I remembered their labels: "Viruses" and "Antidotes." Not only was I itching to find out what Pierpont was up to, but he might have a few more chimps locked away in there. If I walked out now, a dire fate undoubtedly awaited them. I had to find out what was behind that steel door.

I stripped down to my panties and bra, sticking my

clothes, my gun, all four disks, and Panfauna's receipt inside the first locker. Then I slipped inside a Minute Maid colored space suit, pulling on latex gloves while sliding my feet into boots. Hmmm . . . which hood to don? I just planned to step inside and take a quick look, in which case there was little need to waste time inflating my space suit and snapping on the Racal head cover. I peeled down one glove and glanced at my watch. Five minutes and I was out, no matter what. I grabbed the transparent hood with its two purple respirators and made my way over to the door, feeling like a futuristic soldier outfitted for war.

An intercom box was mounted nearby, along with an oblong window which offered a view of what lay in store. I peered into a narrow hallway of cinderblock and steel. Then, pulling firmly on the handle, I stepped over a reinforced metal ledge and entered the room. Invisible pressure slammed the refrigerator door behind me, and I now saw what had been obscured from my view. Rows of stainless steel shower heads lined the ceiling and walls. Clammy fingers of fear slipped inside my suit and clutched me by the throat.

Get a grip! I began to take slow, steady breaths.

I proceeded down the passage to one final metal door which stood silently in wait. I could no longer distinguish the rush of my blood from the thud of each boot as I drew closer to the steel portal, where a white sign with red lettering announced *You Are About To Enter Biohazard Area Four.*

My brain switched on to automatic pilot and my gloved hands latched onto the wheel, spinning the circular handle. The pressurized seal gave way with a hiss and I entered the room. The air-lock door instantly closed behind me.

I found myself in a chamber that was half Julia Child's kitchen and half Frankenstein's lab. The room was awash with shining metal and glass. I walked toward a stainless steel table holding cylindrical glass bottles with metal tops. Each container had several tubes running in and out, though a witches brew of liquid fermented only in one. It emitted a captivating low hum. Next to it sat a Bunsen burner warm enough to alert me that someone had been working in here just recently. I wondered what sort of sinister soup they were cooking up, but the room was silent, unwilling to relinquish its secret. The biggest relief was that there were no animals inside cages or shackled to walls.

I quickly scanned the room, determined to find a clue of some sort. A freezer and refrigerator stood in the far corner and I headed over to investigate.

Instead of Hungry Man entrees, the freezer was filled racks holding tubes of specimens, all marked with different dates. Unfortunately, that didn't provide me with any useful evidence. I pulled out a second metal holder, which proved to be of more interest. The tubes had larger labels, and I lifted one up to eye level. *The Satan Bug*, I read.

My trembling fingers slowly centered the deadly cylinder above an empty slot, and ever so carefully lowered it. Then, I painstakingly slid Pierpont's noxious concoction back inside its frozen vault.

My thoughts began to pirouette in a poisonous ballet. Were F.U. and his cohorts terrorists? I quickly dismissed the idea as completely ludicrous. Yet the only time I'd ever heard of the Satan Bug was in conjunction with genetically engineered viruses. Caught between horror and excitement, I checked out the refrigerator.

Sitting on the bottom shelf were sealed jars similar to

those in Pierpont's office. I picked up one of the glass bottles, staring at its contents.

There was no question that Pierpont was brewing up the ingredients for a biologic Armageddon. I closed the refrigerator, knowing what I'd stumbled upon was way beyond my professional capacity. The most important thing I could do at the moment was simply to get out of here.

My thought was punctuated by a loud burp as the air-lock door swung open, and I spun around to discover I had unexpected company. Martin Pierpont walked inside, dressed in a Tyvek suit and a full Racal hood. He closed the door behind him with his hooks.

"Why is it that you insist on visiting me without an appointment?" he pleasantly inquired.

"Probably because you keep refusing to give me one," I replied, trying to sound more calm than I felt.

Pierpont looked different than I'd ever seen him before—then it hit me. There was no Jimi Hendrix wig stuffed inside his helmet. The man was completely bald.

Pierpont took note of my gaze, and self-consciously reached up to stroke the top of his hood. Jeez! Men and their vanity! At the same time, I caught sight of his other hook. It was locked onto a 9mm revolver.

"It really would have been wiser if you'd waited for an invitation. But now that you're here, I suppose you've already looked around," Pierpont commented with his annoying Mona Lisa smile.

Man, did nothing rattle this guy? "If I say no, do I receive a 'get out of jail free' card?"

Pierpont's smile morphed into a more ominous Cheshire Cat grin. "No. What it means is that I get to put you to work. Actually, your timing couldn't be better. I've been looking for some temporary help."

I wondered if I could push him aside and make a run for the door without getting shot.

"Don't let these hooks of mine fool you. My aim is deadly," he advised as if he'd read my mind, raising the 9mm in my direction.

I took a quick glance around the room. Except for a microscope, there was nothing with which to bop him on the head.

"Would you mind filling me in on what's going on before you start saddling me up with chores?"

"You mean you really don't know?" Pierpont asked in astonishment. "And all this time, I thought you were fairly smart."

That's the other thing about guys. Let them get a gun in their hooks and they begin to feel it's an open invitation to insult you.

"You're in luck today, Agent Porter. It so happens I'd be thrilled to enlighten you on the finer points of my project. Otherwise, how can you truly appreciate what lies in store for you?" He clearly relished the thought.

Pierpont moved toward the stainless steel table. "These bottles are small bioreactors. What you're witnessing are cells that have been infected with a virus, and are now beginning to replicate."

Terrific. "If you don't mind my asking, what type of virus is it?" I inquired, leaning back against the refrigerator door.

"I'm delighted you're showing so much interest. That's the hardest part about this whole thing, you know," he confided. "There are so few people I can include in my work."

The tip of his hook raked along the steel table top as if he were dissecting a patient. This was the happiest I'd ever seen him.

"These biorectors are producing three different genetically engineered strains of the same virus. The basic bacteria is a little something called anthrax."

The word shot through me like a bullet. Anthrax was the most frightening of all biological weapons. Invisible to the eye, a fatal dose is smaller than a speck of dust, and easily inhaled in a single breath. My respiration quickened, suddenly fearful of the very air I was breathing.

Pierpont noted my reaction with enormous satisfaction. "Good. I'm glad to see you understand what I'm dealing with."

"Does F.U. know you're doing this?" was all I could ask.

"Of course! Who do you suppose is sponsoring my work?" he said with amusement. "Krabbs and his associates are the proud owners of my formerly defunct company."

Pierpont moved toward me, and I quickly headed to the other side of the table.

"Then they must be under the impression your work involves something else. Otherwise, why would a group of businessmen have anything to do with the production of anthrax?"

"That's a perfectly valid question," Pierpont responded, "and one which is easily answered. Just think about the world in which we live today. Nuclear arms are no longer the biggest threat we face. That menace has been replaced by germ warfare, precisely because any maniac can concoct a bioweapon simply by getting the recipe off the Internet! Add a beer fermenter, some culture, a gas mask, and you're in business."

I raised an eyebrow at the maniac. "Funny. That's exactly what it appears you've done here."

"No, Agent Porter. You have absolutely no idea what you're looking at. But you will," he added sinisterly.

"The people Krabbs and his associates worry about are not only renegade countries like Iraq and Libya, but terrorists as varied as Hezbollah, Osama bin Laden, and the Aryan Nation. The threat can come from any individual or small organization with a grudge that wants to punish society. What if those who blew up the federal building in Oklahoma had had access to microbial toxins instead of bags of fertilizer? Thousands of lives would have been extinguished. Now take a look at those flasks in front of you," Pierpont instructed.

My gaze became riveted on the bioreactors.

"These are the poor man's nuclear bomb. There's no doubt that a germ attack is going to occur in this country; it's only a matter of time. And when that takes place, what do you think is going to happen to people like you? Let me tell you," he eagerly offered.

I nodded as if fixated by an oncoming accident.

"One day you'll hear a news report about a strange outbreak of a respiratory disease. First locally, and then around the nation. A few hours later, crowds will converge on emergency rooms gasping for breath and complaining of high fever. The government will realize what they're dealing with. But of course, by then they'll have taken all the necessary precautions. Already, important federal officials, as well as FBI and CIA agents, are being inoculated for just such an event. So are those in the Army, Navy and Marine Corps. Possibly even police, fire fighters and health workers will have been vaccinated. Soon after the news breaks, the National Guard will be on the move, declaring martial law over cities and quarantining highways. It will all run fairly smoothly because emergency plans to deal with such an attack have been in place for years." Pierpont paused and smiled. "Oh, but I haven't yet said what will happen to you, have I? People like you will be dead."

I stared at him. "What the hell are you talking about?" I demanded.

Pierpont casually waved his gun in my direction.

"The government has never bothered to create stockpiles of anthrax vaccine for civilian use. For one thing, it's too expensive. For another, it's bureaucratic bumbling at its best. Which means the most you can hope for is a body bag to crawl inside as you suffer an excruciating death. Krabbs and his friends are taking the necessary steps to defend themselves, so that doesn't happen to them."

I waited until my panic had subsided enough so that I could catch my breath. "If what you say is true, then why are you creating viruses instead of developing the vaccine?"

"I'm so glad you asked," Pierpont smiled. "It turns out the Russians recently engineered a new microbe, rendering all existing anthrax vaccine totally useless. Obviously, they're not the only ones creating designer strains. It's quite simple to modify anthrax to outwit what few antitoxins we have. To combat that, I've also been engineering new, improved forms of anthrax in order to develop a broad spectrum antidote. You'll be pleased to learn I've come up with a counteractant which should work against any anthrax strain that could possibly be manufactured."

Pierpont opened the refrigerator and pulled out one of the milkshakes. "This is the part which will interest you the most. I'm now at the final stage of testing."

"Which is why you've been smuggling chimps in over the border," I added.

"Oh, good. You actually *do* know something. Yes, the chimps will be my gold standard test. I plan to infect each with a different strain of anthrax, then I'll have them drink this antidote. Keep your fingers crossed: if they live, that means my work is a success."

"Does that include testing on the infant hybrid you created? Or isn't she quite ready to be killed off yet?" I challenged.

Pierpont's face positively beamed. "So, you've discovered my masterpiece. Isn't she beautiful?"

I couldn't believe what he was saying. "You really *are* crazy. How could you cross humans and apes, solely for the purpose of giving a new species a fatal disease? That's completely psychotic."

Pierpont's smile faded. "You're trying to hurt my feelings, aren't you? I have no intention of infecting her. At least not until she's produced a second generation hybrid all of her own."

"And when you finally develop a hybrid with the same susceptibility to disease as human beings, what then?" I questioned.

"I'll clone it," Pierpont patiently answered, as if teaching a child a science lesson. "If one truly cares about saving human lives, we must discover antidotes for otherwise incurable diseases. Believe me, Agent Porter: I have no qualms about testing on people. But there are all these annoying laws which prevent me from doing so. What I've come up with is the next best solution."

"Are you saying that if your antidote works, it will be made available to the public?" I inquired hopefully.

Pierpont condescendingly shook his head. "Of course not. This medication is purely for the private use of those who are funding the project."

"So much for any grand idea of saving the human race from anthrax. What are *you* getting out of this?"

Pierpont returned the milkshake to the fridge, and headed toward a built-in cabinet opposite the table. "Actually, I negotiated a very satisfactory deal with the conglomerate in which I'll receive royalties from the sale of all hybrids. So you see, I really didn't lie to your friend Lizzie. I *have* been working on cloning."

Pierpont opened the cabinet doors to expose an array of flasks and glassware. Reaching in, he removed a vial filled with a dry pink powder. I caught sight of a rifle on the bottom shelf. It was a duplicate of the gun used to tranquilize the injured antelope on the Happy Hunting Ranch.

Pierpont followed my gaze and nodded. "I'm afraid Tyler proved to be as much of a nuisance as you. He also had to pay the price for learning too much."

"But why did you use succinylcholine to kill him?" I asked, desperately glancing around in the hope of finding some sort of weapon.

"You figured that out, as well? Now I *am* impressed." Pierpont congratulated me. "The animals I work with are unpredictable, so I keep my rifle loaded with a Sucostrin cartridge at all times. I had it with me on the morning Timmy Tom was snooping around. As I said, you never know what you might bump into. It was the first time I've used it on a person, and I'm pleased to report it worked exceptionally well. Since it's a paralyzing agent, his death was appropriately gruesome—though a little too quick for my liking. But don't worry. That's not what I have in store for you."

Pierpont placed his 9mm on the table while he opened the vial in his hook. My adrenaline soared as I grabbed the revolver. God! It felt good to be the one in power!

"Why don't you recap whatever you've got. You won't be needing it where we're going," I instructed.

Showing no fear, Pierpont began to walk toward me.

"I'm warning you to stop, or I swear to God I'll shoot!" I threatened, never having been more serious.

Pierpont's smile turned to a taunt as he continued in my direction.

"It's over, Pierpont!" I cautioned one last time.

But the guy was a certifiable lunatic. He was a mere six feet away, leaving me with no choice. I gritted my teeth and pulled the trigger. I heard the hollow click of an empty chamber—and stared at the man in horror.

"That gun's just a little something I keep on hand for any necessary intimidation. As you can see, it served its purpose well," Pierpont said with a smirk. Then he reached out and ripped off my mask.

There was no time to think, much less react, as the vial's pale pink contents were thrown in my face. My brain screamed at me to hold my breath. Instead, I gasped and inhaled. An Easter parade of tiny spores scrambled down my lungs and swam up my nose, filling my body with a basket of deadly goodies. There was no place to run, much less hide from the cloud of minuscule particles floating around me. The granules coated the inside of my mouth and tickled my throat, as if I'd just polished off some cotton candy. I immediately began to cough.

Pierpont studied my response, as if taking mental notes on a lab animal. "Oh, dear. It appears you've just inhaled my most lethal strain of anthrax. It's one I call the Satan Bug, because it's particularly nasty."

The name high-dived in my brain, heading straight into a pool of sheer terror. "But I saw that in your freezer. It's a liquid," I protested.

Pierpont complacently folded his hooks in front of him. "You received a form that was dried and ground into a fine powder. All the easier to inhale, Agent Porter."

Horror began to wrap around me as tightly as a winding sheet.

"You should begin to feel its effects shortly. Shall I tell you what they will be?" Pierpont's voice cut with the skill of a scalpel. "First your pulse will beat rapidly. Then your temperature will soar. Finally, your lungs will fill with liquid until you can no longer breathe."

My pulse sped up as he spoke and my skin began to sizzle with the intensity of bacon spattering in a frying pan. I stared into his bottle lens glasses in disbelief.

Pierpont smiled from behind his filtered hood. "Death will take a while, giving me time to observe your reactions." His voice coiled as venomously as a snake inside me. "Oh yes . . . that's the other thing. I'm afraid I'll have to withhold the antidote. After all, I do have ethical guidelines I must follow; I couldn't possibly use it on a human until running a final test on the chimps. But before I can test it, you have to die. Then I'll be able to disinfect the room and get on with my work."

My disbelief transformed into boiling rage.

"Like hell you will!" I growled, my anger propelling me toward him. Turning at the last moment, I planted my shoulder directly in his chest and sent Pierpont flying up against the open cabinet. An April shower of glassware tumbled down, including a beaker of liquid which crash-landed on the steel table. Its contents splashed onto the warm Bunsen burner and burst into flames.

"You idiot! That was ether!" Pierpont dashed to put out the fire.

My adrenaline racing like a turbo engine, I sprang for the cabinet and grabbed the dart rifle. Whirling around, I found Pierpont lunging for me, his hooks aimed at my throat. I pulled the trigger and a red-tailed dart hit its mark. It was Pierpont's turn to stare in disbelief.

"You bitch!" he hissed.

"Trust me, I've been called far worse," I assured him, and rushed for the refrigerator as smoke began to fill the room.

Flinging open its door, I reached in only to feel two

sharp hooks clamp onto the back of my suit. Their aluminum tips penetrated the fabric, raking my skin, even as Pierpont's breathing became uneven and labored.

I strained for the rifle, which was lying on the counter. Sensing what I was up to, Pierpont began pulling a hook from my garment, but his prosthesis became entangled in the torn fabric. He gave a hard yank and the hook broke free, just as my hand wrapped around the rifle and I rammed the butt in his stomach. Pierpont fell backward, ripping a hole in my suit.

Seizing two jars of Pierpont's milkshake formula, I stumbled towards the air-lock door. I tried to take one last look back through the haze of smoke, but a lick of flame crackled and danced, obscuring my view. Pierpont was headed right where he belonged: straight into the arms of hell, and out of every chimp's life for good.

I stepped into the shower room, closing the door to Pierpont's lab tightly behind me. My own inferno raged as I stood in the chamber, unsure of what to do. A thunderous pounding at the end of the hall brought me back to my senses. Kitrell was peering in the glass window at me.

"Don't open the door!" I cried out, half in alarm, half in tears. "Pierpont caught me in his lab. I've been infected with anthrax!"

Kitrell's face blanched beneath his forest of beard. His disembodied voice boomed through the intercom. "Listen carefully to me, Rachel, and do exactly as I say. All right?"

I nodded, unable to speak over the sob which was blocking my throat.

"First put down what you've got in your hands. Then stand beneath the shower head closest to you and turn it on."

His voice became my a life preserver as I placed the

bottles in a corner, started the shower and kept my eyes closed. A chemical spray rained down upon my head, washing away the anthrax spores.

"Okay. Now take off the suit and look for a shower with a knob marked 'water spray,'" Kitrell instructed. "There should be a bottle of bleach solution nearby, as well as a bar of soap."

I was grateful my bra and panties were on as I pulled off the gloves, the boots, and self-consciously slipped out of the Tyvek suit. I'd never felt so completely vulnerable.

Dan's voice entered the room once more, this time his tone as soothing as the one he'd used on the coyote. "I'm sorry, Rachel. But I'm afraid the underwear has to go."

"What!"

"Everything you had on in that room has been contaminated. You don't have a choice. First wash yourself down with bleach solution. Then rinse it off and shower again with disinfecting soap. That will keep you from being infectious. Just do it, Rachel. I promise not to look," Kitrell vowed.

My pulse roared with the fury of a Molotov cocktail, and every inch of my skin felt on fire. I glared at Kitrell until he'd turned around, then I stripped out of the last two garments. A rush of water was my only cover as I vigorously scrubbed my hair and flesh as hard as I could. Having finished, I went to retrieve the jars.

"Where are you going?" Dan's voice echoed throughout the chamber in alarm.

Damn it! Of course he was going to snatch a peek, being a typical male.

"That's the antidote," I explained, holding my temper in check. "Pierpont infected me with a mutant strain of anthrax. He planned to use it on the chimps, then give them the antitoxin in those jars as its final trial run." I moved toward the bottles once more.

"You can't, Rachel!"

Dan's voice stopped me dead in my tracks. I turned and stared at the man, no longer caring that I was naked. "What are you talking about? I'll die if I don't take it!"

"Those bottles were in the room with you. They've been exposed."

His words only added to the fire already flaring in my body.

"I'll wash them off," I persisted.

"It makes no difference. They could still be contaminated." Kitrell explained. "Just come out and we'll get you started on a dose of doxycycline, along with a vaccination. We need to leave before anyone else finds us!"

"Didn't you hear what I said? I was infected with a *hybrid* strain of anthrax. The vaccine is totally useless!"

"Then we'll figure something else out. But you can't drink anything from inside that room once it went hot!" Dan insisted.

I knew he was right, and I began what felt like my death march. Each step drummed home the legacy I'd be leaving: a broken relationship, dirty dishes, some secondhand furniture, and an office of messy papers. That's when I remembered Pierpont's compulsively neat office and the mini-refrigerator.

"Wait! I know where there's another batch of antidote!" I shouted in relief. "Pierpont's office is down the hall. You'll know it by the sculpture of a hybrid chimp sitting on the desk. Next to it is a stainless steel fridge containing more of these jars!"

I shoved open the shower room door, determined not to let Pierpont win, and Dan covered me with a towel.

"Get dressed and meet me at the elevator. I'll go find

the antidote. We're getting out of here now," he instructed.

I grabbed Kitrell's arm as he started to leave. "What about the chimps?"

"They're already loaded in the van, along with the baby. Now hurry up!"

I threw on my clothes, stuffing the disks and Panfauna's receipt in my pocket while keeping my .38 revolver firmly in my grip. Kitrell was already holding the elevator door open when I arrived. He slammed his palm against the button and the door closed. Two containers of the antidote sat on the floor, and next to them was Pierpont's laptop computer.

The following moment, the shriek of a fire alarm went off, chasing up the elevator shaft after us. We exited into the lot and dashed toward Lambert's van. The tunnel howled in anger as Kitrell started the engine and our vehicle tore through the black abyss. I pressed the red button we'd passed on our way in, the barn doors flew open, and we peeled across the desert terrain. The van didn't stop until we reached the Flying A ranch house. Then Kitrell slammed on the brakes.

"Drink the antidote, Porter," Dan ordered, picking up the milkshake.

I angrily blinked back the tears which began to well up in my eyes. "What if it doesn't work?" I asked, hating to admit my fear.

"It will, Rachel," Kitrell replied, popping off the jar's lid. "Pierpont tested this stuff. The chimps were just his grand finale. Besides, what have you got to lose?"

I nodded, perfectly aware I'd unwittingly become Pierpont's 'gold standard' test. "All right. As long as you agree that we destroy these." I revealed the three disks labeled "Hybrid Experiment," "Viruses," and "Clones," reserving the one marked "Antidote."

Dan placed the bottle in my hand. "It's a deal."

I drank the chalky liquid, not stopping until I reached the bottom. With every sip I cursed Pierpont, while I prayed his formula proved to be successful. Then, leaving the van, I placed the disks in front of the Suburban's tires and watched as Kitrell ran over them. But even that couldn't quell my rage.

Jerking open the passenger door, I caught a glimpse of Gracie holding her baby, and thought of Pierpont's plans for the helpless infant. Though his disks had been destroyed, his malignant recipes still hid in one last place.

Grabbing hold of the laptop, I pulled it out and swung it against the alarm's concrete post until it smashed into irretrievable bits. Only when Pierpont's demon had been thoroughly exorcised did I climb back inside the van. I was ready to head home.

Epilogue

"**I** don't want to hear any arguments. Just drink," Tia Marta ordered, watching me with an eagle eye.

"Yecchh! What is this stuff?" I lifted my shoulders and shook my head, hoping it would make the aftertaste dissipate faster.

"All you need to know is that it's good for you," Tia Marta scolded. "Besides, I'm making frijoles and enchiladas for lunch. That's better than the hospital food they forced you to eat, isn't it?"

I'd been out of the hospital for a month, but Tia Marta wasn't about to let me forget my one week stay. Especially since she'd been caught trying to sneak in meals. She still insisted I couldn't leave the house without at least one cleansing a day.

A rap on the door revealed that Sonny Harris had stopped by for a visit.

"Got some mail for you," he announced, slipping a can of Tecate beer into my hand.

"Thanks," I said, and quickly took a sip. Tia Marta had banned alcohol, declaring it helped mask any evil spirits that might be lingering. My personal view was that they'd probably appreciate a drink.

"I also brought some peach cobbler," Sonny remarked, displaying a covered dish.

I could tell he'd been spending more time at Miss Mae's by the amount of weight he'd gained.

"Is that you in there, Sonny Harris? Come into the kitchen right this minute!" Tia Marta commanded.

Sonny rolled his eyes and threw me the mail. We both knew she was probably holding an egg in her hand. "By the way, I've got something else to give you after I come back a newly cleansed man."

I began to flip through one envelope after another, my stomach rumbling hungrily at the whiff of enchiladas which floated in the air. The phone rang and, as usual, I secretly hoped it was Santou.

"Let me guess. You've already downed a gallon of creosote tea today." Lizzie's voice giggled.

"Don't forget the quart of honey mesquite and cat claw that Tia Marta brewed," I grumbled.

"Well, I think you deserve time off for good behavior. What say I swing by later and pick you up for a wild Saturday night out on the town?" Lizzie offered.

"I'm not an invalid, you know. I can get around on my own." It wasn't that I minded being pampered; it just made me nervous. I figured my friends knew something about my condition that I didn't.

"I know you can, but I want to show off my minivan. The name of my new nightclub is painted on it," Lizzie bubbled.

"Now all you have to do is start construction, and set an opening date," I teased her.

"Okay. So I'm a little overenthusiastic," Lizzie responded blithely.

After F.U. landed in jail, Lizzie learned he'd secretly placed the majority of his assets in her name. His reasoning had been that if he ever got into trouble, no one could touch his money. Except for his wife, that is.

"I get at least one letter a day from him trying to

convince me it doesn't mean squat that everything is in my name. He says I should know in my heart it's still rightfully his," Lizzie had confided. "I wrote back to him that my heart goes by the name which appears on the checking and savings accounts—and thanks for giving me the Happy Hunting Ranch and the house."

The Happy Hunting Ranch had been turned into a wildlife preserve, where only cameras were allowed to shoot the animals. As for her nightclub, it was guaranteed to be a success. The F.U. Krabbs case had been the biggest thing to hit El Paso in years, and you couldn't buy that kind of publicity.

I agreed to let Lizzie pick me up around six.

Sonny waited until I was off the phone before sticking his head around the corner. "Hey, Rachel. Word on the street is that Admiral Maynard's operation is about to be shut down."

"Who's doing that?" I asked in astonishment.

I'd been trying to put the final nail in Maynard's coffin after finding Panfauna's receipt inside Pierpont's desk, but there wasn't enough evidence. So although I was happy Maynard's primate sweat shop would be folding, I felt short-changed at being left out of the process.

"You're the one closing the bastard down," Sonny said with a wink, and threw me a large manila envelope.

I quickly looked through the contents and found all the paperwork F.U. claimed had been destroyed, detailing every shipment coming through Maynard. Even Timmy Tom's missing papers were included in the lot.

"How did you ever get hold of this?" I inquired incredulously.

"It seems the admiral and his wife discovered the alien father of their daughter's unborn child is really the very human boy next door. They were so angry, they kicked Helen May out of the house. I guess they should have checked her luggage first." He chuckled.

"But that doesn't explain how it came into your hands."

"That's the funny part about this whole thing. I've been teaching Helen May's boyfriend, Billy Bob Holder, how to track. He knew I was a friend of yours, so he and Helen May decided to pass these papers along. I just don't know what you're gonna do with all those monkeys the admiral's got," Sonny added.

I smiled. "Don't worry. I'm sure Lizzie will provide them with temporary housing at the Happy Hunting Ranch."

"In that case, I'll leave the rest of the footwork to you. Just let me know if you need a hand," Sonny replied.

"Will do." I suddenly felt a whole lot better about life.

"I'm going back into the kitchen before Tia Marta gobbles up all the peach cobbler. I *am* invited to stay for lunch, right?" Sonny asked, patting his paunch.

"Absolutely," I replied. "Just give a holler when the enchiladas are ready."

I set the manila envelope aside and went back to sorting through the mail, when my heart came to a stop. In my hand was an envelope with no return address, in unfamiliar handwriting. I carefully ripped it open, and a few photographs fell out. There was also a sheet of paper which beckoned to be read.

Will send you an address where we can be reached as soon as I know it's safe. At which point, we expect a visit! Thanks again for helping me to regain my family. I couldn't have done it without you, Rachel. Enclosed are some photos so that you won't forget us until then.

Dan

I picked up the Polaroids and gazed at the family of man. There was a photo of Dan with Gracie in a pose I'd previously seen, but both were seven years older in this updated version. Man and chimp were touching fingertips in their own private language, with Gracie clearly reveling in her newfound freedom.

I slowly picked up the next picture, anxious to see the photo, yet somewhat afraid. A happy baby girl smiled at me, her inquisitive eyes cornflower blue. She'd never have to worry about spending her life being infected by Pierpont, or making people laugh while trying to balance on roller skates. Gracie and her baby were finally safe.

"Rachel! Lunch is on the table!" Tia Marta called from the kitchen.

I looked at the photos once more, before stashing them safely away. Then I got up to join the people who'd come to form my own family of diverse souls, knowing all was right with the world.